TO HEAL
THE HEART'S EYE

The Stafford Chronicles, Book 2

TO HEAL
THE HEART'S EYE

Patricia Harrison Easton

Servant Publications
Ann Arbor, Michigan

Vine Books is an imprint of Servant Publications especially designed to serve evangelical Christians.

This is a work of fiction. Apart from obvious references to public figures, places, and historical events, all characters and incidents in this novel are the product of the author's imagination. Any similarities to people living or dead are purely coincidental.

Published by Servant Publications
P.O. Box 8617
Ann Arbor, Michigan 48107

Cover design: Paul Higdon
Cover photos: © Superstock. Used by permission.

97 98 99 00   10 9 8 7 6 5 4 3 2 1

Printed in the United States of America
ISBN 0-89283-951-1

Library of Congress Cataloging-in-Publication Data

Easton, Patricia Harrison
To heal the heart's eye / Patricia Harrison Easton.
    p.   cm. — (The Stafford chronicles ; bk. 2)
ISBN 0-89283-951-1
I. Title.   II. Series : Easton, Patricia Harrions. Stafford chronicles ; bk. 2.
PS3555.A7335T6   1997
813'.54—dc21   97-8755
                                                           CIP

The whole point of this life is the healing of the heart's eye through which God is seen.

St. Augustine of Hippo

DEDICATION

For my daughter Liz and son-in-law Chick,
in this the year of their marriage.

May the Lord reside in your hearts so that
through him you can be a source of healing for
each other and those around you.

ONE

Cat O'Reilly searched along the countryside for the mailbox. Dr. Brady had said it was a fancy painted one and she'd spot it right after she drove across the iron bridge. She pushed the brake nearly to the floor before the old truck stopped. It slid a little in the mud that still covered the road from the recent flood. Next to her on the seat a tiny red-and-white terrier opened her only good eye and whined. Cat scratched the old dog behind her ear. "It's all right, Sadie," she said. "Go back to sleep."

Again Cat searched the berm ahead. Just where the road started to curve she thought she saw the entrance to a farm lane. Still, she saw no mailbox, fancy or otherwise.

She took her foot off the brake. With a sputter and cough the truck rolled forward. She gave it some gas, just enough to keep from stalling, and turned onto the lane. This had to be the place. The mailbox probably washed away in the flood.

The truck bounced down the lane over deep ruts, the tracks made by water retreating to the now slowly rolling stream on her right. Even with the signs of the deluge still evident, this place had great natural beauty. But in her less than twenty years on this earth, Cat had learned that beauty wasn't reliable. Most things weren't as they seemed.

The lane turned just ahead. Cat guessed that the house must stand beyond the bend. Her breath caught in her chest. Her stomach clenched. She just had to get this job.

Again she stopped the truck. The old dog rolled onto her back and waved her three good legs in the air. A foul odor filled the cab. "Sadie, sometimes you're downright disgusting," Cat said. Sadie snuggled closer, the stump of her fourth leg digging into Cat's thigh. What if these people didn't like dogs? Or maybe they had dogs of their own and didn't want another one around. The truck convulsed and then stalled. Cat sighed. If her old truck hadn't reached the end of its road, it was darn close to it. As for her, she'd finally run out of luck and money.

She picked up Sadie and hopped out of the truck. No sense flaunting problems right off the bat. Cat carried Sadie to the back of the truck. She'd stash her until the interview was over. She climbed the steps to the door of the camper that served as her home and turned the key in the lock. The rusty, dented door creaked open. Cat gave the windows a quick glance. They were opened enough to give the dog air. Sadie tried to cling to her with her one good front leg as Cat bent to put her inside the camper.

"I promise you won't be in here long, girl. Okay?"

The dog whined but flopped onto the floor. Sadie lowered her small head onto her paw. She looked up at Cat.

"Don't try looking pitiful, Sadie. You just be quiet until they've offered me this job. You hear?"

Before she left, Cat laid a finger on the picture of her mother she'd hung on the wall. A plastic frame protected the faded snapshot of the young and beautiful woman wearing a long sundress, her hair hanging over one shoulder, smiling at the camera as she played her mandolin. Cat had just been a baby when Mamma had died, and that photo and the mandolin was all she had to help remember her. "Bring me luck, Mamma," she said.

Cat hurried back to the cab, hoping the truck would start. After a few cranks it did. With a worrisome rumble and a belch of smoke from under the hood, it bounced toward the house.

What if this wasn't a good place? Lately she'd known only bad. A sign. She needed a sign. She closed her eyes. "Lord Jesus, please, I'm asking for a sign."

She opened her eyes. Nothing. But sometimes a person had to wait awhile for direction. Cat scanned the hillside. Nothing. But no bad signs either—no snakes draped over tree branches … no goat glaring from a rock ledge … no eerie feelings of evil lurking … no soaring bird of prey, like the wide-winged eagle that haunted her dreams at night.

She fingered the wooden cross that hung on the strip of rawhide around her neck. To comfort herself, she said the prayer the old healer woman had taught her. Then taking a deep breath, she let the truck roll around the bend.

The house was even prettier than she'd imagined. A big boxy farmhouse painted tan with green trim. Pots spilling over with deep blue blooms hung from the ceiling of a cozy front porch. Planters filled with pink geraniums and trailing ivy lined the porch rail. High on the hill a barn nestled on a ridge.

She had come to a good place. She could sense it. She stopped the truck. The engine gave another cough and then died. She ran her hands over her hair, smoothing it toward the long braid that hung down her back. She took a deep breath, and another, then wiped her hands on her jeans before climbing the porch steps to knock on the door.

No response came from the house. Cat knocked a little louder. Inside, a dog barked. Cat looked quickly back at the camper. Good. Sadie hadn't answered. Her old ears probably hadn't heard. From inside the house, footsteps padded toward the door. She held her breath as the door opened. She had to be alert should her sign come now. Instead a woman with a wonderful, kind face stood in the doorway smiling at her. This woman was younger than Cat had expected. With her short red hair and rosy cheeks, she was a whole lot prettier, too.

"Afternoon, ma'am," Cat said. "I'm looking for a Mrs. Marty Harris."

"You've found her," Marty said.

"Well, I'm hoping Dr. Brady told you about me 'cause he told me just to come on over. I'm Catherine O'Reilly. But everybody calls me Cat."

Clouds crossed the woman's eyes, but Cat stared right into them without blinking so the woman would see she was honest and could be trusted. Nana always said you could tell a lot about a person by looking in their eyes. Cat liked this woman's eyes. They were the color of moss. There was goodness and loyalty in them. But Cat saw sadness, too, probably for the dead husband Dr. Brady had told her about. "Please, Lord, let her like me," she prayed silently.

"You look very young, Cat," Marty said.

"No, ma'am, I'm nineteen," she replied, looking quickly away so the woman wouldn't catch the lie. Uncle Bud had lied so much about her age she just wasn't sure anymore, except that she was somewhere between seventeen and nineteen. Maybe she really was nineteen. She looked back and saw the woman studying her from head to toe, probably seeing how small and scrawny she was. "And I've been on my own a long time," Cat added.

Mrs. Harris still looked doubtful. Cat didn't usually do much talking—never could see where it did any good—but she guessed now she had some to do. And she'd better make it quick.

"I'm a whole lot stronger than I look and I expect to work hard for my money. I know about horses—been working at the racetrack the last little while, but I know a lot about all kinds of animals. Worked once in a pet store and another time on a working farm that had just about every farm animal you could think of." She stopped to catch her breath. The last wasn't exactly a lie. She'd worked on that farm the first time she'd run off from Uncle Bud. She'd only been a scared little kid of twelve or thirteen. The farm did have all kinds of animals, but Cat had worked in the fields with the pickers. She'd helped bring in first the bean crop and then the tomatoes, day after day in the blistering sun. But Uncle Bud had found her and dragged her off again on the tent circuit. She'd been on her own a mighty long time now. What with her new made-up name, she was sure he'd lost her trail. She'd be safe here. If only …

Mrs. Harris still seemed to be sizing her up. "I need to think about this a minute. I'll get my brother to show you around the barn and explain what we're trying to do here," she said. She turned and called over her shoulder, "Kyle."

A man appeared beside Mrs. Harris. He wore tight Wranglers and one of those big silver cowboy buckles. He was only a bit taller than his sister but younger by several years. In his early thirties, Cat guessed.

"Kyle, this is the girl Cam sent over about working for us," Marty said. "Her name's Catherine, but she says we're to call her Cat."

"Well, hi there, kiddo," he said, throwing an arm around his sister's neck. "Hey, Marty, you can call me anything you want as long as you don't call me late to dinner."

Cat forced her lips to curve upward. She knew a laugh would have been more friendly, but they didn't come easily to her.

"This goof is my brother Kyle. He fancies himself a comedian."

"Now, Marty, I just had to test the kid's sense of humor." He winked at Cat. "You passed, kid—barely, but I caught the smile."

Cat knew her cheeks were red.

"All right, Kyle," Marty said. "Stop teasing and show her the barn."

Kyle shrugged and shook his head. "If I were you, kid, I'd run while I had the chance. My sister is merciless. I'll show you the whip marks on my back." He turned around and started to lift the back of his T-shirt.

Marty smacked him playfully on the shoulder. "You're embarrassing Cat. Just show her around and behave yourself, all right?"

"Come on, Cat. The first thing you have to learn around here is that Marty's the boss," he said, and then continued in a stage whisper. "It makes her feel good, so we all make pretend it's so."

Cat tried to smile again so they'd like her. She wasn't sure yet about Kyle, but she really liked Marty. She fell into step beside this Pennsylvania cowboy. Even though she only came to his shoulder, she pumped her short legs hard to keep up with him as they climbed toward the barn. She suspected Marty was watching. She couldn't let Kyle outstride her. She set her jaw and climbed, moving ahead of him.

"Relax, kid," Kyle said, starting to breathe hard. "If I know my sister, you've got the job."

Cat slowed. All the way to the barn, she listened to Kyle's easy banter about the farm and the animals. At least with him gabbing, she didn't have to make conversation.

Inside the barn, he walked right over to the first stall. A big sorrel horse stood with his head hanging over the opened half of the door. "Marty's been working real hard fixing the place up," Kyle explained. "'Course, being my bossy big sister, she expects all of us to help, too."

Kyle threw his arm around the neck of the horse. He scratched absentmindedly under the horse's mane, and Cat waited for him to continue. "Well, I guess that's all right. Maybe even as it should be. I can't say my old man and I were doing much good by the place until Marty came back last month." Kyle smiled at her. "I'm rambling on. You have any questions you want to ask me?"

Cat shook her head and looked away, pretending to study the barn.

"Oh, so you're the quiet type, huh?"

Cat swallowed hard. "Well ... I mean sometimes I ..."

"That's okay, kid. It will be an absolute relief to have someone around here that doesn't run her mouth all the time. You'll find we Staffords are full of gab."

Cat looked up at Kyle, who had turned to smooth the big horse's mane. She guessed she would come to like this man. His easy ways seemed genuine. And he seemed to care about his sister, this farm, the horse who now nuzzled his cheek. She smiled.

He turned back to her. "Well, that's more like it," he said. "You should smile more often. You're very pretty when you do."

Cat stiffened. Maybe she'd been wrong about him.

"Easy now, girl," Kyle said, taking a step back and throwing his arms wide. "Don't bolt on me. I didn't mean anything by that. I have no idea how old you are, but I know how old I am and I don't hit on children."

Cat could feel the blood pounding in her throat as it rushed to redden her cheeks. If only she could think of something to say. She wanted him to know that she didn't go around thinking all men were after her. She just had to keep on her toes, that was all. She sneaked a look and found him staring at her. She turned to pat the red horse. Her hand shook as she laid it on his muzzle.

"I feel like I'm creeping up on a fawn in the woods. One wrong move and you'll bound away."

Out of the corner of her eye, Cat saw him start to reach toward her. She edged away and he dropped his hand.

"Good grief, girl, I was just going to pat my horse." He backed away again. "Please, look at me," he said, his voice strong, steady, and insistent. Cat forced herself to look right into his eyes and he continued. "I don't know where you've been or what you've been through, but no one here is going to hurt you. I can promise you that."

A huge gangly-legged pup galloped through the door, Marty behind him. The puppy leaped toward them, barking.

"Cody, you fool. Sit!" Kyle commanded. The puppy took a final leap to land beside Kyle and then flopped down, rolling over on his back. "That's not quite what I meant," Kyle said, scratching the pup's speckled belly.

The puppy lolled his head to the side to look up at Cat. She bent to give him a scratch, too. Still on his back, he wiggled toward her and licked her fingers.

"You seem to have Cody's vote," Marty said.

Cat stood. She sensed reluctance in Marty's voice. "I get along real good with animals, ma'am."

"She's got my vote, too, Sis."

"I think you'll do fine, Cat," Marty said.

Cat sighed deeply, then swallowed hard when she realized they must have heard her. It was never good to appear too eager.

"I can't talk about salary yet," Marty continued. "As Dr. Brady must have told you, we're building a therapeutic riding center here and I have to talk to Mr. Marcus, who handles the financial end of the endeavor. Kyle, I also need you to work on some specs for an apartment, say a couple of rooms attached to the new arena."

"I have my camper, ma'am," Cat said. "Just give me a hookup. I don't need more."

Marty gave her a hard look. "Yes, you do. Winters around here can be tough."

Cat looked down at her scuffed boots where the toes curled slightly. The corners of her eyes started to smart. She blinked. They couldn't be tears; she hadn't cried in years.

"Then it's settled," Marty said. "I'm guessing you can start right away."

Cat raised her head and looked Marty right in the eye. "Yes, indeed, I can."

From the far end of the barn, two more dogs tore in at a dead run. One, a shaggy Australian shepherd, had trouble keeping up with the other, a lean but sturdy blue heeler that barked ferociously. The heeler charged right at Cat, who froze with one hand extended.

"Bella, down!" roared Kyle. "Jake, sit."

The heeler dropped but looked ready to spring up in an instant and never took her eyes off Cat. The shaggy shepherd ignored Kyle and shuffled to a tail-wagging stop in front of Cat. She laid a hand on the shepherd's head.

"Kyle, you really have to do something about Bella," Marty said. "She terrifies everyone who comes here."

"It's all right, Mrs. Harris, I'm not afraid of dogs. Let her come and get to know me." Cat reached out her hand. "Come here, Bella." The dog scurried to her, sniffed her hand, and sat down, looking up at Cat, her tail thumping the ground.

"That's amazing," Kyle said. "Bella hates everyone but me."

"I get along good with most animals. And I guess I'd better tell you … I've got a dog of my own. She's just little. And old and crippled. I left her in the camper. She won't be a bother."

The gangly pup rolled to his feet and began to tussle with the shepherd. All three dogs took off after a calico kitten. The kitten leaped onto a post and climbed to the top of a stall. From somewhere in the barn a goat bleated. Marty laughed, a laugh that was even warmer than her smile. "Well, we seem to be running something of a menagerie here, so one more won't matter."

They walked out of the barn into the sunshine. High on the hill two mourning doves lifted off the barn roof. Cat watched them fly toward the woods. Her sign? She knew it was. And she would be safe here and she'd work hard. These were good people in a good place, the kind of place where she could make a life for herself. And they'd let her stay forever … if her luck held and they didn't find out about her.

TWO

Marty watched the girl climb up into her banged-up, rusted-out truck. The engine roared, then rumbled, then died. After several tries it came to life again, and with Kyle directing, Cat drove it around the side of the house to find the electrical hookup for her camper.

Marty wondered for the umpteenth time if she'd made the right decision this afternoon when she'd hired the girl. Everyone else seemed to think so, except Marty's fifteen-year-old son, Jeff, who said, "She is too weird for words, Mom." Of course, Cat had won eight-year-old Annie over with that pitiful one-eyed, three-legged terrier, a Jack Russell type but with dubious parentage.

As for Marty's brother and their dad, Duke, they always led with their hearts, so this poor waif had their vote before she even opened her mouth, which she didn't do often. Marty went to the phone to call Cam Brady and find out what he knew about this Cat O'Reilly.

Cam answered the phone on the second ring.

"All right, buddy, what's the deal on this kid you sent me?" Marty asked.

Cam's sunny chuckle answered. "And hello to you, too."

"This isn't a social call. What do you know about this girl?"

"Actually ... not much. Just that I've watched her with horses at the racetrack and she's good with them. A bad virus swept through the barn where she was working and her horses did better than any of the other grooms' did. She gave them the extra care they needed and ..." Cam hesitated.

"And what?"

"I don't know, just a feeling, but I think some of the guys there were harassing her, not just the other grooms but the boss, too. He is older and married, but he's got a reputation as a womanizer as well as being a cheat on the track. I mean, even if he wasn't bothering her, it's not the kind of place where a kid like her should be working."

"Cam Brady, I've known you all my life and I should have seen this coming. You don't know a thing about her. You found another bird with a broken wing, didn't you? And just like that crazy raccoon you rescued and then gave to Jeff, I'm stuck with her."

"Now, Marty, you do need help and she needed a boost. Seemed perfect to me. Besides, you didn't have to hire her. You could have sent her on her way."

Marty sighed and, in spite of herself, laughed.

"Couldn't do it, could you?" Cam asked.

"No, I couldn't and you knew I wouldn't be able to."

"Actually, yes, I did, and I think it's one of the nicest things about you, old friend," Cam said.

Herman, the abused raccoon, rescued but too habituated to people to be released, peered around the corner of the room. Marty glared at him, and with a squeak, he took off running. "And that's why this farm is filling up with ancient horses due for retirement, all kinds of debilitated animals, and even a psychologically damaged raccoon."

Herman again peeked around the corner. This time Marty bent over and made kissing noises to him. He scurried into her arms and she lifted him into her lap.

"Are you blowing me kisses?" Cam asked.

"Sorry, pal, I'm calling Herman." Marty smoothed the soft, black-tipped silver fur on the raccoon's back. Crazy critter. One minute he acted terrified and the next he fawned all over her. She gently rubbed behind his ears. He purred and curled up into a furry ball.

"You know, Marty, if this kid doesn't work out you can let her go. I didn't ask you to adopt her."

"I know. And I do think she'll probably be fine. It's just that there's a whole lot of misery behind those black eyes of hers, and I'd be more comfortable if I knew something about her background."

Jeff came running into the kitchen to ask when dinner would be ready, so Marty said her goodbyes to Cam and began rifling through the refrigerator to find something for dinner.

Ground meat, ground meat, and more ground meat. Kyle had been real imaginative when he'd gone to the store. She grabbed a package and threw it on the counter. Meatloaf would have to do. She wasn't feeling very creative herself.

And this was exactly the problem. Someone always had something for her to do. She had survived the death of her husband, but she had only just begun to heal. She'd been doomed from the beginning by her name. She was tired of being Martha. She needed to be Mary for a while; she needed space and quiet to sit at the feet of the Lord, trying to discern his will for her, asking him to remove the baggage of grief she carried.

She slammed a bowl on the counter and dumped in the meat, the eggs, instant onion, anything else that came easy to hand that might help. She kneaded the mixture with a vengeance. She certainly didn't need another wounded soul to care for, and this kid's wounds were apparent in every expression that flitted over that tiny heart-shaped face; they shone out of those sorrowful eyes.

When she had the meal well under way, Marty poured herself a glass of iced tea and sneaked into the living room, where she was fairly sure to be alone, especially since she'd removed the television. She sat in her favorite chair and took a deep drink of the amber liquid. She had just picked up the novel she was reading when she heard the screen door slam and Kyle call, "Sis?"

"In here," Marty said, sighing.

Kyle appeared in the doorway, his lopsided grin so like Duke's. "Hey, how about Cat and I go take care of the feeding? I can show her who gets what and then she'll be all set for the morning."

"Great," Marty said. Maybe hiring Cat hadn't been such a bad idea. If she didn't get all entangled in this kid's problems, then having help would give her some "Marty" time.

"Well, then you get a move on, woman. I'm starving. Tit for tat. I feed the animals, you feed me. By the way, Duke told Cat she'd be eating with us. I hope you don't mind."

Marty shot him a glare, but he was gone with no indication he'd caught it. Since when did he think she needed a push to get things going? She was the one who had to keep after the rest of them. She hauled herself to her feet and headed back toward the kitchen.

She waded right in and began the final preparations for dinner. Habit took over as she worked to make the meal a nice one. She had always believed in making mealtimes special for the family, and besides, they might as well present a civilized front for Cat.

But dinner was a disaster right from the beginning. Cat and Kyle walked into the kitchen just as Jeff was saying, "Have you seen that dog of hers? It's only got three legs and it's missing an eye."

Marty arched an eyebrow at him, then tried to rescue the moment as she laughed and said, "And this from the boy who lives with a psychotic raccoon."

"Herman is only neurotic." Jeff flopped onto his chair.

An uneasy silence lasted until Duke sauntered into the room with Annie on his shoulders. As soon as they were all seated, Duke offered the blessing. "Dear Lord, we thank you for this food we are about to receive. We ask that you let it nourish our bodies as your love nourishes our souls. We thank you, too, for this new young person here with us," he said, reaching over to pat Cat on the arm.

Out of the corner of her eye, Marty saw Cat stiffen. She was a strange one. When they all chorused their amens, Cat joined in with more feeling than Marty had heard in her voice all day. That, at least, was a good sign, an obvious indication of some kind of faith. She'd have to remember to ask her if she wanted to go to church with them on Sunday.

The food made the rounds, each of them helping themselves, Cat annoyingly mumbling, "Thank you, ma'am," every time Marty handed her a serving dish.

With forks at the ready, they dug into their food, all except Cat, who forced a tiny spoonful of potatoes between her lips.

"Kyle, pass the meatloaf over here," Marty said. "Cat didn't get any."

"That's okay," Cat said.

"Nonsense, child," Duke said. "We need to get some meat on those bones of yours."

Cat's cheeks turned crimson. She dropped her hands in her lap and didn't take the meat plate Duke held out to her. "I ... I don't eat meat."

"That's a new one. A vegetarian Cat," Jeff whispered to Kyle loud enough for everyone to hear.

"No wonder you're such a tiny thing!" Duke bellowed. He patted his ample belly and sat straighter in his chair. "Your bones never got what they needed to shoot you up right. Now come on. Just try a little piece."

"Dad," Marty warned. "Leave Cat alone. Lots of people are vegetarians these days. I really believe eliminating or limiting meat is a healthy way to eat."

"I just never could eat it," Cat said, stealing a look at Marty.

Marty could feel Duke fidgeting in his chair and gave him a warning look. She had never seen such an incredulous expression on her father's face. The farmer and hunter in him probably couldn't imagine someone actually choosing not to eat meat. Marty decided to drop it. From the look on Cat's face, it was obvious that any further discussion on the subject would ruin the meal for her. She had already stopped eating.

"Lighten up, Dad," Kyle said. "You know Kristen? She doesn't eat meat, either. Lots of people don't these days."

Jeff "humphed" loudly. Cat put down her fork and stared into her plate. Marty's foot hit Kyle's as they both went to kick Jeff under the table.

Now Duke was staring at Kyle. "Kristen? That pretty gal you've been squiring around town? The one who's helping Marty and Sam with the stable? She's one of those vege—whatsits?"

"Vegetarian, Grandpap." Annie looked at Cat and giggled, like she'd been giggling through the whole meal. Cat gave a tiny smile in response.

Marty took her chance and launched into a breathless description of all the wonderful ideas Kristen had for the Center. It worked; Cat was no longer the focus of their attention, but she still didn't eat much—barely enough to survive, Marty judged. She needed to talk to this kid.

"Jeff, will you please do the dishes tonight?" Marty asked, more of a command than a request. It was the least he could do to compensate for his rudeness.

Jeff scowled but rose and carried his dishes to the sink.

"Come on, princess," Duke said to Annie. "How about a game of dominoes?"

As they disappeared around the corner, Kyle pulled himself to his feet. "I'll help old pouty boy," Kyle said. "The two of us are getting pretty good at kitchen duty."

"Good," Marty said. "Come on, Cat, let's sit on the porch. You can tell me about yourself."

The look on Cat's face was one of total discomfort. Mercy would dictate letting the kid off the hook, but Marty had a few questions she needed answered.

On the porch, Marty took her position on the swing. Cat eased into a wicker armchair, perching on the edge as if she were ready for flight.

"So, Cat," Marty began, keeping her voice low and soothing. "Where are you from?"

"West Virginia," the girl answered.

"Then you have family nearby."

Cat just shook her head, her eyes not meeting Marty's.

"No family here? Or no family anywhere?"

Cat set her jaw and met Marty's eyes. Now only her red cheeks showed her discomfort. "Never knew my daddy. Died before I was born."

"What about your mother?"

"Mamma was sick, too. She didn't do so good after Daddy was gone. She died, too."

"Oh, Cat, I'm so sorry." No wonder the child didn't want to talk about herself. "Who raised you?"

Cat hesitated. "A neighbor lady. I called her Nana, but she was no relation. But there's no one else."

This last came in a rush and Marty knew there was more behind it.

Cat stood. "I think I'd better turn in now, ma'am."

"Certainly, Cat," Marty said. "I'm not far from bed myself. It's been a big day for all of us." Cat hurried toward the steps. "Cat?"

The girl stopped and turned back to Marty, her expression hard to read.

Marty smiled. "I'm glad Dr. Brady sent you to us. We're going to get along just fine."

Cat nodded before darting off around the corner of the house toward her trailer.

Marty sat back down on the swing and pushed off with one foot, letting the sway soothe her. Poor kid. Well, okay, so now, in spite of all her good intentions, she was involved. It would be cruel not to be.

Marty couldn't imagine what it would be like to be totally alone in the world. Almost nine months ago when she'd lost her husband, she'd thought she and the kids were all alone, but she'd been wrong. She'd come back home, where Duke and Kyle and all her old friends had been waiting to take her in, to hold her and love her and help her through her grieving. And dear Dan had given her children, their Annie and Jeff, so she'd never really been alone. Not like Cat.

Jeff barged through the kitchen door, letting it bang shut behind him. Marty patted the swing next to her and he squeezed into it. She put her arm around his shoulder. "Have I told you lately how much I love you?"

"Yeah, when you came home this afternoon. Now, don't you go getting weird on me." He stayed snuggled into her shoulder.

Marty relaxed, enjoying the closeness that came rarely these days with her hotshot teenager. But then the recent flood and Annie's hospitalization had been hard on all of them. By the Lord's grace and with each other's help, they'd pulled through just fine. Unlike Cat, who had no one, they had each other.

"Jeff, that poor girl does not have a soul in the world—no relatives anywhere," Marty said. "It just makes me appreciate my family."

"Thanks, Mom. I appreciate you, too. For one thing dinner was better tonight than it's been with Kyle and me cooking."

Marty laughed and they swung on the swing in easy silence, the only sounds the gurgling of the stream and an occasional rustling of the tree leaves as an evening breeze began to blow.

"I don't buy it, Mom," Jeff said.

"What?"

"That she's got no one. Everyone has someone, somewhere. An aunt. An uncle. Cousins. Somebody. She's not telling you the whole story."

"Jeff, what's wrong with you? You aren't usually so tough on people."

"Mom, there's something not right about this girl. I just know it. And she's so dark skinned. Maybe she's an Indian. You know, a Hindu-type Indian. That would explain the no meat."

"I certainly hope, Jeff Harris, that you are not implying that would be a problem."

"Mom, please. You and Dad raised me better than that, but there's something this girl's not telling us and it bugs me."

"Maybe it's none of our business."

Kyle's chuckle came from the doorway. "Well, that's a new one, Sis. Since when did you start keeping your nose out of other people's business?"

"Kyle! You make me sound like Aunt Bertie. I do not pry into other people's affairs."

"Come on, Uncle Kyle, give Mom a break," Jeff said. "Aunt Bertie tries to run the whole town. We're the only ones Mom bosses around."

"That's it," Marty said. She stood and started toward the door. "I'm too tired to sit out here and be insulted by the two of you. Good night." She pulled open the door and turned to smile at them. "And hey, I'm real glad to be home. I love you guys."

Later she lay in the bedroom that had been hers as a girl, listening to the sleeping sighs of her daughter in the next bed and worrying about the strange girl who had come into her life that day. Had God sent her to them because he knew they'd take care of her? Or was Jeff right? If Cat was lying to them, then they'd have to be a bit leery of her. Maybe she was just trying to hide some kind of racially mixed parentage. Then Marty would have to tell her there was no need to, not with them. They weren't bigots. Either way Marty would just have to find out more about her; that was all there was to it.

THREE

Cat jumped from the dank stuffiness of the camper into the cool morning air. As her feet hit the ground she heard a splash behind her. A doe and twin fawns, large but still white speckled across their backs, darted across the creek and up the opposite hillside. A silver-sided trout leaped from the stream. All good omens.

And she hadn't had the dream last night, the horrible nightmare that had plagued her for months. She sniffed, testing the air. Damp ground. Moss growing. Water-logged wood. And something else. Geraniums. Yes, she'd seen them growing in a planter on the porch rail. Sadie whined and she lifted the old dog to the ground.

While Sadie snuffled around in the weeds by the creek bank, Cat studied the house. No signs of anyone else up yet. Good. With a little luck, she'd be well into her work before anyone else showed up at the barn.

Sadie hopped along beside her as Cat climbed the hill to the barn. Mourning doves cooed from the roof. Songbirds twittered in the trees. The sun hung low in the blue-gray sky, not yet hot enough to burn off the dew.

As she got closer to the barn the horses nickered. "I'm coming now," she soothed. "I'm coming." She walked into the barn and the nickering became insistent. Farther down the aisle the goat bleated. "Easy, my friends. Soon enough you'll all have your food." The kittens started toward her but stopped when they saw Sadie. "It's all right," she told them. "Sadie won't hurt you." The kittens approached cautiously. Sadie ignored them, heading off to explore the barn. The kittens rushed forward to mill around Cat's feet.

The tiny calico dug his claws into her jeans and began to climb her leg. "Okay, little one," Cat said, plucking him off her knee. She held him to her chest and rubbed her chin against the kitten's furry head.

On a shelf in the feed room she found the kitty chow and poured a dish for the kittens. She put the little calico down with the others. There now. She could feed the horses without tripping over the kittens. The thought made her shudder. Kittens this little were so vulnerable.

She filled a bucket with grain and tossed in the measuring scoop. The sweet smell of the feed blended with the warm earthy smell of horses and the ripe smell of stored hay. Cat breathed in the familiar odors that both calmed and enlivened her. She moved in and out of each stall with surety. Before dumping the feed into the bucket, she let each horse eat a few mouthfuls from her hands. Each one in turn sniffed and licked her hands, searching for more. And all the while she whispered to them, letting them get to know her as she came to know them. Then she moved on to let them eat in peace.

After she fed Daisy the goat, she sat in the stall, cross-legged in the straw. Goats weren't particular about company while they ate. Not like horses were. Daisy didn't even seem to care when Sadie joined them and curled up in Cat's lap. Cat closed her eyes. "Thank you, Lord. You've brought me to a good place."

By the time Marty walked into the barn, Cat had fed and watered all the animals and was hauling the big blue manure tub to Red's stall to start mucking it out. "My goodness, but you start early," Marty said. "It's just seven."

"Yes, ma'am. I get more done that way."

Marty laughed. "I'm sure you do. I appreciate a self-starter."

Cat's chest expanded in an inward smile as she led Red from his stall. She fastened him into the crossties and dragged the bucket into his stall. She dug right into the job at hand. As she dragged the full container from the stall, she saw Marty watching her.

"I guess we're going to have to get another muck bucket so that two of us can work at once," Marty said.

"There's not so many stalls here to do," Cat said.

"It's easier when we can turn the horses out after they eat, but today I'd rather give the ground some time to dry out. I'll help you with that later. Right now I'm feeling pretty useless. Tell you what ... I have some work at the house this morning and then some calls to make about the therapeutic riding center. I'll be back up in a little while to help you turn the horses out."

When Marty had gone, Cat hurried to finish the stalls. She wanted to be all done, with the aisle swept clean, by the time her boss returned.

But by the time Cat was done and looking for more work, Marty still hadn't returned. Cat stepped outside the barn and looked toward the house. A car was in the driveway. Marty stood on the porch talking to someone. A man. A tall man with gray hair.

No. Not so soon. Not after so many years. Cat could feel sweat beading on her forehead. She turned and ran around the back of the barn. Sadie gave a sharp yip and hobbled after her, so the girl scooped up the small dog and raced across the area where the indoor arena was being built. Mud sucked at her boots, slowing her down. She pumped her shaking legs harder and almost fell. Sadie whined and she clapped a hand over the dog's muzzle. "Quiet, girl. You gotta be quiet." Holding Sadie close, she ran on toward the woods. Uncle Bud may have found her, but she wouldn't let him catch her.

Just as she reached the trees, she glanced at the house. Marty gestured toward the barn and started down a step. Before Uncle Bud could turn and see her, she charged through the underbrush into the woods. Canes of pricker bushes whipped at her face and arms. Again Sadie whined. Letting go of the dog's muzzle, Cat shielded her face and her dog with an outstretched hand as she charged on. When she was deep enough into the trees not to be seen, she stopped. The scratches on her arms stung. She could feel the sticky warmth of blood. But she didn't look. Sadie squirmed and Cat loosened her too-tight hold, lifting the dog like a baby against her shoulder. As Cat willed Sadie to be quiet, she could feel the dog snuggle against her.

Cat leaned back against a tree, afraid to move, almost afraid to breathe for fear she'd be heard. She had no idea how long she stood like that before she heard Marty's voice calling her from the barn. Cat squeezed her eyes shut and buried her face against Sadie's side. When she opened her eyes again and looked upward, a crow peered down at her from a branch not far above.

Everybody back home knew about crows; they were messengers of evil. She forced herself to stare into the crow's eyes and shivered. She silently commanded him not to give her away. The crow looked back with his beady black eyes. He cocked his head first one way then another. Finally, he hopped to a higher branch and then flew deeper into the woods.

Cat slumped to the ground, her back still against the tree. Sadie's warm tongue licked her hand. Rhythmically she stroked Sadie's back as her own shaking eased and her breath returned to normal. But behind her breastbone, her heart still pounded hard.

No one called her, but Uncle Bud was still near. She could feel his presence. She eased to her feet. A deer path lay on the other side of some undergrowth. Still clutching Sadie, Cat waded through the briars. When she reached the path, she crept away from the barn. Toward what? She didn't know or care.

The path wound through tall pine trees. Cat followed it, moving silently like the Delaware Indian who had been her great-grandfather. The path led to a clearing. Cat looked up at the ring of tall pines, and a sense of peace crept into her heart. She'd be safe here. She sank down onto the bed of dry brown pine needles.

Sadie wiggled in her arms. She freed the dog, who sniffed, circled, and then lay down beside her. Cat's mind raced. How had Uncle Bud found her? How did he always find her? But this time it had been years. She had been so careful to erase all trace of herself. She'd even bought a phony driver's license from some creep at the track. Katie Parker no longer existed.

It had been so long since Cat had even thought the name. Now it bombarded her with images. Katie Parker—a little girl in a ruffled white dress ... a makeshift stage in a tent ... or in a field ... or on the altar of some church ... all the hopeful ill waiting for their miracle ... all waiting for Katie. Cat again began to shiver. She willed the memories away, but they kept coming....

"I can't do it, Uncle Bud," the little girl cried.

Before she could jump away he grabbed her arm and twisted. He didn't slap her face anymore. Makeup didn't cover those red welts and bruises. Katie clenched her jaw, grinding her teeth. She wouldn't cry. She wouldn't.

"Now, you listen here, you worthless brat," Uncle Bud hissed in her ear. Katie could smell the peppermint on his breath, and also the whiskey smell he was trying to cover. "If you don't go out there and give those folks what they've come for, I'll beat the tar out of you. You understand that, don't you, you ..." He twisted her arm again.

A lady with curly hair the color of sunflowers pulled Katie away. Her bracelets jingled as she put her arms around the little girl. "Get out of here, Bud Parker. Let me talk to her," the woman snapped.

"There now, girl," the woman soothed as she lifted the little girl onto her lap. Katie liked this woman. She smelled like lilacs.

She was better than the usual sort Uncle Bud picked up on the road, and she'd been with them longer than most. "Now, Katie, you don't need to worry. I heard him talking to the boys and everything's taken care of. They've got a few ringers in the crowd. All you got to do is pretend to fix 'em up. Their crutches will fall away. Everyone will cheer and we can go home."

Katie shook her head. "No," she said. The lady didn't understand. It was all that sorrowfulness and pain, all those people who really needed help. When Katie was out there on stage she felt it. Almost like it was hers.

"Now, darlin', listen to me." The woman held Katie close. "You know what Bud's like. He's not going to give up 'til you do what he wants. The harder you make it on him, the tougher he'll be on us after the show."

Katie buried her face against the woman's shoulder. The nice lady rocked Katie in her arms and laid a tear-soaked cheek against Katie's forehead. But Katie didn't cry. She knew the woman was right. She pulled away and climbed off her lap. "I'll do it," she whispered. "Because you want me to."

"No, honey girl, I don't want you to," the woman said. "But I don't think you have much of a choice in the matter."

So Katie went out on stage and faced all the yearning sorrow of the hurting crowd. She begged God to help her. She did her best. She did it for God and for the nice lady. But the next day the woman was gone, and Uncle Bud was meaner than ever.

"Cat," called Marty, from far away but closer than before. "Cat, where are you?"

"No," Cat whispered. "No." She curled around Sadie, hiding her face against the dog's side. She shut her eyes tight and prayed they wouldn't find her here.

FOUR

Cat opened her eyes. She had no idea how long she'd lain on the forest floor. A pretty good while, she guessed. Sadie had long since wandered off to sniff the weeds across the clearing. Cat sat up, crossing her legs under her, but they felt cramped. She pulled herself to her feet and stretched. Safe.

She'd creep to the edge of the woods. Make sure the car was gone and then she'd go back to work. But what would she tell Mrs. Harris?

Voices and hoofbeats in the woods on the hill above startled her. The voices were getting closer. First Mrs. Harris. Then a man's voice, but not Uncle Bud's. That voice she knew. His throaty drawl lurked in her memory just below awareness, waiting to catch her off guard.

She had to be careful. Even now, what would Mrs. Harris think, finding her here? Cat dashed across the clearing and grabbed Sadie, looking for a route of escape. She was about to plunge through the underbrush when she saw a path leading away from the clearing. She took it at a run.

She ran until she could no longer hear the voices or the horses' hooves. She slowed as the path wound steadily downhill. Pines and sometimes a spindly-trunked hardwood rose on either side. The path ended in a bright meadow just above the farmhouse. The strange car was still parked in front. Cat studied it. Uncle Bud never drove a car that fancy. At least, not since they'd hit hard times. Why had she been so certain the gray-haired man was Uncle Bud? She had to get a grip on herself. She'd acted like a total fool. If she could just make it back to the barn unseen, then at least no one would know about it.

Below her, near the house, Jeff was clearing debris from the recent flood. He didn't like her. She had to be extra careful around people like that. She crept along the edge of the woods, keeping to the shade, hiding from the light. When she rounded a bend where trees hid her from the house, she dashed uphill toward the barn.

She burst, out of breath, into the barn. Halfway down the aisle, Annie brushed her ancient pony.

"Whew," said the little girl. "I thought you were Mom. She thinks I'm still resting in the house."

Cat filled her lungs with air, willing herself to sound relaxed. "I think your mother will be here soon."

Annie frowned. "It's all right. I mean, she didn't really say I couldn't come to the barn. It's just …"

Cat walked toward the little girl. The calico kitten, Lucky, sat on the shelf beside the extra brushes looking warily at Sadie. Ignoring the kitten, the dog flopped down and curled up against the wall. Cat picked up a brush and went to work on the pony's other side. She smiled at Annie. Annie was gentle, kind, and good. Cat couldn't explain it, but she just knew things about people. Nana said it was part of her gift.

"Mom worries a lot," Annie said. "And I've been sick. I drank some water with some kind of germ in it and had to go to the hospital and the bridge was flooded, so Mom had to carry me out and she was scared."

Annie didn't seem to need a response. Cat kept brushing her side of the pony and listened. She could just imagine Mrs. Harris scaling the steep hillside behind the house with Annie. No doubt about it, her new boss was a woman to be reckoned with. Cat didn't find the thought comforting. As Annie talked on, Cat looked up into the little girl's still-pale face.

"I missed Cocoa too much to stay all day at the house. And Lucky's my favorite kitten. I think she was missing me, because she's been sticking right with me, like Sadie does with you," Annie said. "I told Grandpap where I was going and he said it was fine. But Mom ... I guess she worries so much because my dad died."

The silence that followed tugged at Cat. She looked up and saw Annie watching her. "I know," Cat said softly. She studied the child's face, looking deep into her eyes, seeking what was behind them. Cat smiled. "You're not going to die. You're all better now."

Annie smiled back. "I know. I keep telling everyone that."

"So here you are, Cat," Duke boomed as he shuffled breathless into the barn. "Where have you been? Marty was looking for you, young lady."

Cat pulled away from the pony. How could she possibly explain why she'd run to the woods?

Duke came toward them huffing and puffing. Cat's mind raced for an explanation.

"Ha! From the looks of you, girl, you must have been in the woods. You've got pine needles stuck in your hair," Duke said. He slumped down onto the bench by the tack room door. Sweat beaded his forehead, but at least he seemed to be catching his breath.

Cat ran her hands over her hair. Pine needles fell against her shoulders and onto the floor. "Your woods are beautiful," she said.

"So you're an explorer, are you? When I was young, I took to the woods every chance I got. Did you see the big pine clearing? That was always one of my favorite places," he said.

"Mom showed me that," Annie said. "She likes it, too."

"She used to call it her woodland cathedral," Duke said. He mopped his bald head with a handkerchief.

Cat heard hoofbeats approaching the barn. She gathered up some of the extra brushes from the shelf by the crossties and headed toward the tack room. She hadn't had to lie to Mr. Stafford or Annie, but Mrs. Harris had a powerful curiosity. She wouldn't let Cat off so easily.

Inside the tack room, Cat heard the metallic clip-clop of horseshoes on the asphalt aisle. She busied herself straightening the grooming tools on their shelf.

"Annie, what are you doing? You should be taking it easy for another day or so," Marty said, an edge of worry in her tone.

"I'll go back down soon, Mom. I just had to see Cocoa and my kittens and Daisy."

Cat heard the warm ripple of Mrs. Harris' laugh. "You know, I do believe you have more color in your cheeks."

"She looks like the picture of health to me," said the man's voice Cat had heard in the woods.

"That she does," Duke said. "And thank the Lord for it."

"I can see Cat hasn't shown up yet," Marty said, the edge back in her tone. "I can't imagine where that girl has gone. I'm not sure—"

"Relax now, Marty," Duke said. "She's back. She just went for a walk in the woods."

Cat slipped from the tack room. "I hope you don't mind, Mrs. Harris," she said, hurrying to Marty's side to take the saddle she was pulling off the bay mare.

"Of course, I don't mind," Marty said. "You had already done your work. It's just that I didn't know where you'd gone. My goodness, your arms are all scratched up."

"It's nothing, ma'am. I just tangled with a pricker bush."

"There's some hydrogen peroxide in the first-aid kit. That's the one mounted on the wall in the tack room. Better put some on the cuts," Marty fussed.

Cat felt the warmth coming to her cheeks. She sneaked a look at the man unsaddling the gray mare. Like Uncle Bud he had gray hair, was tall and thin. The man smiled at her. Cat got the same kind of feeling from him that she got from Annie. This man was nothing like Uncle Bud. "Hello, sir," she said.

"Cat, this is Sam Marcus," Marty said. "I was calling you to meet him. Sam's foundation is funding our Center."

"Please, Cat, call me Sam," he said. His voice was strong, but kind and filled with good intentions. "And welcome aboard. We've got big plans, and we're going to need your help."

"Yes, sir, Mrs. Harris has told me." Cat hauled the saddle into the tack room. She hefted it over her head onto its rack, then returned to fetch Mr. Marcus' saddle to show him she was a good worker.

"I've got it, Cat," he said. "Good exercise for me."

Cat hurried to the gray mare's stall and got her halter. She then replaced the mare's bridle with the fancy leather halter and snapped a lead rope to the brass ring. She scratched the mare's forehead. The mare lowered her head and moved it against Cat's fingers. Cat sensed that the horse was steady and reliable, just like her owner. Cat usually had no trouble figuring out animals or people; Mrs. Harris, however, was proving a tougher case.

Sam took the lead rope from Cat. "Well, I thank you and Grandma thanks you. Don't you, old girl?" Sam said, rubbing the mare's neck. Grandma lifted her head and curled her lip. "See there? She's thanking you herself."

Cat hung the bridle in the tack room and hurried to help Mrs. Harris, but Marty had already taken the bay mare to her stall. Cat grabbed the broom and swept up the hair on the floor around the pony.

"Doesn't she look beautiful, Cat?" Annie asked.

Cat looked at the sunken-eyed, swaybacked pony. Still, the pony's coat had a good shine to it. And gloss rarely showed on age-faded brown. Cocoa's white mane and tail hung thick and knot-free. Her full forelock fluffed straight down the center of her tiny face. "Sure does," Cat said.

"Cat," Marty called. "Let's turn Red and these others out. The ground's still too wet to leave them out all day. I don't want the pasture torn up, but I do want them to be able to move around for a while."

"I'll help you," Sam said, heading for the old racing mare's stall.

Cat had just picked up a lead rope when Sam called. "I think we've got a problem here."

Cat knew the minute she stepped into Glory Girl's stall that something was seriously wrong. The mare stood with her head drooped between her knees. Half of her breakfast still lay in her feed tub. Her hay had been scattered, but not much had been eaten. The mare nipped at her sweat-soaked side. "Colic," Cat said as Marty bustled into the stall. Marty began to check for herself, but Cat was sure it was colic. Not good anytime, but worse in an old horse like Glory Girl.

"Hold her head, Cat," Marty said.

Cat took the mare by her halter. Marty laid her ear against the mare's flank. Cat scanned the straw. "Mrs. Harris, I cleaned her stall early this morning. I'm not seeing any manure here."

"I'll bet we've got a blockage," Marty said. She went to the stall door. "Duke, run to the house and call Cam. Tell him to get out here on the double. We've got trouble. Colic with a possible impaction." She took the lead rope from Sam and hooked it to the mare's halter. "Cat, you get her moving. I'll get an injection of pain killer ready."

Cat took the lead rope and led the old mare down the aisle. By the time she had turned and brought her back to the stall, Marty stood waiting with the injection and an alcohol swab. Without the least hesitation, Marty swabbed the mare's neck and plunged the needle into her muscle.

"Cat, let me take her," Marty said, taking the lead rope and handing Cat the empty syringe and swab. "This is the best we can do for her until Cam gets here." Marty pulled on the mare. With a groan the old mare started walking up the aisle again.

While Mrs. Harris was taking care of Glory Girl, Cat with Sam's help turned the other horses out in the hillside pasture. Cat's mind raced. Right now the mare wasn't too bad, just starting into it. She didn't think it was a serious blockage. But what if Dr. Brady didn't get there in time? No, she wouldn't think about that. He had to.

"I need some help in here," Marty yelled.

Cat took off at a dead run. As she rounded the corner into the barn, she saw the mare sink to the ground. Annie ran to help.

"Stay back, Annie," Marty yelled.

Cat hurried to catch the little girl's arm. "If the mare starts to roll around, you could get kicked."

Annie backed off to the bench. Cat rushed to Marty, who hauled on the lead rope. The muscles in Marty's arms lifted hard and defined on her forearms. Cat reached to help. Like her, Marty was stronger than she looked. Finally, by clapping and shouting and prodding they got the mare back on her feet.

"I sure hope Duke's been able to get ahold of Cam," Sam said.

So did Cat. They needed Dr. Brady now. If the mare would just keep moving, she might pass the impaction. If she went down again and refused to get up.... Cat laid her hand against the mare's side. She tried to focus but there was too much confusion. She needed to get the mare alone, close her eyes, concentrate only on the mare, say the prayer. Then she might know how much time they had. She couldn't let the mare die without trying to help. But then Mrs. Harris, Mr. Marcus, all of them, would know about her. She'd only just come here; she wanted more time.

Duke, red-faced and gasping for air, stumbled into the barn. "I got him," he puffed. "He's not far from here." Duke threw himself down on the bench and leaned back against the wall. His chest rose and fell rapidly. "Should be here in about ..." he took several deep breaths before going on, "ten minutes."

Cat turned back to the mare. She'd hold 'til Dr. Brady got there. She shut her eyes. *Thank you, Lord. Oh, I thank you for not making me reveal myself,* she prayed silently. When she opened her eyes, she saw Duke, his eyes closed, his chest still heaving. The color in his face had faded to storm cloud gray. She started toward him. He couldn't wait; he needed help right now.

FIVE

Cat squeezed next to Duke on the bench. He hardly seemed to notice she was there. His lips moved but Cat couldn't make out what he said. She leaned closer.

"I just need a minute," he said.

Cat took his hand. She could almost feel the life oozing out of him. She fought to recall the ancient words, the holy words from Ezekiel. Nana said it wasn't the words that mattered; she could call on the Lord in her own way. But Cat had never tried without the special prayer. And now her mind was blank. "Please, my Lord Jesus," she whispered. The words came back in a rush as clear as the day the old healer woman had taught them to her. She said them as quietly as she could. Her hands grew warm and she could feel the Lord working through her.

Duke's eyes fluttered opened. He looked at her, confused. She let go of his hand. She shot a glance over her shoulder. Marty, Sam, and Annie were busy with Glory Girl. And Duke didn't seem to realize what had happened.

"My goodness," he said. "I was feeling pretty poorly there for a minute." He looked hard at Cat.

"That's why I came over. You didn't look so good."

"All of a sudden like, I felt fine," he said. "Strange."

Cat stood. "Sometimes it happens like that." She looked straight into his eyes and willed him to accept that simple explanation.

"Well, I guess so." He still looked powerfully puzzled.

Cat jumped to her feet. "I'd better get back to help with the mare."

"You do that, girl," Duke said. "I'll go watch for Cam."

By the time Dr. Brady arrived, both crises were over. Duke's cheeks were petunia pink again and Glory Girl had passed a huge pile of manure. Dr. Brady checked the mare anyway.

"I'd like to tube her and get some mineral oil into her system. If she's thinking about blocking up again that will help."

Dr. Brady had come into the barn prepared. Cat stepped forward to help. "That's all right, Cat," Marty said. "I'll hold her."

Cat stood with Sam and watched as Dr. Brady ran the rubber tubing through Glory Girl's nostril, feeling her throat to make sure it went where it should. The mare pulled back and tried to shake her head. Instantly, Marty adjusted to hold her tighter, talking soothingly the whole while. Glory calmed down and Dr. Brady continued to push the tube toward her stomach. Sam turned away.

"I don't think I want to watch this," he said.

Even Cat winced when Dr. Brady blew in the tube and then put it to his nose, sniffing for the rank stomach gas to be sure he hadn't run the tube into the mare's lungs, instead of her stomach. But Marty never flinched. She held Glory firmly, as the container of mineral oil flowed into the mare. The only sign Cat saw that Mrs. Harris was at all nervous was the way her shoulders relaxed when the tube was withdrawn. It occurred to Cat that her boss was one of those women whose strength showed most in an emergency.

Dr. Brady turned to Cat. "Now, Cat, you keep an eye on her stall. You'll soon get an idea of how much manure she usually passes. If that changes, call me."

Cat nodded. She liked Dr. Brady. He was smart and, from what she'd seen at the track, the best vet around. Unlike some men, he didn't parade his virtues like a badge. Most men didn't have as much goodness as he did to be flaunting anyway. And she knew he walked easy with the Lord. She'd heard him whispering a prayer as he treated one of the racehorses a while back.

"Well, if we're all done here," Marty said. "Let's go down to the house and I'll fix everyone some lunch."

"Go ahead, ma'am," Cat said after everyone had agreed. "I have a few more things to do up here first."

"I don't starve my help," Marty said. "Do what you have to and then hurry down because I will be waiting lunch for you."

Cat watched them go and sank down on the bench. Truth to tell, she was wrung out and needed some time alone. She wished Mrs. Harris would quit pushing all this togetherness stuff. Couldn't she tell how uncomfortable all the fuss made her?

Through the open barn door, she saw Dr. Brady watching Mrs. Harris as they walked down the hill. Mrs. Harris was a take-charge lady, strong of body and mind. But as smart as she was, she still missed some things that were right under her nose. Like the fact that Dr. Brady really cared about her. And that Annie was healthy now, but her father wasn't. Well, he was now, but he hadn't been.

Cat shook her head. Mrs. Harris would take some getting used to. Cat pulled herself to her feet to sweep the barn aisle. She still felt weak and shaky. Back when she was a little kid, healing didn't take so much out of her. Used to be each time she felt wonderful—grateful to God and exultant like the angels. She was still thankful, mightily so. She knew the Lord, for reasons of his own, didn't always answer her prayer. Uncle Bud had never understood that. He thought it was something she could just turn on and off, like a faucet. She'd had quite a few hidings over it. Maybe that's where the exaltation went. Or maybe she'd just plumb worn out.

Her stomach growled. Maybe Mrs. Harris was right and some lunch would help. But down at the house, the gabby group around the kitchen table only taxed her further. At least Kyle wasn't there to tease, but Jeff's sour looks kept her on edge. The only time that kid looked even halfway pleasant was when he was talking to Dr. Brady. Cat caught the drift that Dr. Brady, in addition to his regular patients, also took care of sick wild creatures. Jeff helped out once in a while. Maybe Cat needed to give Jeff some time. Maybe he was better than he seemed.

"And, Cat, what were you doing in the woods earlier?" Mrs. Harris asked.

"Now, when you were a young girl, and you'd go disappearing on your mamma and me, what would you have said?" Duke asked.

"I guess I'd have said, 'On a beautiful day like today, who needs a reason?'" Marty said. Her lovely green eyes shone, predicting a smile even before her lips curved upward.

"I rest my case," Duke answered.

Cat wasn't aware she'd asked him to handle her case. Still she was grateful to have the discussion ended.

Halfway through the meal, Dr. Brady's beeper went off. He thanked everyone and left, giving Marty an extra long look that only Cat seemed to notice. As the others finished eating and wandered off, Sam spoke up. "Cat, why don't you stick around a minute? Marty and I want to discuss your terms of employment, make sure everything's all right with you."

Cat sat uneasily on the edge of her seat. All she wanted was a place to stay where she could care for animals, a place where she and Sadie would be welcome. She thought of Jeff. She thought of Mrs. Harris' probing. Well, if not welcomed, at least a place where she'd be safe. All this talk was unnecessary. The money didn't mean much. As long as she had enough to send Nana every month. A little extra for food for her and Sadie.

"Now, I've done some checking and I know we can't pay what you were making at the racetrack," Sam said. "Their salaries are high."

When Sam named the salary figure, Cat's jaw dropped. They

were going to pay her more—much more—than she'd been making at the racetrack. Just as she'd guessed, that weasel boss of hers had been cheating her. Probably charging the owners the full amount and pocketing the rest, because he knew she'd have never asked anyone else what they were getting.

"Will that be all right with you, Cat?" Marty asked.

"That's more than fine, ma'am. Sir."

"Of course, you can continue to take your meals with us, if you like."

"I don't want to be a problem. I have a hot plate in the camper."

"If you can put up with our chaos and my cooking, you're welcome to eat with us," Marty said. "At least, until the apartment is finished."

"And honestly, Cat," Sam said, "after we get running we may find we can pay you more. We just aren't sure about how much everything's going to cost. How many riders we will get. Lots of things are up in the air right now."

"I'm content, sir," Cat mumbled, standing. "Mrs. Harris, what would you like me to do for the rest of the afternoon?"

The chores Marty asked for were easily accomplished in an hour. Cat sat in the barn until feeding time; then she brought the horses in from the field and fed them, finishing well before she was expected at the house for dinner.

She went to the camper to change her shirt and wash up and saw Sadie sitting outside. The dog whined, and Cat gave her a boost up the steps. Cat just wanted to crawl into bed. She'd had more than enough for one day.

She still couldn't shake the feeling that Uncle Bud was near, at least closer than he'd been in a long time. She knew that if Duke had any notion of what just happened to him in that barn, he'd sing it to the hills, and Uncle Bud would be on her trail like a hound after a chain-gang runaway. She shouldn't have taken such a risk. Well, she'd had to, that was all.

It wouldn't happen again, though. She wasn't going to blow her chances here. This job paid more than any she'd ever had. If she could, she'd try to get to a pay phone tomorrow to call Nana. She'd be able to send her more each month. 'Course Nana didn't want any of it. Cat sent it anyway, faithful every month, no matter what. After all, Nana had done without to keep her fed when she was little. She'd even tried as hard as she could to keep Uncle Bud from taking Cat away. 'Course nobody could do anything about that with him being blood kin and all. Maybe if the social workers had known what a snake he was …

The stuffy air in the camper grew heavier. Cat cranked the windows wider. Above her out of an open bedroom window, a woman wailed the blues from some scratchy old recording. Cat stopped to listen. It was the music she'd grown up on.

She picked up her mother's mandolin. Battered and worn, it still had fine tone. According to Nana, that day when her mother had given her up, she'd left the mandolin, too, telling Nana to be sure her baby girl learned to play. That old instrument and the faded snapshot of her mother were all she had left of her family. After leaving her at Nana's, Mamma had gone right home and burned their place to the ground before walking off into the forest. Nana had said it was because she knew she was dying and that's where she wanted to face the Lord, in the forest she loved. Cat liked to imagine that Mamma had burned the place so Bud wouldn't get his hands on it.

Cat sat down and softly picked the strings, playing along with the familiar song. Nana's nephew Samuel had given her lessons, starting her off on a tiny kid's guitar and then switching to the mandolin. She'd got the basics before Bud dragged her off. The rest she'd gone and worked out herself.

Nana had said that Cat's mamma played the blues better than

any white woman she'd ever heard. Nana said all the sadness that had been heaped on Mamma had given her the right and the savvy. Cat leaned back and worked the strings, humming softly with the song. The way she figured it, she'd earned the right to sing the blues, just like her mamma had.

S I X

Marty stared at the patterns on the ceiling made by moon-light shining through the swaying tree branches. In the bed next to her, Annie snored softly, the snoring something new since her illness. But it wasn't Annie's little snores that kept Marty watching the leafy patterns. Tonight her life lay heavy on her mind. She sighed deeply. On the rag rug between the beds, Cody raised his head off his paws and looked at her, head cocked to one side.

Marty slipped out of bed and the dog rose to greet her, his overlong tail swinging back and forth. With one hand under his chin, she stroked his head with the other. He looked at her adoringly out of his white-rimmed, almost human eyes. She grabbed her robe and, with the big pup padding beside her, crept down the steps. She put a sturdy mug of water into the microwave and sat, patting Cody's head, which he rested in her lap.

Her hands were warmed by his soft hair as she mindlessly stroked the white-streaked gray of his head. Although it sur-prised her, his simple affection was important to her. She some-times thought his love was the only one out of all of theirs that was simple, straightforward, and undemanding. He asked noth-ing of her except food in his bowl, water in his dish, and an occasional pat on the head. For the little she gave him, he adored her.

The microwave alarm sounded. Marty kissed Cody on the bridge of his nose and made herself a cup of chamomile tea with honey, her mother's favorite remedy for sleeplessness.

She settled onto the porch swing. With a jump that set the

swing rocking and the tea splashing, Cody landed beside her. He immediately dropped to his belly with his head in her lap. She laughed softly and held the tea to the side so she wouldn't drip on them. Together they swayed and Marty sipped her tea.

Fear of making the wrong choices gnawed at her. The last important decision she'd made was to leave this place and go to college. She'd fled, hoping never to return. She rarely had. There had been no decision involved in her marriage to Dan. She'd dreamed a long time about someone like him, someone kind and intelligent, someone with a good future far from this cultural backwater where she'd been raised, someone who could give her a life of art and culture.

There'd been a lot of hoping while she waited for the handsome teaching assistant to notice her. Her feelings for him grew quickly, but not because of any conscious decision on her part. They were the natural consequence of the kind of man Dan was, and again she began to hope, this time that he would somehow love her as much as she was coming to love him. The swing had almost stopped and Marty pushed off with one foot, setting it again in motion.

He proposed right after he'd been offered the full-time instructor's position at the university. Her answer came instantaneously from her heart and soul, not from a decision, but as the inevitable result of her love for him. And the children? No, they weren't a decision either. She and Dan wanted children and assumed that when you were married they came when they would, and they had. Now that Dan was gone, she wished they'd been a bit more deliberate about it. She'd have liked one or two more, not just for themselves, but also as pieces of Dan for her to hold on to.

An owl called from the creek bank. Cody snapped to attention, his ears cocked. She patted his head. "Just an old hoot owl, boy," she murmured. He relaxed his head again on her lap.

After Dan's death, her homecoming hadn't been a decision either. Where else could she have gone on the little money she'd had left? She knew now it had been the right thing to do. Maybe if she'd have actively chosen it, she'd feel it was a better fit. The barn loomed in the shadows on the hillside, the skeletal framework for the arena stark against the moonlight.

Now her life was going in another direction she hadn't chosen. If Sam and her friend Gayle hadn't pushed this thing with the therapeutic riding center and Sam hadn't found a way to fund it, she wouldn't be doing it. The thought caused more anxiety than any she'd had all evening. She took a long drink of her cooling tea. It didn't soothe her. She was so excited about using her teaching skills and her horse knowledge together to benefit special-needs kids. What if something at this late stage went wrong? With the licensing or the insurance? Could she set things right? Did she even know how?

Marty wasn't sure. It seemed that everything, even wonderful things like the Center, just came and imposed themselves on her without her actively choosing them. She always had followed Dan's lead. But then, he'd been a good leader. Now she was in charge, or should be. Maybe this is what it meant to turn her life over to God. Still, God helped those who helped themselves. She'd been raised on that ethic. It was just that right now it all seemed to be such a struggle. And what was it God wanted from her anyway? Sometimes she was so confused.

From the side of the house where Cat had parked her truck and camper, she heard mellow chords of someone playing a mandolin, so softly she almost thought she imagined it. But no, there it was again, haunting and sad like Cat herself. Cat hadn't said anything about being musical. But then Marty suspected that there was a lot they'd never know about this strange creature. That was another question plaguing Marty, one she swung hot and cold on as often as it forced itself into her mind. Just because Cam Brady had found this kid and the kid had shown up, why had Marty felt she had to hire her? Was it just another nondecision?

The slap of the screen door jarred her. Duke shuffled across the porch in his pj's. "Hi, Dad," Marty said.

Duke pushed Cody to the floor and sat beside Marty on the swing. "You, too, huh?" He pushed off to set the swing in motion again.

"Yeah, I can't sleep, but this isn't like you. We usually have trouble keeping you awake," she teased.

"Something happened to me today, Marty. Something strange and frightening. I swear I was fixin' to have a cardiac arrest. You know when Glory Girl was sick and I'd run down to call Cam? When I came back into the barn, I couldn't get my breath. I had an awful pain in the middle of my back and was real sick to my stomach. My whole field of vision started to close in, you know, in swirls almost like the end of a cartoon."

Marty tightened her arm around his shoulder. "Dad, why didn't you say something? But you feel fine now, don't you? I mean, you seem good."

"That's the funny thing about it. All of a sudden like, I was fine."

Marty sighed. "Dad! You were probably just hyperventilating. Heart attacks don't just spontaneously go away."

"I know they don't usually, girl, but I think the Lord gave me another chance. Trouble is, I don't know for what." Duke pushed off with his foot again.

They swung in silence. Marty didn't want to discourage him. Her dad needed something to get him going. What better than a mission from God, whether real or imagined?

"Do you think the Lord could have something he wants me to do?" Duke asked.

Marty had never heard such genuine innocence in an adult's

voice. She laid her head on her father's shoulder. "Oh, Dad, I don't know, but I imagine he could. I was wondering the same thing about myself. I find it hard to follow God's lead when I have no idea what he might want from me."

Duke gave a low chuckle. "Life's big mystery, huh? But, Marty, you shouldn't be pushing yourself. You're still grieving Dan. I know you're a strong woman. I admire how you've taken charge...."

"You're kidding, right?" Marty pushed back and looked hard at her father to see if he was teasing her.

"No, I've watched you grabbing life by the horns, working hard to carve a life for you and your children."

He meant it. She should have known; Duke rarely teased. "It's a good act, Dad," Marty said with a sigh. Still she was perversely glad her confusion and indecision weren't as evident as she'd believed.

Her father hugged her tight and kissed her temple. "No need to act, daughter. You're with family who loves you. Give yourself the time you need to heal."

Marty just nodded. She laid her head against her father's chest and swung in silence, listening to the steady beat of his heart. A breeze rustled the leaves and patterns danced in the moonglow on the lawn. The quiet bubbling of the stream, instead of soothing her as it usually did, stirred her anxieties. Taking time to heal wasn't a luxury she could afford; her responsibilities to the children, for the animals she kept acquiring, for the business she was starting, and even, in some ways, to her father and brother wouldn't go away while she withdrew to mend.

From the side lawn, Cat's camper door banged shut. Marty waited but wherever Cat was going, she didn't come their way. She heard a splash. "She shouldn't be swimming this late at night with no one knowing she's in the water...." Marty started to rise, but her father pulled her back.

"We know," he said. "Let the child be, Marty. I remember when you would sneak out to take a swim on a warm evening. Your mamma and I would just lie awake until we heard you come in and knew you were safe."

Marty settled back onto the swing, remembering the feel of the satiny cool water on her sweat-soaked skin. Cody jumped to his feet and started off the porch. "Cody, down," she ordered. "You let her be, too."

Duke nodded his approval.

"She's a strange one, Dad."

"More sad, I think. A poor little sad one who's not known much love, I'm afraid."

"That may be, but I get the feeling she's running from something. Whatever it is, it's caused a lot of misery for her and I'm just hoping it doesn't follow her here. Frankly, we don't need any more trouble. The kid will continue to bother me until I figure her out."

"Marty, you've got to quit picking at her and crowding her. She's poised to bolt like some spooky colt."

"I wish I could believe she was that domesticated. I'd say she's poised for flight like some wild bird."

"Doesn't matter what kind of creature she seems like, she's still just a kid and she's scared and sad." Duke yawned. "I think I might be able to sleep now." He kissed the top of Marty's head. "See you in the morning, my girl."

"'Night, Dad." As Marty watched him go, a heaviness settled into her muscles. All she'd need to do was snuggle under the soft sheets of her bed and she would probably be asleep in no time. But she couldn't go as long as Cat was swimming. That had always been the number one house rule: no one swims alone unless someone else is nearby to get help should it be needed. Well, she'd give her a few more minutes.

Marty's head slumped forward, startling her awake. The porch swing wobbled as she jerked herself upright. How long had she been sleeping? Cat. She listened but heard no splashing.

Marty hurried around the side of the house, stopping in the shadows to look toward the water. Cat sat on the big rock in the center of the stream, her head thrown back, looking at the star-studded sky. While Marty watched, Cat slid into the water and, sleek as an otter, swam to the shore. She pulled herself up the bank and shook herself, the moonlight catching the droplets of water flung from her long dark hair. Her little dog rose from the bank. Cat leaped into a run and, with the dog hobbling behind, dashed for the camper.

Marty stepped back into the shadows. When she heard the slap of the camper door, she softly called Cody and headed for the house. Sad the child might be, but also strange and feral. As for Marty's other worries about the girl, she'd have to let them go for another time if she hoped to get any sleep tonight.

SEVEN

On Monday morning Kyle's work crew showed up before eight to work on the indoor arena. With relief in her heart, Marty watched them pull up to the house and climb the hill. This was good. Before the rains and the flood, her lackluster builders had wandered in piecemeal every morning. Little work got done with their late arrivals, long beer-swilling lunches, and early departures. Kyle had promised to take charge, and it looked like he had. Even Jeff was up on the hill, carrying lumber.

Marty counted this as one of the wonders of the summer. When she and her family had arrived in early June, Kyle and Jeff had hardly been the best of friends. In fact, Marty had spent the early part of the summer either trying to keep the two of them away from each other or serving as a referee when she couldn't.

All morning long Marty delighted in the staccato rapping of the workmen's hammers. Cat was taking care of the barn work, so Marty could give some much-needed attention to the house. While Annie dusted, Marty ran the vacuum. Surprisingly, now that she had the time to do it, she didn't feel overburdened and resentful. It also did her heart good to see her little girl smiling and energetic, bouncing from room to room.

"Mom, we're all done, so I'm going up to the barn," Annie called. "Okay?"

"Go ahead, sweetie," Marty said. "I've got some paperwork to do. Tell Kyle I'll have lunch ready at noon. Make sure Cat knows she should come, too."

After Annie left, Marty worked up estimates and potential schedules for Sam, who was eager to get on with the realities of the Center. She'd already begun her training with Joanne, the licensed therapeutic riding instructor. Two nights a week she went to McFarland, the center east of Pittsburgh where her mentor, Joanne, worked. As soon as Kyle and the crew finished the arena, Joanne would come here until Marty got her license.

Marty was excited about the prospect of having her own center. In the short time she'd been doing this, she'd seen miracles happen—an autistic child who only spoke when he was on horseback, a young mother with multiple sclerosis who had been able to put her walker away when she began to ride, a four-teen-year-old girl with cerebral palsy who had never slept through the night until she began to ride six months ago. Right now these miracles were for Joanne's riders. Soon miracles would be happening right here at Stafford Farm.

Marty sat up straighter and sighed. These thoughts, instead of cheering her, brought impatience. She'd missed a whole week of working with Joanne. The arena was way behind, set back by the rains and even more by their undisciplined crew. Sure, Kyle and the boys were trying to make good now, but if they'd been working like this all along....

And now she had to stop, with loads of paperwork left undone, and feed them. She had tried to explain to Kyle that workmen usually brought their own lunch. "Aw, come on, Sis," he'd said. "Most of these guys live alone. I said we'd feed them." Which meant *she* had to feed them.

She left her papers scattered on the dining room table and walked into the kitchen. Duke stood at the sink, washing tomatoes. Marty shook her head. How like him—too impatient to wait and have lunch with everyone else. And he'd planted himself right where she needed to be.

"Thought I'd help get the food ready," he said with a grin. "Looks like we've got some hard-working boys up there and they're bound to be hungry."

Humbled, she gave him a hug. It was time to get off this emotional roller coaster she'd been on. It impaired her judgment. "Thanks, Dad." And why did his behavior surprise her? She'd seen this change coming over the past few days, ever since he'd had that heart scare on Thursday. He'd even been the first one ready for church yesterday morning. No matter how many times Marty tried to explain that heart attacks don't just go away by themselves, and they certainly don't leave a person feeling better than before, he was convinced he'd had "an encounter with death." Whatever happened, real or imagined, had wrought amazing effects.

Marty took a head of lettuce from the refrigerator and squeezed in next to her father to wash it. Duke, usually on the gloomy side, whistled softly as he sliced the tomatoes onto a plate. Marty stole a look at her father. His cheeks were colored a healthy pink and his expression was cheerful. Maybe something miraculous *had* happened to him.

Duke quit slicing and, with the broad-bladed knife still in his hand, gave his pants a hitch. Tomato seeds dripped from the knife to the floor and the knife tip nearly gouged the cupboard door.

Marty grabbed a few paper towels and bent to wipe up the mess. As Duke headed to the table with the plate full of tomatoes, he almost stepped on her hand. He didn't seem to notice. As his large, flat feet plodded past, Marty saw that he had on one white athletic sock and one of gray wool. The bottoms of his pant legs were frayed and stained. Duke certainly hadn't been completely transformed by his experience.

Just as Marty finished pouring pitchers of lemonade and iced tea, the boisterous group filed into the kitchen, jostling and carrying on as they took turns washing their hands at the sink. Cat was the last to arrive, staring at the floor, looking miserable. Everyone crowded around the table. After a somewhat overlong grace by Duke, everyone dug into the food, except Cat, who just picked at some fruit and cheese.

The five-man work crew, all Kyle's rodeo or drinking buddies, laughed and teased and told jokes. Even Marty found their high spirits contagious.

Davey, the youngest of the group, probably no more than twenty, flirted with Cat. The more he tried to get her into a conversation, the more deeply red her cheeks became and the more she squirmed in her chair. Jeff found this very funny and went off into a fit of laughter. Cat set her jaw and stared at her plate.

Pete, Kyle's partner in the carpentry business and on the team-roping circuit, smacked Davey on the back of the head. "Listen up, you oversexed, hardly-out-of-diapers Romeo, you're making the young lady uncomfortable. The poor little thing can hardly eat with you bothering her. Knock it off."

Davey laughed and rubbed the back of his head. "Hey, man, you can't blame a guy for trying."

Everyone laughed but Cat. The conversation moved away from her, and Marty saw her begin to eat more quickly. It wasn't long before she excused herself and fled out the kitchen door.

Jeff had to get ready for band camp, so he wasn't far behind her. He came back into the kitchen, cleaned up and carrying his saxophone, all of which made him the butt of their jokes.

"Laugh all you want," Jeff said. "But musicians get the babes."

Marty smiled. At least one young lady seemed smitten; her friend Gayle's lovely niece had been coming around quite regularly. The sound of a car crunching over the gravel drive sent him running for his ride, with catcalls and hoots following him.

Marty looked around the table. This was good. Jeff no longer sulking. Kyle hard at work. Annie healthy. Duke up and engaging life. A work crew ready and willing to complete her arena. She almost felt content. Almost.

The moment she acknowledged her discomfort, it began to swell, slowly but inevitably, like bread dough set to rise. As Marty cleared the table, Annie and Duke jumped to help. "Hey, Sis," Kyle said, after ushering his workmen from the kitchen. "If you're going into town this afternoon, could you stop at the auto supply? I need a few things to get Cat's truck running."

"Sam's due late this afternoon, but I can run in now. You guys ate me out of house and home, so I need to stop at the grocery store before dinner, and I have a few things to pick up at Patterson's Hardware."

Kyle grabbed a piece of paper and wrote a list. "Cat was trying to get into town yesterday morning while you guys were at church and her old clunker wouldn't start."

So that was why Cat had turned down Marty's invitation to attend church with them. She hadn't explained, just mumbled, "No, thank you, ma'am." Marty's curiosity was piqued. What had Cat wanted to do in town that was so important?

Kyle handed the list to Marty. "I think this ought to take care of it. I'm doing the repairs, and I told her you'd just take the cost of the parts off her next check. They shouldn't be much."

Marty looked at the list. No, they didn't look costly. But Kyle shouldn't have offered without checking with her. She didn't want to get into giving loans against future pay and such nonsense. She gave him a look with one eyebrow raised.

"Come on, Sis, lighten up. You know you'd have offered to help her out." Kyle gave Marty a one-armed hug around her shoulders. "While you're at it, you could take her with you. I don't know what she wanted to get in town, but she was pretty upset when the truck wouldn't start."

"Since when did you become Mr. Helpful? And why do you think I wouldn't have offered to take her myself?"

"It's obvious this kid bugs you. You're not easy around her like you are with most people."

"Nonsense. I wouldn't have hired her if I felt that way."

Kyle gave her a kiss on the cheek. "Whatever," he said, and headed out the door after his crew.

Marty ground her teeth. How typical of him to just saunter out without giving her time to explain herself. She banged the cupboard door shut.

"Hey," Duke protested. "I was just going to put this bowl away. What's eating you?"

"Nothing," Marty snapped. "Annie, be careful with those glasses." She took the stack of three glasses Annie was lifting toward the shelf.

"Mom, I could have done it," Annie said.

Marty looked at Annie's face, the hurt written all over it. "I'm sorry, Annie. Of course you could have. Listen, let's leave this and go into town. All three of us, and we'll ask Cat. Okay?"

"I think I'll skip," Duke said. "My show's on in a little while, so you go on. I'll finish cleaning up."

Marty chose not to protest, but the irony of the situation did amuse her. For a man who claimed to have had a miraculous reprieve from death and to now be searching for his "mission from God," he apparently didn't feel he needed to change his routine to accomplish it. Ever since he'd retired from the mine, Duke had followed the same routine—trashy talk shows in the morning, his soap operas in the afternoon, a nap before dinner, and sitcoms all evening. He'd been less rigid about it recently, going to the barn with Annie when one of the shows failed to grab his interest. She tried to get him to stretch a little, but she just wasn't up to the struggle today. "That will be great, Dad," Marty said.

"Pick me up some of my newspapers while you're at the store," he said and turned back to the sink.

"There's precious little 'news' in those rags, Dad," Marty snapped. She grabbed her purse and walked out the door, followed by a giggling Annie. Duke knew how she felt about those dreadful tabloids. She really didn't even want them in the house where the children could read such hateful, distorted garbage.

"Annie, run and see if Cat wants to come with us," Marty said. "I think I heard her go to her camper after lunch."

Annie ran around the side of the house and soon returned with Cat. For the whole short ride to town, Marty listened to Annie's gay chatter and Cat's one-word responses, glad that she wasn't expected to participate in the girls' conversation. The day had started so well and now, for reasons she couldn't quite get a hold on, she felt downright peevish. And she hated it when other people behaved this way and she tried to keep it to herself.

She tried repeating the Serenity Prayer, the one their pastor had given his sermon on yesterday. *God, grant me the serenity to accept the things I cannot change,* she prayed silently. But she was unable to go on. That was the problem. She didn't seem to be able to change anything, and a lot of it she simply did not want to accept. A phrase began to form at the edge of her consciousness ... "Turn it over."

That was one of those shibboleths that sounded easy, but Marty didn't really even know how to begin. She remembered a prayer that had come to her during one of her most frightening moments when Annie was sick. *Lord, please, show me your ways,* she prayed, trying to engage not just her head but also her heart and soul. *Thy will, not my will, be done.*

But the trouble was, turning over her will took more trust than she had right now. True, he'd spared Annie, but he'd also taken Dan from her.

Perhaps if she could just discern what the Lord had in mind for her, all her doubts and fears would vanish. She tried to concentrate.

On the street far ahead of them, a car pulled away from the

curb in front of the hardware store. What luck. She stepped on the gas to assure she'd be first to the parking spot. She'd have to get back to her prayer later.

EIGHT

Annie seemed determined to be Cat's guide to the town of Clayton. As soon as she could, Cat escaped to the pay phone at the service station. She lined up her change in front of her and dialed. After many rings, Nana answered.

"Nana, hi. It's me," she said.

"Darling child, I'd been thinking you'd dropped off the edge of the earth again," the old woman said.

Cat could hear the pleasure in Nana's voice and imagined the wide smile on her broad face, her soft eyes, and her skin the color of melted chocolate. "No, I'm still in the same area, south of Pittsburgh, but I've changed jobs." The corners of her eyes stung. She squeezed them tight. The only time she even came close to crying was when she talked to Nana. Pure lonesomeness, she guessed.

"Not because of trouble, I hope."

"No, I've gone to a better place is all. One of the track vets recommended me to a lady who is starting up a center where handicapped people can ride horses. They say it's real good for them. Called therapeutic riding."

"I do believe I've read something about that. What a wonderful place for you. You could sure do the Lord's work at a place like that, Katie. Yes, you could."

Heaviness wrapped itself around Cat's heart. She had never told Nana that she didn't use her gift anymore, not unless she absolutely had to. "Well, anyway, the people are nice. They're even making an apartment for me."

"Oh my, tell me all about it."

And Cat did, but only the good parts—no need to tell that Jeff didn't like her and Marty didn't seem to be too sure about her. Cat always left out the bad parts when she talked to Nana. Nana had never known about the time she'd had to pull her knife on that man up in Erie, or that she'd spent a good part of the last months avoiding the boss when he got drunk and came looking for romance. Why worry Nana over stuff Cat could handle herself? At least she wasn't dealing with a situation like either of those other two. At least, now she was safe, even if not entirely welcomed.

Coin after coin clinked its way through the telephone as Cat gave Nana her news. "And I'm getting paid better, so I can send more money."

"Oh, my darling, I keep telling you. I'm doing fine. You keep your money. I got my social security, and that's plenty for me."

Cat felt a tap on her arm and looked to see Annie standing beside her. "I'd better go, okay? I'll call next week." She turned to Annie. "Tell your mom I'll be right there, okay?" She watched as Annie ran off. "Nana, I've got to get going," Cat said.

"Listen, Katie, I've got to tell you that your lowlife, belly-crawling snake of an uncle has been by looking for you."

Cat's hand started to shake. Her throat froze. Just as she'd thought. She always knew when he was stirring.

"You still there, Katie?" asked Nana.

"I'm ... yeah, I'm here," she croaked.

"Don't worry, child. He's been asking all over, but nobody told him nothing. 'Course, nobody but me really knows for sure where you are and you know I won't tell, not even in the face of death. I promise you that, little one."

"I know, Nana. I love you. I'll be fine."

They said quick goodbyes and Cat, her knees still shaky, crossed the street and slid into the backseat of Mrs. Harris' car.

He wouldn't find her. Even if he somehow tricked Nana, Nana only knew she was somewhere south of Pittsburgh.

Mrs. Harris' next stop was the auto supply store, but Cat couldn't attend to the job at hand. Fear put her mind into flight. Her breath came in short, shallow gasps, a cold sweat trickled down between her shoulders. Her hands felt numb as she clutched Kyle's list.

Inside the store she gave the list to Mrs. Harris, who handed it to the stockboy. He filled the order. Cat didn't even pay much attention to the bill. Like a robot she walked to the car and crawled into the backseat. She only half listened to Annie's chatter and Mrs. Harris' comments. The little girl never seemed to need more than a smile or a nod. Cat wasn't sure she could give Annie more.

They arrived at the farm close enough to feeding time that Cat was able to thank Mrs. Harris quickly for the ride and the salary advance to buy her truck parts, then make a dash for the camper. She let Sadie loose, and the two of them headed for the barn. Once inside, she sat in the hay stall, holding Sadie close to her until her breathing became regular. "Sadie girl, we've got to keep our eyes peeled and our ears opened," she whispered. And Cat herself would have to tune into her "feelings."

She brought the horses in from the field and watered them, stopping to pat each one. The bay quarter horse, Sassy, leaned her nose forward as she did with Marty when she wanted a kiss. Cat leaned her cheek against the fuzzy warmth of the mare. Sassy blew short breaths against her cheek. Cat felt herself relaxing. She gave the mare a kiss and dragged the hose to the next stall.

By the time she was finished, she wasn't as panicky. She called to Sadie and left the barn. Mr. Marcus' car was parked in front of the house. At least she recognized it this time. And she wouldn't again mistake him for Uncle Bud.

She took a deep breath. The heaviness of August was giving way to the crispness of September. Annie had said that next week, just after Labor Day, she'd start her new school. Jeff, too, Cat guessed. She hoped he appreciated it as much as Annie seemed to. Snotty kid had no idea what it was like not to have the chance to go to school. Cat sure did. There certainly had been nothing regular about her education. When they were on the road, Uncle Bud got around to it when he could. Usually whatever lady friend he had at the time handled the schooling. Whenever they got back home, she always had a terrible time trying to catch up with her class in the little country school. The teachers didn't bother with her, knowing she'd soon be gone again. Left to her own, she caught what she could. Sums had come of necessity when Cat had headed out on her own. And she was good enough to make sure nobody cheated her. She'd learned to read and took comfort in books. She could even write pretty well. Her spelling wasn't the best, but she managed.

She checked the sky. The sun was on its downward arc but still high. Plenty of time until dinner. She'd just fetch her book, sit outside, and read a bit. She slipped around the side of the house and into the camper, pretty sure no one had seen her. She didn't need any well-meaning conversation from Duke Stafford, Annie, or Mr. Marcus. And she wasn't up to any prying, well intentioned or otherwise, from Mrs. Harris.

She pulled the soft-edged paperback from under her pillow. It was the fifth book she'd read about the Murphy family. She'd found the first in a used book store near the track. She'd gone to the big bookstore in the mall looking for the others. They were little kids' books, probably for children about Annie's age. She didn't care. They were about a nice family with four kids. All kinds of funny things happened to them. But no matter what kind of trouble they got into, it always turned out all right.

Cat jumped out of the camper and sat on the ground on the

far side of her truck, hidden from anyone coming toward the house. She faced the stream, listening to it gurgle and smelling the damp earth and moss of its banks. Sadie curled up in her lap. She stroked the dog's coat as she read. The faint hum of voices came from inside the house. Probably Mrs. Harris and Mr. Marcus meeting in the dining room. The windows to that room were on the other side of the camper. Well, never mind, they couldn't see her.

She smiled as she read about Collette Murphy's mishaps, this one getting her into trouble with her mother. Yet Mrs. Murphy never yelled at her, and Collette never got a beating. She got sent to her room, or sometimes she had to do some chore or wasn't allowed to go somewhere she wanted to. That was all. Cat felt certain her own mother would have been like Mrs. Murphy.

The slap of the porch door distracted Cat. She could hear the voices clearly now—Mrs. Harris and Mr. Marcus.

"So how is your helper working out?" asked Mr. Marcus.

"She's all right, I guess. I certainly can't complain about her work," Mrs. Harris answered. "Our Cat may be as small as a kitten, but she works like a tiger."

Cat stopped reading.

"Then why do I detect a tone of misgiving here?"

"I don't know, Sam. It's nothing I can put my finger on, but something's not right. Jeff thinks she's hiding something. Whatever it is, it probably isn't any of our business, but ... I don't know."

"Out with it, Marty. What don't you know?"

"Well, for one thing, she claims not to have any family anywhere, and yet she was desperate to make a phone call today. She was practically dancing a jig until she found a way to slip across the street and get away from Annie and me. And then when she came back, she was obviously upset."

Sam laughed. "She's a pretty young lady, Marty. Did you consider that it might be boyfriend trouble?"

Marty chuckled. "Of course not. That would be too simple an explanation for my twisted mind. Like I said, whatever is bothering her is probably none of our business."

"So then you think she'll work out?"

"I hope so. She seems to be smart enough, but she's obviously uneducated. She's so antisocial I'm afraid she won't be able to deal with our riders once the Center opens. And you know Cam is sending some boarders to us, some 4-H-ers who want to keep their horses somewhere with an indoor arena. She'll really have to interact with those kids. I may need someone with a bit more savvy and sophistication. I guess we'll just have to wait and see how she handles it."

Their voices became fainter as they moved away. Cat tried to forget what she'd heard and get back into her book, but a moment later she closed it. It wasn't that Mrs. Harris didn't like her. She said she hoped it would work out. She had a lot of doubts, though. Cat guessed "antisocial" meant she didn't like people much. Well, she didn't. But she did love animals. And she liked children. And they liked her. Couldn't Mrs. Harris see how well she got along with Annie? She'd be fine with the kids. And she'd try real hard with the adults. She couldn't do anything about the education. It wasn't her fault that Uncle Bud had been so slipshod with her schooling.

Cat opened the book again. She held Sadie close, and although she tried to be amused by the story, it had lost some of its magic for her. A girl her age shouldn't be reading a little kid's book anyway.

NINE

Cat rose to her feet. She'd take a walk until dinner. As she rounded the back of the truck she almost ran into Mrs. Harris.

"Oh, Cat," Marty said. "I thought you were at the barn."

Cat just shook her head and looked away. Down the lane Mr. Marcus' fancy car rolled around the bend out of sight.

"Oh, dear," Marty said. "You heard my conversation with Sam, didn't you?"

Cat could feel the blood rush to her cheeks. She nodded.

"I am really sorry. That was very insensitive of me. But maybe it's important that we have these concerns in the open. Now we can talk about them."

Cat looked at Mrs. Harris. The woman looked so sincere, but she was as pushy as a train conductor. Nobody got a free ride, and nothing passed her notice.

"So do you think you can handle having to deal with customers?"

"I think I can ... well enough. I didn't think the job called for me to become their best friend."

Marty laughed, right out loud, startling Cat. "You're right. It doesn't. And as long as you take care of the horses and aren't afraid to interact with the customers strictly in a business sense, then I think you'll be fine. I'm very pleased with how you handle the animals, Cat. I've meant to tell you that."

"Thank you, ma'am."

"And, Cat, please quit calling me 'ma'am' and 'Mrs. Harris.' You're making me feel ancient."

Cat nodded. She'd try, but somehow she couldn't call this woman by her first name. And "hey, you" wasn't very polite.

"What are you reading?" Marty asked, reaching for the book.

Cat had no choice but to hand it to her. Did the woman have to pry into everything?

"I love these books!" Marty said. "Annie and I read the whole series together. They are such fun." She handed the book back to Cat. "We have the rest of them if you want to borrow any."

"Thank you," Cat said, swallowing the "ma'am" before it escaped. "I do like to read."

Marty looked away from Cat toward the creek, the pink in her cheeks deepening. "It wasn't very fair of me to make a comment about your education, was it?"

"I'd have had a lot more schooling if I could have. I've tried on my own, you know, to learn things … read stuff."

"Cat, our living room is filled with bookcases. Anytime you want, just come on in and get any book that appeals to you. All right?"

Cat nodded and bit the inside of her lip. She didn't understand this woman at all. First she seemed to bad-mouth her, then she offered a gift beyond price, one that demanded something in return. "Today in town … I wasn't talking to a boyfriend. Don't have a boyfriend, and I'm not so sure I want one."

"Cat, I was out of line. That is none of my business." Marty seemed uncomfortable. "I have a tendency to try to run everyone's business. I'm trying not to, honestly. As my brother likes to tell me, 'God doesn't need my help to run the universe.'"

"But I want you to know," Cat went on. "I call my Nana every week. You know, the lady who raised me. The one I told you about."

This time Marty just nodded and for a moment seemed to have nothing to say. Then she offered, "I was just going to take a short walk along the creek. Want to join me?"

"Sure. Just let me put my book away." Cat tossed the book in the camper and joined Marty by the creek bed. For a while they walked in silence beside the rushing water. Downstream, Cody charged from behind some bushes, giving Sadie a quick sniff. The little terrier snapped and growled, and the big dog backed down.

"Cody, you are a case," Marty said. Cody, tail wagging, fell into step beside Marty. Sadie huddled closer to Cat. With three short steps and a hop, she stayed right with them.

Cat watched the stream rolling over submerged rocks, listened to its music, smelled its freshness. They followed its course toward the main road. She loved how the hills on either side and behind them seemed to protect the hollow.

Where the creek narrowed, Marty bent over a washed-up log. "Come on, Cat, help me with this."

Together they lifted a section of split tree trunk upright on the bank. Marty wiggled it back and forth, positioning it. "On three, let it go so it falls to the other side," Marty said. "One ... two ... three!" The log crashed across the creek, flat side up. "There." Marty stood on the log and gave a bounce. The log stayed firm. Cody charged ahead of her and scaled the hillside, then turned and barked. "Come on," Marty said, walking carefully across the makeshift bridge. "I want to show you something."

Cat followed with Sadie close behind. They crossed the creek and then scrambled up the hillside to a rock ledge below an overhang. Too shallow to be called a cave, it hung on the hillside almost hidden from below by trees. It was a place of quiet and wonder.

"When I was a kid, I used to sneak up here when I wanted to hide from everybody," Marty said. "This is where I came to read and weave my dreams. Back then I was very unhappy. I couldn't wait until I got old enough to head off into the wide world. I was sure anyplace was better than this farm."

"Was it?" Cat asked.

"In many ways, yes, it was—for me. I needed more than this place offered. And remember, I was a very happily married woman." Marty sighed, but a slight smile curled the corners of her lips. "What I've found since I came back is that many of my memories from here are happy ones. I had left a lot behind that I'd been missing. Does that make any sense?"

Cat nodded but didn't really understand. She couldn't imagine anyone ever wanting to leave this place. Marty had come from a good family. All right, so maybe they weren't as perfect as the Murphys in the book, but Cat would have given anything to have a family like the Staffords. "It's real pretty up here," she offered.

"Well, you feel free to come here whenever you want. I suspect you're a lot like I was and need a good bit of private time. My kids don't know about this place, so you can hide out whenever you want."

Cat groped for the right words, but none would come. Maybe there were no exact right words when someone was showing you a kindness. "Thanks ... Marty," Cat said, the name now sounding comfortable on her tongue.

"You're welcome," Marty said, with a broad smile and a sharp nod of her head, as though she considered the matter settled.

Well, Cat guessed something had been. At least, it seemed as if they'd agreed to try to get along, to somehow make things work. For her part, Cat prayed they would. Usually she didn't give two hoots about what people thought of her, but this woman was different. The realization surprised Cat; she wanted Marty to like her.

"Well, good then," Marty said. "But I'd better get back and

finish dinner." She climbed off the ledge and started down the hillside.

Cat followed. "I'd be real happy to give you a hand ... I mean, if you could use one."

"Are you kidding? I can always use a hand when it comes to feeding this crew," Marty said.

Back in the kitchen, Cat sliced tomatoes. She spread them fanned and fancy across a pretty blue-and-white plate. Marty husked the corn and put it on to steam. Annie burst into the kitchen with Duke right behind her. Jake and Bella, tails wagging, followed them.

"Dogs outside," Marty ordered.

After the dogs had been banished, Duke and Annie set the table. Cat poured the drinks and Marty pulled the breaded chicken breasts and a potato casserole from the oven.

Jeff and Kyle came on the first call and soon all were seated around the table. For a moment, Cat felt part of a family. And this time nobody even commented when she passed on the chicken.

"Hey, Cat, you got a phone call," Kyle said.

Cat stared at him. How could Uncle Bud have found her already? Her heart pounded so loudly she was sure everyone would hear.

Kyle kept cutting his chicken. "Your old boss from the racetrack. Seems someone told him you came here. He sounded drunk. He said to tell you he's really short of help and he'd be willing to give you a fifty-percent raise to come back."

Cat almost laughed. Even with that big raise she was making more here. Not that she'd even consider working again for that skunk. She caught Kyle looking at her and smiled.

Kyle winked. "That's what I thought. I told him he'd better look for someone else. We weren't about to let you go."

"That's right," Duke echoed.

"You wouldn't really leave us, would you, Cat?" asked Annie.

Cat shot a look at Marty. Marty smiled, a private kind of smile, like a smile between friends.

"I just got here, Annie," Cat said. "I'm not planning on going anywhere."

"Oh, my gosh," Jeff said. "She talks."

Cat stole a look his way. He wasn't smiling, but he wasn't looking spiteful either.

"Of course she talks," Duke said. "When we give her a chance to get a word in edgewise."

Cat took a bite of the creamy potato casserole. She'd never tasted anything so good. But then, until now she hadn't been able to taste anything she'd eaten at this table. All she'd ever thought about was getting away from the whole noisy, nosey bunch of them. Given time, they really weren't so hard to get used to. Cat settled in and enjoyed her meal.

Cat even stayed long after she was done eating. She listened to them chatter while they all waited for Duke to finish. Finally, Duke pushed his chair back from the table. He patted his belly and gave a burp. "Lovely dinner, Marty," he said.

Cat heard the sound of tires rolling down the gravel lane. Then a car door. The dogs, Bella loudest of all, barked a warning.

Kyle jumped to his feet. "Bella!" he shouted before he even opened the door.

Cat turned to look. Through the window and across the porch she saw a stout, gray-haired woman swing a bulky purse and whack Bella right across the chops.

Duke let out a roar. "That Bertie! She's something else."

Kyle threw the door open and Bella charged through to cower behind him. "For Pete's sake, Aunt Bertie," he said. "You've terrified my dog."

Cat heard the stomp of the woman's steps as she crossed the

porch. Aunt Bertie strode into the kitchen, her purse now hooked over her elbow, a pie held high in her other hand. She glared at Kyle. "Well, it's about time someone did. That beast is a terror." She turned to survey the room. When her glance lit on Annie, the woman's face softened. She rushed forward and set the pie down right in front of Annie. "This is for the little one," she said, wrapping both arms around Annie and kissing the girl on the top of her head. "And you don't have to share it if you don't want to."

But Duke already had a finger in the syrupy pools of juice along the crust. "Black raspberry," he declared. "Bertie, you know that's my favorite."

Now the woman leveled a glare at Duke. "I assure you, Duke Stafford, if I ever did know such a detail, I have long forgotten it. This pie was baked for my great-niece." She lowered herself into Kyle's chair. "Well, it looks like I've timed my visit perfectly. Just in time for dessert." She patted Annie's hand.

"Can I share if I want to, Aunt Bertie?" Annie asked.

"Certainly, my dear, the choice is yours."

"Then I want everyone to have some." Annie smiled like a princess granting a blessing.

Aunt Bertie's eyes came to rest on Cat. Cat squirmed in her seat. "Is no one going to introduce me?" Aunt Bertie asked.

Marty's laugh seemed to circle the room. "If you'll give me a chance," she said. "Cat, this is my favorite aunt, Bertie Crawford. Bertie, this is Cat O'Reilly, who will help me with the Center."

Bertie leaned toward Cat and smiled. "Truthfully, dear, I'm the only aunt she has left, but she is my favorite niece and I have several." She turned to Marty. "And I already knew about Miss O'Reilly because I had to take Digger ..." Mrs. Crawford looked back to Cat. "He's my basset hound. He's old like me and has heart trouble. Anyway I had to take him to Cam for his checkup and he filled me in on what's been going on around here. If I had to wait for any of you to give me a call, I'd never know anything."

Duke served the pie and Mrs. Crawford chattered on. The family added their two cents' worth whenever she gave them a chance. Cat listened and ate the pie with no thoughts of escape.

By the time the aunt left she was insisting that Cat call her Aunt Bertie. Cat smiled, feeling the color rush to her cheeks. "Thank you, ma'am," she said. "I'd be proud to."

Bertie turned to Marty. "She's polite. That's important when you're running a business and have to deal with customers."

Marty grinned at Cat. "I was just telling her this afternoon that I'm sure she'll do fine here."

That night Cat fell into a deep sleep with Sadie curled next to her on the pillow. She didn't wake once during the night. The horrible dream stayed away, and by morning she was pretty well convinced that if her luck kept running like this, she had nothing to worry about.

TEN

The leaves began to show their fall colors. First the locusts turned yellow-green. Then the big maple down by the house showed a frosting of red along the top. Cat's phone calls to Nana brought good news. Uncle Bud wasn't around hounding anyone for information about her. Nana thought he'd given up.

Throughout September the weather held; no heavy rains, but each day seemed to dawn a little cooler than the one before. Slowly the arena began to take shape—first the roof and then the sides and insulation. By the end of September, the work crew had moved inside and were putting on the finishing touches. Even Cat's apartment, attached to the back of the arena, was nearly completed. When Kyle's girlfriend Kristen had stepped in to help with the decorating touches, the work had gone even faster. Cat noticed that the crew worked even harder, each of them trying to impress pretty Kristen.

On the first of October, Cat was in the barn getting three stalls ready. Three 4-H-ers were moving their horses in that afternoon after school. Cat fluffed the straw in the last stall. Perfect. She stepped into the aisle and surveyed the barn, then took a deep whiff of the scent from the linseed oil she'd rubbed on the stall doors. She loved their golden shine. Not even one cobweb hung in the rafters. And as soon as she swept in front of this stall, not a strand of straw would litter the floor.

Through the open door at the end of the aisle, she looked into the arena. She could see Kyle and Pete carrying lumber. They'd have to get it cleared out by five. Marty was giving some town kids lessons then. No doubt about it, this place was thriving.

Eleven stalls in use. Nine still empty. Cat was sure that when word got around they'd fill up. Then Marty had said she'd get help for Cat. The thought made her chuckle. She'd never been a boss before.

"Cat, come here," Kyle called. When she got to him, he headed off toward the apartment. "Decision time, kiddo."

Cat followed to the far end of the arena out the door and around the side where they'd built her new apartment. Kyle flung open the door and gestured her through.

Cat just stared. Pete and one of the other guys were installing the kitchen. A real kitchen with a stove and refrigerator, and linoleum that looked like real wooden planks on the floor. The linoleum was the same throughout the three rooms. She sniffed the newness.

"Pete and I just realized that we designed this with just a counter separating the kitchen and the living room, but we could totally close in the kitchen. So the choice is yours. Do you want to leave it open with a counter, or do we throw up a wall and enclose the kitchen?"

Cat smiled and shrugged. She'd love it either way.

"Listen, kiddo, you're the one who's going to live here. And you'd better get used to making decisions, because Kristen is coming over tonight with some wallpaper books." Kyle laughed. "I even got her to agree to help hang the stuff."

Cat walked over to Kyle and looked toward the living room. Next to the door, a big square window offered a view of the hill behind and the woods. "Don't close it in," she said, her voice sounding tiny even to her own ears.

"Good choice," Pete said. "You can look out your window while you're in your kitchen. How about we make this into a breakfast bar?" He bent over a tablet and started to sketch. He pushed the tablet toward Kyle.

"And then on the living room side, we could build in a drop-down table. Like this...." Kyle took up the pencil. "That way she'd have a table when she wanted one but could fold it out of the way when she wanted more room in the living room."

They both turned to Cat, big grins across their faces. Cat's throat clogged. All she could manage was a nod. She spun away from them and hurried into the bedroom. Kyle followed her.

"So what do you think?" he asked.

Cat took in the room. She'd last seen it a week ago. Now it was finished with a big sliding-door closet on one end. A window just like in the living room. The floor had been cleaned and the walls prepared for paint or paper, whatever she wanted. Just this room alone was twice as big as her camper. And throughout the whole place, they'd gone way beyond "make do," even beyond sufficient. Cat had never known better than "make do" her whole life. "I ... I really like it," she said, her voice hoarse.

Kyle nodded. "Good." He looked as though she'd just given him a present. He started to turn away.

Without thinking about it, Cat reached out. She touched his arm. In an instant, her hand sprang back. But Kyle was already turning back to her. "Thanks," she whispered.

He reached out as if to throw an arm around her, but instead patted her shoulder. "No problem, kid," he said with a wink.

Cat ducked her head and darted back to the barn. She'd always wanted a big brother. This one wasn't perfect. He drank too much, and only worked to buy more time to play. He teased and sometimes joked when he should be serious. Still, she'd have been pleased to have a brother just like him.

Two weeks later, Marty and Sam took her to pick out some furniture. Cat crawled into the backseat of Sam's car with Annie and Sam's granddaughter Lisa. "No," Lisa said. "Cat has to be in the middle."

Annie laughed and crawled over Cat's lap. Cat smiled at the girls as they nestled against her. "We know a secret," Lisa said with a giggle.

"Shhh!" said Annie. "No telling, Lisa. Remember?"

Lisa shook her head. Her wide grin pushed her chubby cheeks against her eyes, making them almost disappear. She hugged Cat's arm. "Get a grip, Annie." She shook her head hard. "I won't spoil the surprise. Cat's my favorite."

"Hey!" Sam said. "I thought I was your favorite."

"And what about me?" Marty said.

"Yeah," said Annie. "And me, too."

"Grampy, you're my grandpa. That's better than favorite. The rest of you are all my favorites," Lisa said, hugging Cat's arm harder.

Cat patted Lisa's arm, wishing she could be as trusting and open as Lisa. Like the other Down's syndrome children Cat had met on her trips with Marty to McFarland, Lisa was friendly and affectionate and trusting.

Annie inched across the seat closer to Cat. Cat slid an arm around her shoulders. These two little girls had crept into Cat's heart almost without her knowing it. She loved the warmth of them snuggled against her. When she'd first met Lisa, Cat had pulled away, uncomfortable with her clinging. But slowly, like frost disappearing from a windowpane, Lisa had melted something inside her.

At the store, Lisa and Annie hurried through the rows of beds and sofas and chairs, exclaiming, "How about this one?" or "Oh! I like this one." Cat tried to pay attention to Marty and Sam. They insisted she help pick out the furniture.

Cat almost laughed when Sam said, "I really wish we'd have been able to budget more for this, Cat, but we should be able to get you what you need." The amount of money they had to spend was more money than Cat spent on herself in a year.

The problem was she couldn't decide. With the wallpaper and paint, she'd finally just let Kristen choose. How could she make a decision when everything was so beautiful and cost so much more than she'd ever expected? Besides, what if she picked the most expensive items? Then they might think she'd turned greedy. Truth was, they could stop anytime and she'd still be grateful her whole life for all they'd done for her. She swallowed hard.

"Well, which sofa do you like best?" Sam asked.

"They're all so nice," Cat said.

Marty gave her one of her "I think I can fix this" looks. "How about if Sam and I pick three and you tell us which one you like best?"

"That'd be easier," Cat said.

An hour later they all piled back into Sam's car. In just three days a sofa, some chairs, a double bed, and a dresser would be delivered to the farm. Cat slipped her arms around the little girls and held them close. In three days, she'd move into her apartment. It was almost more than she could bear.

As they started down the farm lane, Marty was the first to notice lights on in the barn. "That's strange," she said. "Cat, did any of our boarders say they were coming back tonight?"

"No. They know to tell us if they're coming late."

"Sam, we'd better drive up there and see what's going on."

Sam turned left onto the asphalt drive that had recently been cut along the ridge that ran from the lane to the barn. When Sam stopped the car, they all piled out, but no one seemed to be in the barn. Cat made a quick check. All the horses were still bedded down for the night, just as she'd left them.

"Cat, maybe Kyle's still working on the apartment. Better check," Marty said.

Cat strode across the arena with Annie and Lisa following. Lisa giggled and Annie shushed her. Cat opened the back door. The light from the apartment window shone a rectangle of white on the ground. Cat tried the door. It opened on an apartment filled with people. "Surprise!" they yelled.

Cat's knees buckled and she almost went down. Annie and Lisa rushed forward to hug her. "I told you there was a surprise," Lisa said.

Cat stared. It wasn't her birthday. That was in May. At least, that's when she and Nana had always celebrated it. So what were all these people doing here? The entire family, including Aunt Bertie, the guys from the work crew, Dr. Brady and his little girl Kika, the boarders, Gayle, Mac, Luke, and Christy Morgan from the next farm, and Kristen all stood there as though they were waiting for her to say something. Marty and Sam came up behind her.

Kristen rushed forward. "So smile, will you," she said. "It's a housewarming party."

Lisa pushed Cat into the room. "And we get to help you open the presents," Lisa said.

In the corner, a stack of packages wrapped in joyful colors reached halfway to the ceiling. Lisa and Annie pushed Cat in that direction. As they passed the table, Cat stopped. Plates of cookies, a punch bowl, and a big rectangular cake filled the table. On the cake someone had painted an icing picture of the barn and the arena with her apartment on the end. She looked more closely. From the window of the apartment a tiny face with a red icing smile peered out. Her. That was her.

Cat looked around the room into all the faces grinning back at her. Her eyes burned. For the first time in years, she wasn't sure she could banish the tears.

Marty pushed through the crowd to her side. "Hey," she said. "This is supposed to make you happy."

"I am," Cat said. "I'll be right back, everyone." She ran from the apartment, past the glow of light to the edge of the dark field. She took deep breaths and squeezed her eyes shut until she was certain she wouldn't cry. All these years she'd toughened herself against the meanness in the world. Nobody got to her before she saw them coming. Well, she sure hadn't expected this one and she'd almost lost it ... ambushed by kindness.

ELEVEN

Marty made one more round of the barn. Good. All the spit and polish they'd been pouring into the place showed. Today was the day. Today the Lisa Center at Stafford Farm officially opened, only a week after the target date of October 15. "Cat, make sure Aunt Bertie brought the paper cups for the punch," she called.

"She did, Marty," Cat said, from where she and Duke worked to hang a banner across the end of the aisle.

"For heaven's sake, Marty," Duke puffed. "You've been riding close herd on all of us for days now. I promise you no one forgot anything."

The sound of hammering came from the front of the barn. Marty squeezed her eyes shut and prayed for patience. She'd been telling Kyle to get their sign up all week. Typical! Here he was with their guests due any moment, up on a ladder with only Kristen to help him heft the heavy sign into place.

Gayle Morgan—Marty's dearest friend since childhood, her neighbor, and now the Center's volunteer coordinator—gave her a hug. "Everything is perfect. Kyle will have the sign up before anyone gets here and if he doesn't, so what? Stop worrying."

"I can't help it." Marty wished she could be more like Gayle—so calm, so sure, so strong in love and faith. She looked at her friend and tried to smile. "The punch! Did anyone make the punch?"

Gayle laughed. "Yes indeed. Grandma Morgan's famous fruit punch. I made it myself, but I'll check and make sure it hasn't gone anywhere. While I'm at it, I'll make sure the youngsters are arranging the cookies to your specifications."

"I know I'm awful," Marty wailed.

"Not awful, just terribly fussy. You should be enjoying yourself. You've worked so hard to make this happen. Lighten up, friend."

"I'll try," Marty promised. As Gayle walked off, Marty looked at her watch. The first guests would be arriving in twenty minutes. Gayle was right. They were ready for them. But she couldn't forget that many of these guests were the VIPs—backers who had donated money or given free advertising, the mayor, the town council, people from the newspaper as well as the volunteers, the physical therapists, the few adult riders who had signed up ... everyone. Everyone except the kids. The kids' first sessions would start tomorrow.

The therapists had nixed having the kids attend the party, although Marty had so wanted them. To her they were the reason for all the work she had been doing for the past months. But as the head therapist had patiently reminded her, the kids wouldn't be coming here to play. They were coming to work and work hard. No sense starting them out thinking their time was all fun and games. Let the fun part come as a surprise and as a result of the work, Joanne had told her.

Gayle waved to her from the office and reception area. Marty hurried over. "What's wrong?" she asked.

Gayle laughed. "Nothing." She put her arm through Marty's and pulled her close. "You're standing there looking panic-stricken. Come and have a drink of punch."

"I'd choke on it," Marty said.

Inside the office, Aunt Bertie ladled the punch into plastic cups. Gayle's daughter Christy arranged cookies on a tray. Even Jeff helped, setting out paper plates and napkins with blue-eyed, honey-haired Rachel, the two of them paying more attention to each other than their tasks.

"Where's Annie?" Marty asked.

"Sam and Lisa made a run into town for more ice. Annie went with them," Gayle said.

"I told her she could go, Mom," Jeff said, "and that I'd tell you where she went."

Marty leaned into Gayle. "I can't believe this is finally real."

"Now, Marty, the Lord's been taking care of this since the beginning. Of course it's real!" Gayle said.

Marty wished she could be as firm in her faith as Gayle. She figured if there were modern saints, Gayle was one of them, although Gayle would vehemently deny it. But then humility was just another one of her virtues. "Friend," Marty said, "you are one of the great blessings of my life."

By the time Sam returned, Kyle and Kristen had the sign hung, the table was set and the refreshments ready. Duke and Cat had hung all the colorful "Welcome to the Lisa Center at Stafford Farm" banners.

The first guests to arrive were the Cramers—Joel, Amy, and their daughter, Casey. Not only was Joel the pastor of the church Marty attended, but Amy, an accomplished artist, had created the logo for the Center. Casey immediately charged across the room to be with Jeff and Rachel.

"I think you know everybody," Marty said, "except maybe Cat and Kristen." Marty gestured to each of the girls as she said their names. "Kristen and Cat, this is Joel and Amy Cramer."

Everyone said their hellos, Kristen warmly, a brilliant smile lighting her face. Marty noticed Kyle watching Kristen with a look of softness and vulnerability she'd never seen on his face. Uh-oh, little brother was getting in deep. And no wonder. Kristen was beautiful and bright and caring.

Cat looked uncomfortable, and Marty was certain she would have loved to escape.

"Cat," Joel said, "I'm sure we've met before."

"I don't think so, sir. Marty's been asking me to come to church, but see, I'm a Baptist."

Joel laughed. "I may be the Methodist pastor here, but I know a lot of people in other denominations."

Cat blushed a deep red and looked over her shoulder as if seeking an escape route.

"I'm not sure where it was, but I know I've met you somewhere," Joel insisted.

Gayle's husband, Mac, burst through the door. "Well, glory hallelujah! The big opening has finally arrived!" His son, Luke, pushed into the room after him. The mayor of Clayton and his wife strolled in right behind them, followed by Joanne from McFarland and two of the therapists. Through the open door Marty saw a steady line of cars climbing the drive. She blinked back tears.

Sam slipped a fatherly arm around her shoulder. "This is a time for smiles," he said.

"I know. I'm just so happy." Marty gave him a hug.

And by the end of the afternoon, Marty was even happier. Several of the big supporters had pledged additional money to the foundation to support the Center and had promised to encourage their friends to donate. And everyone seemed to have a good time.

The Cramers and the Morgans, and Cam Brady, who had arrived late as usual, stayed to help clean up. Marty noticed Joel talking to Cat, who had begun to look desperate again. The poor kid. She did have trouble dealing with strangers.

Marty went to bail her out. "Cat, why don't you get Lisa and Annie to help you feed."

Relief washed over Cat's face. She grabbed the little girls' hands and headed toward the feed room.

"Annie and Lisa," Marty called. "You two stay out of the way when Cat's bringing the horses in from the field."

"Marty, it's driving me crazy trying to figure out where I met that girl," Joel said. "I never forget a face."

Amy patted his arm. "Well, you turned forty last month. Maybe your memory is going."

Everyone laughed.

"I'd call that a challenge," Cam said. "Actually, knowing Joel, he won't rest until he figures out where he's met Cat."

"No, my wife can tease all she wants, but a pastor only gains respect and credibility with age."

Marty enjoyed their friendly bantering as they cleaned away what was left of the reception. All her nervousness had been for nothing. It had been a beautiful day, the appropriate beginning for a wonderful undertaking. Would she ever learn how to hand all that worry over to God?

The door to the room flew open and Annie and Lisa rushed in. "Dr. Brady, Cat says come quick! Sassy's hurt real bad!" Annie cried around sobs.

Marty and Cam ran out of the barn to the field, the rest following. Just over a hilly rise, Sassy struggled to her feet with Cat standing by her head. As Marty and Cam ran toward them the mare took a step forward, limping badly on her right front leg.

They had to push past the other horses to get through the gate. "You go on," Kyle called. "We'll put these guys in their stalls."

Everyone but Marty, Cam, and Mac stayed to help Kyle. Marty stole a look at Mac and saw fear in his eyes. Sassy was his, just on loan to Marty, and he made no bones about the fact he loved that mare just like he'd loved her mother before her.

"Don't move her, Cat," Cam called as they hurried toward her. Cat stopped, her hand on the mare's neck. The mare stopped with her.

"What happened?" Marty asked as Cam bent to check the leg.

"I whistled ... you know, like I always do ... for the horses to come on in and get fed. Well, they came charging and bucking. Then a sharp breeze blew some leaves. Sass, just playing, spooked and bucked, but she must have hit a hole 'cause she fell ... hard."

Mac walked behind them. "It's a hole all right," he said.

"I just checked this field yesterday," Cat protested.

"It's fresh dug, Cat. Not your fault. Blasted groundhogs!" Mac spat.

Cam ran his hand down Sassy's leg, from her knee to her ankle, again and again. He stood, looking troubled. "Let's see if she'll walk to the barn."

It was slow going but the mare climbed the hill to the barn. With every painful step, Marty winced. Poor Mac, he looked as if he were going to cry. Cat had gone pale, and trembled with anxiety.

Cam ran to his truck to get the portable X-ray machine and wheeled it into the barn. Annie and Lisa ran right beside him. Everyone gathered around. The other horses whinnied and banged their stall doors, demanding dinner. Sam and Kyle left to feed them.

Annie clung to Marty's side and Marty put an arm around her, patting her on the back. Annie pulled on Marty's sleeve. "Mom, I heard a really loud crack when she fell—like all her bones broke."

"Well, Annie, this machine will let us know if she broke anything," Cam said. "But I doubt it, the way she walked up the hill."

"And she always was a terrible baby. The slightest bump and she'd limp for a week," Mac said. The mare, calmer now, nuzzled his cheek. He leaned into her and stroked her jaw, worry still evident on his face.

Cam positioned the machine to take X-rays. He shooed

everyone out of range. Marty stepped back from the scene to collect her thoughts. If she hadn't, she wouldn't have noticed Cat, her eyes shut tight, lips moving. On the opposite side of the mare, Joel stared at Cat, an expression of recognition on his face. When Cat opened her eyes, she spun away from Joel and bolted toward Marty.

"I'd better help Sam finish the feeding, Marty," Cat mumbled. And she was gone, scurrying down the barn aisle.

Joel started after her. Cat looked over her shoulder and started to run through the barn, into the arena and out the other end.

Marty stared in amazement. Now what was going on with that odd child? Her instinct was to follow Cat and get to the bottom of this, but it would have to wait. Right now Sassy and the X-ray Cam had gone to develop took priority.

TWELVE

Cat ran all the way into her apartment. She slammed the door behind her and bolted it. She leaned against it, breathing hard, praying he wouldn't follow her. He knew. He hadn't at first. She was sure of that, but she had seen it in his eyes when he remembered. Right off, she'd known who he was. The years hadn't changed him much.

She felt the vibrations of his step before she heard his knock. "It's Joel Cramer," he called. "Please let me in. I have to talk to you."

Every muscle in Cat's body stiffened. Words froze in her throat. "Go away," she mouthed, shaking her head.

"Please, I understand. I just want to talk to you."

Cat shook her head—back and forth, back and forth. She stopped listening to his appeals. Slowly she backed away from the door. She crossed the living room and went into her bedroom. She shut that door behind her and slid down until she sat on the floor, her back against it. No, she wouldn't open the door. She wouldn't answer him. He thought he knew who she was, but he couldn't prove it. It was just his word against hers.

She remembered when she'd met him. How long ago? Eight years ago? Ten? She hadn't been very old, but she'd never forget him or the men he'd come with, an angry group of ministers determined to prove she was a fraud. Where had that been? Illinois? Indiana? The places from those years all ran together. But that night—wherever it had been—Cat remembered well.

Katie had noticed them right away when they'd walked into the tent. They walked woodenly, all stiff legs and tight shoulders in their fancy suits. But she'd been expecting them. Uncle Bud had told her, and then threatened her. "No funny stuff tonight, missy. You be at your best or we're liable to be run out of town on a rail."

She'd tried real hard that night, but the Lord hadn't given her any miracles, except for one old man, the one who had walked up onto the stage as if nothing was wrong. But Katie felt his pain. She prayed especially hard for him. She felt God's power working through her, and when she let go of his hands, he smiled. That did nothing for the crowd, because only Katie and the old man knew how sick he'd been. That's how it was lots of times. But that wasn't the way Uncle Bud or the crowd wanted it.

Of course, Uncle Bud had his usual plants in the audience. He decided that night not to go with the wheelchair lady. She'd been seen standing outside the tent before the show, smoking a cigarette and talking to the ticket seller. Probably drunk again. The teenager who faked the stutter almost laughed in the middle of his speech. It had been a bad night.

Katie wasn't surprised when the men showed up at the trailer door. Uncle Bud told them to go away. The show was over. They insisted on seeing Katie. He refused. Katie heard one of the men tell Uncle Bud he wouldn't like what he saw in the paper if he didn't let them in.

"I got this space for three more nights, fellas. Why don't you give us a break and just go about your business?" Uncle Bud said in that oily voice he used when he wanted something. Katie peeked out the door around her uncle.

"Well, sir, earlier in the tent you claimed to be doing the Lord's work. Now that means we're in the same business. We're ministers in this town, and we don't want you giving the Lord's business a bad name," said the young man Katie now knew to be Joel Cramer. "Believe me, sir, if our letter is printed in the paper, there will be no point in you staying for even one more night."

Uncle Bud gave a deep sigh and opened the door. "Well, since you put it so persuasively, gentlemen, do come in."

He held the door wide and the five men crowded in. Uncle Bud motioned them to the kitchen, where they took the four chairs and the stool. Uncle Bud leaned against the sink. "So just what can we do for you all?" he asked.

"We'd like to talk to Katie," one of the older men said, his voice kind as he looked at her.

Katie stood before them, biting her lip. She recited the Twenty-third Psalm in her head: *The Lord is my shepherd. I shall not want ... please, Lord, don't let me cry.... He maketh me to lie down in green pastures....*

And the questioning began. It wasn't so different from the other times in other towns.... "Well, Katie, so you have the power to heal people, do you?" ... "How do you do this?" ... "So, if you say the words right in your heart, can you heal anyone you want?" ... "How does Jesus let you know who he wants to heal?" ... On and on, around and around, until she usually became confused and said something she didn't mean because she misunderstood what they were asking.

But this time it ended differently. The young man, Joel Cramer, bent and looked right into her eyes. He had kind eyes, so Katie looked deep into them. "You believe in our Lord Jesus Christ, don't you, Katie?"

"Yes, sir," she said.

"What do you think he wants of you?"

"He wants me to touch people and say the words so he can make them better," she said. "See, they don't know the special prayer, so I have to say it for them."

"What are the words, Katie?"

She looked again hard into his eyes. Maybe ... no, she'd

promised. "They're from the Bible. The healer lady back home taught them to me. Only I can't tell anyone, 'cause I promised. If I tell, she said, God will be mad and he won't let me help him anymore."

The man sat back in his chair and sighed. "Katie, I don't believe God could ever get that angry with you. You are one of his special children, remember that." Joel smiled and reached out to touch her cheek.

The touch only lasted a moment and then Joel stood with the others to go. From the place where his fingers had rested, pain shot through the side of Katie's head across her forehead and down her other cheek. She reeled back, but the men were now talking to Uncle Bud.

They asked him to come outside, where they could speak to him alone. Katie crept to the opened window but only heard part of what they said. Words and phrases, many of which she didn't understand, like "exploitation" and "child labor and education laws" and "working a con," hung in the damp evening air.

Soon they left and walked toward the few parked cars left in the lot. Uncle Bud stomped off toward the camper where the wheelchair lady stayed. Katie slipped out of the trailer and followed Joel Cramer. He said his goodbyes and broke away from the others to walk to his car. Just as he reached for the door handle, she called, "Mister?"

He turned and smiled again—that gentle smile. This time Katie saw the pain in his eyes. He crouched down so that he was eye level with her. "What is it, Katie?" he asked.

She stepped forward and placed her hands on his temples. She recited the ancient words of the prayer in her heart asking Jesus to heal this man. She felt the warmth spread from the center of her soul down her arms into the man. "Amen and thank you, Jesus," she said. Then she turned and went back to the trailer. At the door she looked back toward the lot. The man was sitting in the dirt, staring after her.

Sometime in the middle of the night Uncle Bud came back. Katie smelled the whiskey on his breath when he wakened her. "Come on, brat, we're getting out of here...."

Cat could still hear Joel at the door. He spoke a little louder. "Please, listen, I mean you no harm ... how could I? If you ever need anything, call me. I've left my card here by the door. I don't know what's going on, but as far as I'm concerned your name is Cat and you work for Marty. I won't say any different."

After it had been quiet for a very long time, Cat crept into the living room. She pulled the curtain aside and peeked out the window. He was gone. She opened the door and snatched the business card he'd left on the doormat.

She stared, memorizing the phone number before putting it in her dresser drawer. Could she trust him? Maybe. Years ago she'd believed he was a good man. She had no reason now to think differently, just more evidence of his kindness. And he was Casey's father. That had been a surprise. Cat liked Casey. She was one of the nicest of the kids who came around. On the outside she seemed all spunky and sassy, but inside she was gentle and kind. Cat could tell by the way she treated the animals and the younger kids.

But people were unpredictable. Some people just had to meddle where it wasn't their business. Marty was like that sometimes. And if she and Joel teamed up it could be trouble. Cat sure didn't need anyone messing in her life right now, trying to fix it. For the first time ever, it didn't need fixing. At least, it hadn't before this afternoon, and if her luck held that X-ray wouldn't show anything. But she knew from experience that X-rays didn't lie.

THIRTEEN

When Cat finally left the apartment and went back to check on Sassy, the Cramers had gone. So had most everyone else except the family, Sam and Lisa, Gayle and Mac, and Kristen. Sassy stood in the crossties with Mac running cold water from the hose over her front leg.

"Cat, where have you been?" Marty asked.

"I had to go to my apartment for a minute."

"It was more than a minute, Cat. I could have used your help with this mare," Marty said, spitting the words hot and sharp from her mouth.

Cat went to take the hose from Mac. "It's all right," he said. "I've got it covered."

"What did Dr. Brady say?" Cat asked, hating the tremble she heard in her voice.

"He says it's a miracle if her leg's not broken, but he doesn't think it is. After all, she did walk in from the field on her own," Marty said.

"But, Mom," Annie wailed. "She was limping bad."

"Not like she would have been had it been broken," Mac said. "Like I said before, she's always been a real sissy about pain. I think we're looking at a bad sprain, that's all." He squinted at the leg as if he could see through the skin.

Kyle crouched in front of the mare and looked, too. "At least the cold water is keeping the swelling down."

Cat didn't need to look. There wouldn't be any swelling. The mare would be fine.

When Dr. Brady came back into the barn with the X-ray, Cat knew there would be trouble. She slipped away from all of them, hoping they didn't notice, hoping no questions would be asked. She busied herself sweeping outside the feed room. She couldn't hear what they were saying, but when she looked over her shoulder she could see the agitation in their poses as they stood around Dr. Brady and the X-ray.

"Cat, come here, please," Marty said.

A sigh racked her body. She had made up her mind. No matter what, she wouldn't lie. Marty had been too good to her. Still she couldn't tell her with all these people around.

Dr. Brady held the X-ray to the light. He pointed out the crack and the thickening areas around it. "It doesn't make any sense, but what I'm seeing is a fracture that is already healing, what I'd expect to see a month from now," he said, pointing to places where the bone seemed to be thicker at each end of the crack.

Cat nodded and tried to look innocent.

Everyone started to talk at once, firing questions at Dr. Brady, offering impossible explanations. Dr. Brady just kept shrugging and saying, "Actually, I don't know."

"Just a minute, everyone," Marty said. "Cat, tell us again exactly what you saw."

Cat felt herself growing small inside, shriveling back into a frightened little girl. So often she'd been questioned, by ministers, by town officials, by reporters. No one wanted to believe that one so small could have such a gift. Usually they left thinking she was a liar and a fraud. But it wasn't much better when they believed her. She didn't care much about the doubters. But she did care about the others, the ones who could have been friends, the ones who pulled away when they found out about her. She was too different, an oddball, a freak. She'd learned to steel herself to it, not expect anyone to understand. But she'd let her guard down this time. She didn't want these people to stop liking her.

Cat took a deep breath. "Well, like I told you, Sass was running and carrying on. Then she spooked. She fell in that hole. Landed hard."

"Did you hear the crack like Annie did?" Dr. Brady asked.

"Yes, sir, but at first I thought it might just have been how she landed. She went down like she was shot." All true. Cat might escape this time if they kept up this line of questioning.

"Did she get up on her own?" Marty asked.

Cat chewed her bottom lip. Marty was getting closer to the truth. The trick here was to answer the question carefully and offer nothing extra. "No, Marty, I helped her."

"Well, really, from that point on, we could see you. You were steadying her head," Marty said.

"And she was limping then, but not bad enough for me to suspect a break if Annie hadn't said something about the crack," Cam said.

"Could something be wrong with the X-ray?" Marty asked.

"Sometimes the image isn't clear enough for an accurate diagnosis, but this one is crystal clear. Beyond all reason, it shows a healing fracture." Cam shook his head and ran his hand over his bearded chin. "I mean, I guess maybe it could be the X-ray, but ... well, actually, I don't know. But regardless, I'd better cast this leg. Jeff, come and help me get my supplies from the truck." The two of them wandered off.

"Marty, if you're done with me, I'd better be getting back to work." Cat said.

Marty looked at her watch. "Oh, my goodness, yes. We all had. This place has to be in top shape by tomorrow morning when our first lessons arrive."

The next morning Cat woke up extra early and fed the animals. Poor Sassy looked uncomfortable, especially with the cradle around her neck to keep her from chewing the cast. Cat spent a few minutes cuddling her and then threw an extra flake of hay in the corner hay rack.

After the horses had eaten, Cat turned out the ones that

weren't to be used for lessons or whose owners wouldn't be coming to ride them. All the rest, including Sassy, stayed in after their breakfast. She hurried to clean the stalls.

While she worked, Dr. Brady and Marty came into the barn to check Sassy. They huddled together over her leg. Dr. Brady took more X-rays. To Cat's great relief they ignored her and let her go about her business.

Joanne arrived from McFarland well before the first riders. One by one, they drifted into the barn—Kyle, Annie, and then Jeff, followed a few minutes later by Sam and Lisa. Even Duke showed up to help, with a clean shirt on and a grin on his face, though it was early for him.

Two physical therapists from the hospital arrived and then the four volunteers who were scheduled to help. Cat had Glory Girl and one of the donor horses, Max, groomed and ready. They stood tied in the arena, each with a sheepskin across their back held in place with an elastic belly band.

With Kyle's help, Cat rolled the mounting block into place. She heard a car pulling up to the office door. Joanne, the other therapists, and Marty hustled off to greet their first rider.

Annie came into the arena carrying Lucky. Cody followed all dressed up with a red bandanna around his neck for the big day. As the kitten's tail swished back and forth under Annie's arm, the pup would give it an occasional lick. When Cody saw Sadie sitting beside Cat, he gave a yelp. Sadie jumped to her feet and leaped at Cody's new collar. As Cody ran through the arena toward the woods, Sadie hung by her teeth from the bandanna, her front foot off the ground, giving huge kangaroo hops with her hind legs when they chanced to hit the ground. Cat smiled. Even Sadie had made friends here.

"Cat, bring Glory to the mounting block," Marty called over the intercom.

Annie giggled. "She could have just opened the door and asked you."

"Naw," Jeff said, from his perch on the mounting block. "It makes her feel like a big shot to use that thing."

Cat led the mare to the mounting block—wide wooden steps and a platform that Kyle had built. A tiny blonde girl, much smaller than Annie but about the same age, Cat guessed, stood in the office doorway. Using a walker, she struggled toward them. She walked on her toes, her movements jerky, her mouth twisted with effort. Every few steps she stopped to rest. When she did, her eyes immediately lifted to the mare and a huge smile lit her face.

A woman with the same pale hair, brown eyes, and bright smile walked beside the girl. "Julie was so excited about this she couldn't sleep last night," the woman said.

Julie stopped again and smiled. Only a brief rest this time and then she moved her thin legs faster, hurrying the last few steps to the block. Joanne and one of the therapists came beside her as she reached the step. They each took her by the elbow as Julie pushed free of the walker.

Cat caught her breath with each labored step the child took. She wanted to put her arms around Julie, lift her to the platform, and then onto the horse. But she knew better. Even this struggle was part of the therapy.

When they reached the top of the platform, Marty signaled Cat to lead Glory forward. As she did, Glory lowered her big homely head to the tiny trembling hand Julie held out. "Julie, this is Glory Girl," Marty said. "We call her Glory, for short." Glory stuck her nose right in the little girl's face, blowing gentle puffs of air, checking her out. A tiny giggle, hardly more than a whisper, came from Julie.

"All right," Joanne said. "I can tell you two are going to get along just fine. Let's get you aboard."

Cat led Glory forward a step so that Julie faced her flank. The therapist put Julie's hands high on Glory's sheepskin-covered back. "Now you pull yourself on while we lift, Julie," she said. It looked to Cat as if Julie just gripped the sheepskin while the other two lifted her on, but no matter. The way her face lit up once she was on that horse's back and sitting upright, Cat figured it didn't matter how she got there.

Joanne and Marty showed Julie how to sit and hold the reins. A volunteer came forward to lead. Another stepped into place on one side of the mare, the third walked around to the other side. The side-walkers supported Julie's legs at the knee and ankle. "Now, Julie, what did we tell you to say when you were ready to go?" Joanne asked.

Cat saw by the excitement in Julie's eyes that she knew, but it still took some time for her to get the words out. Finally, they came, small and quiet, but triumphant, "Walk on, please!"

"That's the way!" Joanne cheered, nodding to the leader who stepped right out. The first session had begun.

Cat looked around her at these people she had come to care for. Tears glistened in the corners of Marty's eyes. And Sam's, too. Duke blew his nose noisily. Kyle cleared his throat. Annie hugged her brother. Cat thought Jeff's eyes were a bit shiny, too. He put on his cool teenage mask and, with a laugh, tousled Annie's hair. It was a good thing Kristen hadn't shown up; she'd be blubbering all over the place.

"Next horse, please," called the other therapist. Holding her hand, a little boy with the blunt features of a Down's syndrome child waved at Cat. She smiled and waved back. The boy was already so excited he bounced and squirmed. If he smiled any wider, his cheeks might burst.

Cat rubbed a finger hard under her nose. She went to get Max, who was scheduled for this lesson. This was no time for her to get all mushy like the rest of them. She had work to do.

FOURTEEN

Marty rubbed her neck and flexed her shoulders. She had always considered herself a physically strong person, but no doubt about it, she needed to get in better shape. A week of tugging and lifting and side-walking with her riders—both the therapeutic riders and the general lesson kids—had taken its toll. She took a sip of tea from her mug and settled onto the porch swing. What a treat to have such a mild evening in late October. She smiled as she pushed off to start the swing's gentle sway. Her children were out for the evening, Annie in town playing with Jennifer Patterson, Jeff with Rachel and their gang at the movies in Washington.

In the past seven days she'd cared for twenty-five therapeutic riders, nine adults and sixteen children. Either Joanne or her assistant had been present at each one, but in order to learn, Marty had walked side by side through each one. The volunteers were wonderful. Only a few didn't show or came an hour or more later than they were supposed to.

She was grateful that Joanne had scheduled breaks in the week. The Lisa Center, which was the official title of the therapeutic riding branch of her business, operated on Mondays, Wednesdays, Fridays, and Saturdays. They hadn't filled all of their slots yet, but Marty was aware of how lucky they were to be associated with McFarland and the hospital, both of which had waiting lists and had been looking for another facility.

On the off times, she'd scheduled her nine general riding lessons with the boarders and kids from town. Those sessions had been physically less demanding and, while not as gratifying, were fun and profitable as well.

The screen door squeaked and Duke walked toward her carrying a can of red soda pop. Cody bolted out the door before it slammed shut and charged toward Marty, dropping at her feet.

Marty scratched the dog's neck and gave his side a pat. She nodded toward her dad's pop can. "That stuff's not good for you," she said, keeping her voice soft. She didn't have it in her to let his indulgence go unnoticed, but neither did she want a hassle, not tonight.

"A little treat won't hurt me," he said, settling into the armchair across from her. "Not as hard as I worked all week."

"You sure did, Dad." Marty smiled at him. "Thanks for all your help."

Duke nodded and took a sip of his pop. "It was a good week, wasn't it?"

"Sure was. The best."

"I was thinking ... so many of the kids come early and have nothing to do while they're waiting. And then, too, we've got all their brothers and sisters running around. Maybe I could set up a little zoo for them, you know. We've got Daisy, the two ponies, and the kittens, and that raccoon of Jeff's. Come spring we should have some ducklings."

Marty stifled the grin she felt working its way to her lips. Obviously, Duke had been thinking about this for a while now. "I think that's a nice idea, Dad. We'll have to find a place that's out of the way but still close enough for the kids to get to easily."

Duke shifted to the edge of his chair and leaned forward. "I figure Annie would like to help. Maybe Cat."

"Well now, Annie will be in school during some of the weekday lessons. And the program needs Cat," Marty said.

"Well, honestly, I can handle it alone. I just wanted your permission. You're the big shot around here now."

Duke looked at Marty with a look of such intense love, she glanced away.

"I'm real proud of you, girl," he said.

"Thanks, Dad," she said, her throat filling so she couldn't say more.

"Lots of people in your situation … losing your husband and all … would have just sat down to feel sorry for themselves. I know I did. I plain couldn't cope without your mother. But look at you. You've done better than just cope. You've turned to something that I think is real important. What I've seen this week with those little kids … well, it matters, you know." He reached in the pocket of his baggy jeans and pulled out a hanky. He blew his nose loudly. "And you know all of this lit a fire under me, too. I just … I don't know, I'm not too good with saying things right, but I feel real good about all of it, you know?"

"You should, Dad. You've been a part of it since day one. This is still your place. I may run the stable and the Center, but you're the boss at Stafford Farm. And you were the one who invited me to come home."

Duke gave a short laugh. "Well, stubborn as you are, I knew you'd never ask. I figured you and the kids needed to be with family."

Marty nodded and took another sip of tea. Duke was right; she never would have asked, even though her financial situation, while not desperate, had been tight, and moving home meant she'd have more than enough money to raise and educate the children. Duke knew it, too, but he never threw that up to her, never made her feel as though she had accepted his charity. What a bullheaded woman she'd been. She hadn't even known how much she'd needed her family and old friends. In Washington, D.C., after Dan's death, her wounds had just been festering. Now with all this love around her, she'd begun to heal. If only it wasn't such a slow process.

Sadie rushed up on the porch, her small stub of a tail

wagging. Cat stepped out of the shadows behind her. "Hi," she said.

"Hi, yourself," Marty said.

"What's a pretty young girl like you doing home alone on a Friday night?" Duke asked.

"You're always saying things like that," Cat teased back. "Believe me, I've had enough trouble in my life without going out on a Friday looking for more."

"Besides, she's not alone," Marty said. "She's with us. Right, Cat?"

"That's right." Cat settled onto the porch sofa. Sadie, tired of trying to get Cody's attention, jumped up beside her. "Beautiful night," she said.

"Sure is," Marty answered. "Want a cup of tea or some juice?"

"Not now, thanks."

Marty leaned back into the swing and pushed off again. She liked the fact that Cat now felt comfortable enough to seek their company. Still, she had to be lonely sometimes. "Thanksgiving is just around the corner, Cat. The Center will be closed that weekend. Would you like some time off to visit Nana?"

"No," she said. "I mean ... we aren't much for celebrating the holidays and all. Besides, there'll still be plenty of work to do here even without the Center being open. All the boarders will be out to ride on the weekend, and it's your holiday, too. I won't go off and leave you stuck."

"Cat, you're entitled to time off."

"The agreement was Tuesdays and half-days on Sunday. That's fine with me." Cat squirmed on the cushions.

Marty backed off. She'd learned over the last months not to probe too deeply into those unexplainable dark corners of Cat's mind. Besides, if she waited, Cat sometimes opened up a little and gave Marty a glimpse into her reasoning. But Cat said nothing more. "Well then," Marty said. "You will have Thanksgiving dinner with us."

"I'd like that," Cat said, bending to fuss with Sadie's collar.

"And why don't you invite your Nana up here for the feast," Duke coaxed. "Marty makes the best stuffing."

Cat shook her head. "Nana's arthritis has been bothering her. She's probably not up to travel, but thanks anyway," Cat murmured.

Marty watched Cat's face screw up as though she were thinking hard about something far away. "Maybe I'll take that Saturday and Sunday off and go see her," Cat said at last. "If that's all right."

"Of course, it's all right," Marty said. "With the kids off school through Monday, I'll have plenty of help."

They settled into an easy silence, Marty feeling a sense of rightness about the exchange.

After a minute or so, Duke started to hum. "Isn't that what you were playing the other night, Cat?"

"It's a mountain tune I know. I might have been playing it the other night, but I didn't know anyone was listening."

"I hear you up there playing on nice nights. I leave my bedroom window open a crack just so I don't miss you. Why don't you go and get that instrument and play for us?" Duke said.

"I'm not very good."

"What I've heard comes down off that hill as soft and sweet as my mamma's lullabies. I'd sure love to hear it tonight."

"Dad's right, Cat. Some music would be just the thing," Marty said.

Cat gave a shrug. "Well, I feel real silly, but all right." She ordered Sadie to stay and took off up the hill toward her apartment.

"You know, Marty," Duke said, his eyes following Cat up the hill, "thinking about all the kids that have gone through here this week, I believe that one may need us more than any of the others."

"I've thought that myself, Dad," Marty said, and rose to go make another cup of tea.

When she returned, Cat had settled onto a chair and was tuning her mandolin. Even in the dull glow of the porch lamp Marty could see that the instrument was old and well made. "What a gorgeous instrument," she said.

Cat smiled. "Nana says my grandpa made it. After he passed, it belonged to my mamma. It's all I've got left of them." She worked the strings, the rich sound filling the air.

"My husband played the guitar, or maybe I should say tried to play the guitar," Marty said. She smiled, remembering. "He was a college student in the early seventies. Guitar-playing, folk-song-singing guys were very popular with the women. I think that's why he took it up. He told me once that the oils from his hands over time would permeate the wood of the guitar's neck and make the instrument's sound uniquely his own."

Cat nodded. "I've heard that before, too. I hope it's true. Nana said my mamma played and sang like an angel." She began to play a tune, a sweet and haunting ballad that Marty vaguely recalled singing in high school. Marty hummed along, singing the few words she remembered. When the song was over, Duke smiled. "Yes, sir, that was nice."

Cat picked out another tune, a lively jig.

"'The Irish Washerwoman,' right?" Marty asked.

"Oh, I don't know the name, but I like it," Cat said.

"And so do I," Duke said.

After Cat played a few more songs, a car pulled onto the gravel lane. Pudgy Patterson drove up to the house with his daughter and Annie. One of the nicest things Marty found about coming home was watching her children make friends with children whose parents were her old friends, like Darla and

Pudgy Patterson. It gave her a feeling of solid rootedness.

Pudgy hefted his bulk to the ground with a grunt. "Here she is. Miss Annie. Delivered as promised."

Annie and Jennifer bounced up the porch steps. Annie waved a newspaper at her grandfather. "Here you go, Grandpap," Annie said. "Me and Jennifer went over to Raynak's to buy some candy and they had just gotten your paper, so I got it for you."

Duke took the paper. "Hot dog, the new *Roving Star.*" He gave Annie a hug. "What a good granddaughter I have."

Marty looked at Pudgy and shook her head. "I can't believe he reads those rags," she said.

"Look at them sometimes myself, Marty," Pudgy said. "Especially when it's about alien abductions and possessions. I love to see what kind of misdeeds people are blaming on poor defenseless aliens." He gave a hearty laugh and settled onto the porch step. "Sure is a gorgeous night."

Annie and Jennifer squeezed in next to Cat. "Oh, Cat, were you making music?" Annie asked. "Please, play something."

But Cat just squirmed on the step, ignoring the girls. Her eyes darted from Duke, who sat with the paper up to his face, to Marty, and then toward her apartment on the hill. "I think I'd best be getting to bed. Sorry." She jumped to her feet and, like a pheasant flushed out of hiding, fled.

"Gee, I hope we didn't scare her off," Pudgy said.

"No, she's real shy, that's all," Marty said, watching her go. "Honestly, she's been getting better. And she certainly should be used to the Patterson family by now. I don't know what spooked her tonight." One thing Marty knew for sure, something more than the appearance of Pudgy and the girls had driven Cat off.

FIFTEEN

Cat turned out all the lights in her apartment. She had left kind of abruptly. This way if they came checking on her they'd think she was sleeping. She curled into the armchair, waiting in the darkness, holding Sadie close. She had to get to town to get one of those papers. She opened the window a crack and listened. After a while she heard a car start. *Good, the Pattersons must be leaving.* She waited a bit longer. The air coming through the crack was chilly now as the night edged on.

She slipped from the apartment to the edge of the hillside. Below her the porch lights were still lit, but no one sat on the porch. Jeff was still out, but it was well before his curfew. As for Kyle, on Friday nights he usually crawled in closer to dawn. The downstairs was dark, but a few lights glowed from the upstairs windows. *Duke, Annie, and Marty must be getting ready for bed.* It was their custom to read awhile before turning out the lights. Cat bit her lip. Duke was no doubt reading that awful paper.

With the headlights and motor off, Cat let her truck roll down the hill. The driveway to the barn hugged the hillside. Because of the configuration of the land and the placement of several large trees, it was only visible from the porch for a short distance. No one looking out of a window would see her. With their windows closed, they shouldn't hear her. The drive entered the lane on the far side of the bend, out of sight of the house.

As the truck dropped onto the lane, Cat started the engine. When she got to the road, she pulled on the lights. By her figuring she still had a half hour before Raynak's eleven o'clock closing time. The country road wound long and lonely in front of her. She made it to Raynak's in ten minutes.

The rack with the *Roving Star* stood right by the check-out. The pictures of smiling children stared at her. In shocking red the headline glared: THE PRODIGIES—WHERE ARE THEY NOW? A leaden lump formed in her chest. There was Katie Parker—the only one not smiling—staring from the bottom center of the sheet.

Mrs. Raynak was behind the counter. "Well, my goodness, Cat, this is late for you," she said.

"Yes, ma'am." Cat had to think fast. She couldn't just grab a paper and leave. "I've come to get some milk for breakfast." She headed for the cooler at the back of the store. She knew Mrs. Raynak was smiling after her. The darn woman was so friendly. Cat used to think it was neat that Mrs. Raynak knew everyone by name. Now Cat just wished she could disappear.

She loaded up on milk, orange juice, and some bread. At the counter she listened to Mrs. Raynak chatting on about the beautiful weather. As the woman reached for the final item, Cat threw the paper on the counter. Mrs. Raynak scooped it up without looking at it. She tossed it into the bag with the other items.

Cat called good-bye more cheerfully than she'd said hello and made her escape. She only got as far as the parking lot before she was stopped. Jeff, Rachel, Casey, and another of their friends, a kid named Hap, piled out of Casey's parents' Chevy sedan. "Hey, Cat," called Casey, "what are you doing here?"

"Just getting some stuff for breakfast," she mumbled, moving toward the truck. She hopped in and started the motor. "See you," she called and took off, even though Casey had a hand raised and Jeff was calling to her.

The trip home seemed a lot longer than the trip in, even though the clock showed different. As she drove past, she checked the house. The upstairs lights were out. Good. They'd gone to bed. Cat hurried into her apartment. She ripped the bag trying to get at the newspaper. She sank down at the kitchen table and opened it. There she was with big round eyes, staring darkly. She studied the old photo. It was pretty fuzzy, and in it she looked to be about ten years old. Maybe no one would recognize her.

She read the captions under the pictures. The Asian boy was listed as a violin prodigy. The pretty blonde girl was some kind of math genius who had gone to college at the age of twelve. The curly-headed, freckled boy was a chess master who had beaten a famous Russian player. On and on … a six-year-old who had mastered four languages, a thirteen-year-old sculptor, some pale sunken-cheeked boy they called the human computer … until she came back to Katie Parker, listed as a miracle healer.

She opened the paper. The story covered all of page two and most of page three. They had tracked down some of the children pictured. The blonde girl taught at Harvard. The Asian boy played fiddle in a country band. The human computer was in a mental hospital. The artist was still carving things. They hadn't been able to find the chess master, or the girl who spoke all the languages, or Katie Parker, the miracle healer. The article then listed dozens of other children like them, children with gifts, who had disappeared over the last fifty years.

The reporter went on to quote articles written in the fifties and sixties that claimed the earlier kids had been kidnapped into Russia. He didn't believe the Russian connection. He thought they were being held prisoner and studied by some top secret branch of the U.S. government. As uncomfortable as she was by the whole thing, Cat had to smile. She just couldn't imagine herself as a government guinea pig. At least, this guy was a little saner than the newsman who came poking around when she was little trying to prove she was an alien.

She continued to read and her smile disappeared. The reporter had interviewed Uncle Bud. "Naw, the kid's still around somewhere," Uncle Bud had said. "I know she talks to the old woman who raised her, so she's still on the planet." At the end of the column a plea from Uncle Bud was printed: "Katie, if you read this, please come home. I'm sick, real sick. I need you." At the end of the article, Cat saw in block print, "ANYONE KNOWING THE WHEREABOUTS OF ANY OF THESE YOUNG PEOPLE CALL ..." and a phone number.

An asterisk beside the number led Cat to the bottom of the page. When she read the notice there she nearly choked—"A two-hundred-dollar reward is offered for information that will lead to the recovery of Katie Parker."

Cat slammed the paper onto the table. The recovery of Katie Parker! Ha! She was recovering very nicely, and would continue to recover as long as she kept away from that rat of an uncle. A knock on the door startled Cat. She jumped to her feet in a panic, looking for someplace to hide the paper. She opened the freezer and stuffed it beside the ice cube trays.

When she opened the door, Jeff and Casey stood on the stoop, looking sheepish.

"Hi," Casey said. "Jeff wants to ask you something, but you ran off before we could. We dropped Rachel and Hap off at their houses in town and hurried out here to catch you before you went to bed." She smiled and her whole face seemed to bloom, one of the reasons Cat liked Casey.

Jeff cleared his throat. "Well, you could at least ask us in," he said.

"Sure," Cat mumbled, stepping aside. She frowned as they settled onto either end of the couch as though they had arrived for a long visit.

"Cat, we've heard you playing your mandolin," Jeff said. "When you play outside your apartment, we can hear you down at the house."

Casey laughed. "Yeah, and sometimes we sneak a little closer to hear better, too."

Jeff looked apologetic, but still Cat found herself getting defensive. Duke leaving his window open was one thing, but was everybody snooping on her? The music was hers—her comfort, her tie to her home, hers to share only when she chose. She set her jaw.

"Aw, man," Jeff said, "will you get that look off your face? We just want to ask if you'd teach us some of your music."

Casey leaned forward, her elbows on her knees. "Cat, you know we have this band. Well, we started out playing jazz and we still do, but we've started doing some bluegrass and you're really good. We'd love it if you would help us."

Cat shook her head. "Thanks, but I don't know..." She was flattered, but she had a lot more on her mind tonight. Maybe she could tell them she'd think about it and they'd go away.

"Look," Jeff blurted, his face red. "I just have to know how to play some of those tunes. I've got my dad's old acoustic guitar. I've never played it much, but hearing you ... I want to play your songs on his guitar. I've been trying to pick them out, but I can't get them right." He stared at Cat. He looked like a little boy begging for candy. "Look, I know I've been a real jerk and haven't been very nice to you, but..."

"It's not that..." Cat started. She thought of her own beautiful mamma, her long brown hair sweeping forward as she bent over the mandolin, playing each note perfectly. Nana said her mamma had been that good. Cat was nowhere near as good as her mamma had been. She looked from Jeff to Casey, her expression almost as eager as his. "My music has always been something special, private. I only share it every once in awhile. I'm just not comfortable..."

Casey held up a hand to stop her. "I'm sorry to interrupt, Cat, but my dad always says that when God gives a special gift, that gift is for sharing. And the way you play that mandolin, you've been given the gift of music. Please share it with us."

Cat looked away from them. Guilt floated to the surface. Her music wasn't the only gift Cat had tried to hide. And the other one was far more important. She looked hard at Jeff. She'd heard him banging angry rhythms on those African drums of his, and she'd recognized tones of both sorrow and joy when he played the saxophone. He knew how music soothed a hurting heart, just as she did.

On lonely nights, Cat picked up her mandolin to play, conjuring up all the images she had of her poor dear mother—Mamma, who had sung and played like the angels ... Mamma, who although sick and worn out had struggled to care for her until she just couldn't anymore ... Mamma, whose last act was to make sure her baby girl was safe. Some nights her mamma's mandolin music was all that could comfort Cat enough to allow her to sleep.

"All right, but just you two, no one else," Cat said. "The mandolin isn't the same as a guitar, but it's close enough. I learned first on a guitar, so we'll work it out. Now would you two get out of here and let me get some sleep? It's nearly midnight."

Casey jumped up. "Thanks, Cat. You're wonderful!" She bounced toward the door.

Jeff hung back, his hands in his jeans pockets, looking down at his shoes. "Thanks, Cat. I just really need to learn to play my dad's guitar, you know."

Cat sighed, letting her defensiveness flow from her with her breath. "I understand. It's my mother's mandolin."

His head shot up and he gave her a wry smile, blinking rapidly but not fast enough to hide the tears shimmering in the corners of his eyes. He was a good kid at heart, like his Uncle Kyle. Cat felt as if she'd just adopted another brother. Maybe that's what she was doing here, adopting an entire family, a family that seemed to want to claim her, too.

She got ready for bed and in no time burrowed under her covers. Sadie jumped up beside her. Cat looked at the little dog's stump of a leg and remembered. She'd found Sadie bloody, limp, and nearly lifeless, lying in the manure wagon at the track where she'd been dumped. If Cat hadn't used her gift, Sadie would have died. And Duke might have. And Sassy? Well, who knew, but Cat was sure she'd helped the mare. Surely it was nothing to share her music.

"Katie, if you read this, please come home," Uncle Bud had said. But what he didn't know was that she was home, as long as they'd have her, and as long as he didn't interfere. But Uncle Bud would probably like nothing more than to jump in with both boots and mess it up for her. He probably wasn't even sick. He'd just used it to con that fool reporter into searching for her. But what if he really was sick? The thought caused odd feelings to swirl inside her. If he died, she'd be free. But could she just let him die?

Her heart pounded and her throat felt tight. Her breath came in short, shallow gasps. She propped her pillows against her headboard, turned on her light, and sat up to think. In the months she'd been here, she'd been getting better about old Bud. Lately, the mere thought of him hadn't sent her running to hide. So why was she panicking now?

She knew. She'd known since the night they'd thrown the party for her. With every day she spent here, she grew more into these people and this place. For the first time in her life she had something to lose.

SIXTEEN

The next morning after Cat fed and turned the horses out, she hurried to the apartment. She still had plenty of time before the first riders arrived, and she had to talk to Nana.

Nana answered on the second ring.

"Nana, hi." Cat tried to keep her voice level. No need to get Nana fretting right off the bat.

"My darling girl, I was just thinking about you." Nana's voice sounded like sunshine.

It only took a few minutes to share the news of the last four days since Cat had talked to her. "Nana, listen," Cat said. "Uncle Bud's at it again. He was talking to some reporter from one of those gossip papers."

"When is the Lord going to deliver us from that man?" Nana asked with a deep sigh. "God, forgive me. I really wish him no harm, but he is a thorn in my hide."

"Mine, too. This time it's worse than usual. The article listed a number and Bud's put up a two-hundred-dollar reward for information about me."

"My goodness," Nana said. "Now that's puzzling."

Cat waited for Nana to explain.

"Bud's so tight, he squeaks when he walks. I can't believe he'd put up that kind of money. What's he hope to gain? Surely he doesn't think he can force you back on the road. Not at your age."

Cat's stomach clenched. Nana was right. "He says he's sick and needs me."

"I'll see what I can find out, but he hasn't been around in a while," Nana said.

"Uncle Bud told the reporter that he knew I still talked to you."

"You know Samuel's got a big mouth, sweetie. If he wasn't my dead sister's boy, I'd disown him."

Cat smiled. She remembered Samuel's gentle hands over hers as he positioned her fingers on that kiddie guitar, and how he came later to help her with her music whenever he could. "Samuel's okay, Nana. Just don't tell him anything you don't want the world to know. And make sure no one gets hold of my phone number. All right?"

"I've got it hid in a plastic bag at the bottom of my flour bin and stored in my memory, too. No need to worry. Praise God, my memory hasn't failed me yet."

Cat relaxed a bit. If Uncle Bud had any clue as to where to find her, he never would have offered money. Nana was right. The man made Scrooge look generous. With the release of fear, Cat's heart filled with a rush of sadness. She missed Nana. Still, if Bud was snooping around at all, there was no way she could go home. "Nana, if I send you the money, could you get a bus and come up here for Thanksgiving?"

"That's a mighty tempting invitation. Especially seeing as how I'm missing you something terrible. I haven't really made plans yet, though the cousins and I usually get together then. I'm sure they'd understand," Nana said.

Cat kept quiet and let Nana continue to talk herself into coming. She looked up and saw the clock on the stove. "Nana, I've got to scoot. We've got two therapeutic riders due in a half hour. You check the bus schedule to Washington, Pennsylvania. That's the closest to where I am. I'll call you back next week."

"Well, let me think some more on it, but I surely am tempted...."

"I want you to come and meet my family here," Cat said.

After Cat got off the phone, and even while she readied the horses for the first lessons, her own words warmed her—"my family here." For that's how she was coming to look at them. And families stuck together, as Nana had always stuck with her. Nana had always been more family to her than Bud, her true blood relative. She just knew that Marty and Nana would hit it off.

But when Duke walked into the barn, she snapped back to reality. He'd read the article, she felt sure. She searched his face for signs of trouble. Did he know?

"And how is our gifted girl this morning?" he asked.

Cat's heart pounded.

"I sure did enjoy last evening," he continued. "I believe music is one of the Lord's great blessings. And you've got the gift, girl."

Cat smiled and relaxed.

"Now, how about helping me out here a minute," he said. Puffing, he hurried toward Daisy's stall. "Animals are another of his blessings, so I'm going to set up a little petting zoo for the youngsters. You know, for when they're waiting for their lessons. For the brothers and sisters, too. I feel kind of bad they don't get to ride. Annie's on her way up here and so is Jeff, but they're pokey this morning."

Cat hurried to him, glad to help. He obviously hadn't connected her to the girl in the picture. "Why don't we use the foaling stall?" Cat suggested. "It will only take a few minutes to remove the divider and open it up."

"Good idea," Duke said.

Just as Cat came from the tack room with the stepladder, Jeff walked into the barn. He held his raccoon in a pet carrier. Through the wire net door Cat could see the poor thing weaving back and forth.

"I figure Herman will be calmed down by the time the kids get here. If he gets all freaky on us, I'll just take him back to the house," Jeff said.

"For now, give him to your grandpap and help me get rid of

this divider," Cat bossed, figuring after last night she had the right. "Duke, let us do this. You catch your breath."

In no time, the two of them slid the two-by-fours from the brackets. The two stalls became the large foaling stall. As Cat led Daisy to the stall, Annie rushed in with a brightly colored sign proclaiming "Zoo Room." Jeff helped her tack it to the door.

By the time Julie and Davey arrived for their lessons, Annie had rounded up the kittens. Jeff had Herman calmed down enough to allow Davey's small stubby fingers to stroke his fur. Herman reached up and took Davey's glasses. The little boy laughed, his face squinching up so tight his eyes disappeared.

All morning long kids went in and out of the zoo room. Around noon, during a half-hour break in the lesson schedule, Cat went to check on Duke's zoo. As she came around the corner, she heard Jeff yell and saw Herman coming at a dead run, chittering as he went. Jeff charged after him, but the raccoon had too much of a head start.

Cat dropped to her knees. The frightened raccoon made a beeline for her and climbed right up into her arms. As she wrapped her arms around him, he hid his head in the crook of her elbow.

"Thanks, Cat," Jeff said. He reached for Herman, whose tiny paws clung to Cat and refused to be pried loose.

"What happened?" Cat asked.

"The one therapist brought her daughter today. The kid tried to pick Herman up. When he backed away, she grabbed for him. You know what a chicken he can be. I thought we'd lost him."

Cat carried Herman to the zoo room and sat a few minutes with him until he loosened his hold. She handed him back to Jeff. Immediately he ducked his head under Jeff's elbow.

Cat knew his story. Dr. Brady had found him chained to a porch where someone had used him for B.B. gun practice. That's the kind of bad scare that left scars much deeper than the skin. "He'll come around in time, Jeff. Just keep letting him know he can trust you."

Jeff gave her a long stare. "What I want to know is why he ran to you? Usually I'm the only one he'll come to when he's scared."

Cat shrugged.

"In case you haven't noticed, Mr. Smarty," Annie piped up from the corner where she sat cuddling her kittens, "all the animals love Cat."

Cat laid a hand on Annie's soft brown curls. "That's because I love all animals, Annie. That's what wins them, knowing you love them."

For the afternoon lessons, Marty was short one volunteer, so Cat helped in addition to getting the horses ready. She led Glory for Angie, a five-year-old Down's syndrome girl who sang cowboy songs while she rode.

She side-walked with Jim, a silent, remote autistic boy. She could feel the tension in the leg she braced, and ached for him. She had known a time of being locked in silence inside herself. She prayed for him as she walked, but the healing warmth did not come. Still, by the end of the lesson, Jim's leg had relaxed. And when he dismounted, he leaned forward and kissed Max on the nose. He smiled and whispered, "Thank you."

She had learned not to question God about such things. Besides, Cat had come to see that the Lord had provided for all kinds of healing. And maybe he'd set her down in this place to show her another. In fact, she was pretty sure that, even without any healing miracle, Jim walked away from Max much less woodenly than he'd marched to the mounting block to start his lesson.

By the end of the day, their busiest of the week, Cat was exhausted. But when Jeff showed up at her door with the guitar, she couldn't turn him away.

"Casey's busy tonight," he said. "But she already knows a bit about the guitar, so maybe if you worked with me...."

"Sure," Cat said, fetching her instrument.

Jeff was so eager to learn. She had no words for much of what she had to teach him. Still, he caught on quickly when she demonstrated.

After an hour or so, he was picking out the notes to the simple piece all by himself. "Good," Cat said. "Now practice it until you know the notes by heart. Then you can worry about getting the rhythm right."

Jeff smiled at her and started to say something, his cheeks turning red. He looked back down at his guitar. The phone rang and Cat went to answer it.

"Hey, is my son still up there pestering you?" Marty's warm laugh sounded on the other end of the line.

"He's not bothering me. We're just working on some music."

"Well, I was too pooped to cook tonight and the pizza man just arrived with dinner. Send him on down and you come with him. Kyle must have been hungry, because he ordered enough to feed an army."

"We'll be right there," Cat said.

Again Marty laughed. "Do you know that's the first time I didn't have to coax you into accepting an invitation?"

Cat hesitated before answering. "I guess you're right. I think it's because I now know you mean it." She got off the phone and, with Jeff chatting away beside her, headed down the hill to the farmhouse.

Just before they reached the porch, Jeff grabbed Cat's arm, stopping her. "Cat, I wanted to tell you ..." He shook his head. "Aw, man, this is tougher than I thought it would be ... look, I'm really sorry ... you know, for being so nasty to you when you first came."

Cat could feel her cheeks getting hot, but she nodded to let him know she accepted his apology.

"But you don't know the half of it. I bad-mouthed you to Mom. I told her not to trust you. I thought you weren't being square with us. I never gave you a chance."

Cat held out her hand. "So come on, shake. It's all over. We're friends."

Jeff pumped her hand, grinning. "Thanks, Cat. You're the best."

But Cat knew she wasn't. As they climbed the porch steps, she remembered the night before, the awful article in that dreadful paper, and how she'd run, afraid the truth was closing in on her. Jeff was right—she had never been totally square with them. And if she cared about these people as much as she thought she did, it was time she trusted them with the truth. The thought stopped her dead in her tracks.

SEVENTEEN

On the Wednesday before Thanksgiving, Cat sat in her truck in Raynak's parking lot, waiting for Jeff to return from the hardware store. She leafed through the latest edition of the *Roving Star.* There was a letter to the editor from some man in North Dakota who claimed to know the exact location of the government compound that held the young prodigies prisoner. Other than that, no news on October's big story. It looked as though it would all blow over.

Still Cat knew she should come clean with the family. She'd started to—several times—but somehow the timing never seemed right. Although she knew it was the right thing to do, part of her argued that it might not be necessary. Nana had said Bud had come back home but wasn't bothering anybody. Nana would arrive tomorrow in the early afternoon. Cat had told her about her new name and that no one here knew about her. Nana wouldn't give her away.

She jumped when Jeff opened the passenger door.

He pointed to the newspaper. "Aw, man, Cat, don't you start reading that garbage, too. It's bad enough that Grandpap does," he said.

Cat stuffed the paper between her seat and the door. "I usually don't," she muttered. "Did you get what Kristen needs?"

Jeff looked into the big paper bag on his lap. "I sure hope so," he said. "I got the last fake pumpkin in the place and an extra large supply of hot glue."

"And the staples?"

"Enough to keep her staple gun loaded well into the new year."

Cat smiled. "It's going to be a great float."

"Is it really a float? I mean, we're talking about a hay wagon pulled by a team of work horses loaded with a bunch of kids dressed like Indians and Pilgrims. I'm not sure that's a float," Jeff said.

"I don't know what else to call it," Cat mused.

"I guess it's as close to a float as we'll see in the Clayton Holiday Parade tomorrow," he said. "And I do have to admit it looks pretty good."

When they got back to the farm, the float looked even better than when they had left. The Morgans' big flatbed hay wagon had been pulled into the indoor arena, where it had been transformed. Kristen, looking like a model posing for an L.L. Bean catalog, draped a garland of artificial fall leaves studded with wax fruits and vegetables around the base of the wagon. Kyle had finished the big wooden feast table. Annie and Lisa, helped by Rachel, Casey, and some of the other 4-H kids, worked on making the Pilgrim hats and Indian headdresses.

"What do you think?" Marty asked.

Cat smiled and nodded. "The kids will love it."

"They will, won't they?" Sam said with that look of contentment on his face that Cat loved.

By evening Marty had summoned the troops. All the close friends and neighbors—the Morgans, the Cramers, the Pattersons, Dr. Brady and his little girl, Kika—hurried to finish the Center's entry in the town's holiday parade. Cat had been sent to the store two more times. Finally, they all stood back and admired their work. Cat, feeling wonderfully happy, stepped back farther and watched all of them.

"Come here, girls," Gayle Morgan called. Annie, Jennifer, Kika, and Lisa stopped playing with the kittens and ran to her. She fastened Pilgrim hats on Kika and Annie. On Jennifer and Lisa she tied Indian headdresses. "Get up there now so we can see what it looks like."

Cat helped the little girls onto the wagon, and they took their places around the roughhewn table. Kristen had borrowed some fake food from a grocery store. A big rubber turkey and a huge plastic haunch of beef rested in the center of the table. Kristen and Kyle stood squabbling, with Kristen insisting that the roast "would too" pass for venison. A cornucopia overflowing with brightly colored plastic fruits and vegetables filled one end of the table. A huge basket sat on the other end. It was filled with bags of candy to be thrown to the children watching the parade.

Kristen had raided a local theater company. She'd talked them into lending her a stuffed deer, an eight-point buck. The buck had been fastened into place behind the driver's seat of the wagon, his glassy eyes staring from behind a fake maple tree. The tree looked real right down to the wrinkles in the bark and the red fall leaves.

"Kristen, it's gorgeous," Marty said.

"You haven't seen it all yet, Sis," Kyle said. He pulled her around to the back of the wagon. Cat followed with the rest of them. "Now just wait here," Kyle ordered. He and Jeff walked over to the scrap lumber pile and returned with a big square piece of plywood painted with a colonial village scene. They turned the wood around. Painted in all the rich colors of fall, it announced, "The Lisa Center at Stafford Farm wishes you a happy and blessed holiday season."

"I love it!" Marty cried. She hugged Kristen. "You did that, didn't you?"

Kristen nodded, pride shining out of her big gray eyes. Kristen deserved to be proud. She'd designed and done most of the work on the float. Cat was proud, too, because Kristen was her friend. The thought surprised her. She knew most young girls simply took for granted their many girl friends, but she'd never had a friend before. She smiled as Kristen hurried past her to help Jeff hold the sign against the back of the wagon while Kyle hammered it into place. One side provided the perfect backdrop for their Thanksgiving scene and the other proclaimed their greetings to everyone.

Cat wished Nana had been able to arrive today. She would have loved this. But the best she'd been able to do was the bus that would leave from Beckley early tomorrow and arrive late afternoon in Washington.

"Joel, let's christen the float like they do ships," Gayle said. "Come on, say a prayer to launch her."

He waved his arms for all to gather around. Cat found herself between Kristen and Lisa. They took her hands in theirs to complete the circle that formed beside the wagon. As Joel began to pray, Cat bowed her head and listened.

"Heavenly Father, for so much we are grateful," Joel began. "Thank you for the success of this Center. Thank you for moving Sam and Marty to begin this endeavor. Bless them and their families who have done most of the work here. Thank you for sending us dear Kristen, whose fund-raising efforts and ideas have helped it to bloom."

Without thinking, Cat smiled at Kristen and squeezed her hand. Kristen leaned into her and squeezed back. Still smiling, Cat again bowed her head.

"We remember also all who donated time and money from the goodness of their hearts," Joel prayed. "For all of us, thank you for letting us be a part of your healing grace for those who come here. Use us and this float as you will. Thank you, too, for giving us to each other. May we always count our love for each other as one of your many blessings. Amen."

Cat was sorry when the prayer was over. She wanted to stay in that circle and hold on to these people. She said a private prayer of her own, thanking God for setting her down here in this good place with such good people, people who had given her a life that was so much more than anything she'd ever thought possible.

Everybody started to buzz with their own concerns and the moment was broken. Kristen fretted that they didn't have enough bags of candy. Kyle promised to drive by the store and get more. The little girls ran off to play. The older kids—Jeff, Casey, Rachel, and Luke and Christy Morgan—begged off to drive into town to get some ice cream. The adults excused them.

"Hey, Cat, why don't you come with us?" Casey called.

Cat shook her head. "Thanks anyway," she called. "I still have some work to finish up."

Casey hurried over. "Come on, Cat. All you do is work. You're still a kid, you know. Besides Luke says he thinks you're kind of cute."

Cat felt the heat rush to her cheeks. She'd probably turned beet red.

"Oh, so you think he's cute, too," Casey whispered.

"I do not!" Cat sputtered. "He's just a kid."

"Cat, you can't be more than nineteen or twenty. Luke's twenty."

Cat just shook her head. She could never explain to Casey. Casey saw everything in such simple terms. Cat and Luke may have lived the same number of years, but she was ages older. Maybe someday it would be nice to have someone like Luke to care for her, but not now, no way. Right now the thought just scared her. "Thanks, Casey, but you're going to have to fix him up with someone else."

"Well, to be honest, he's got a girl friend. But none of us like her, so I thought it was worth a try."

Cat laughed. "That kind of trouble I don't need."

The kids took off and Cat wandered over to say good night to everyone else. She'd promised Marty she'd bring a vegetable dish to dinner tomorrow and she wanted to get it made.

Kristen bounced up to her first. "Guess what? Everyone has

decided we're all going to have Thanksgiving together up at the church."

They all seemed to talk at once as they worked out the details. Only Sam and Lisa had family plans that couldn't be changed. The rest of them were to bring all the food they prepared up to the church in the late afternoon.

"The parade will be over by noon. How about we meet around three?" Amy Cramer offered.

"Cat, what time is Nana arriving?" Joel asked.

"Her bus is due in at 4:05, but it could be late," Cat said. "Don't worry about us. She wouldn't want you to change your plans."

"So let's say we meet at the church between four-thirty and five," Joel said. "Cat, you get there when you can. We wouldn't dream of starting without you."

The next day Cat arrived early at the bus station, hoping to will the bus into being on time. The parade had been wonderful, almost as magical as the night before. She had never really felt part of a group before ... never. The best she'd ever known, except for her relationship with Nana and Nana's family, had been an occasional moment of being comfortable with a random kind stranger. She was glad Nana was coming to be part of their holiday and to meet the wonderful people who were part of Cat's life now.

The bus pulled in on time and Cat struggled for patience as it began to unload. Mostly smiling faces leaped down the ramp into the arms of waiting family. An occasional sorrowful soul walked past everyone and headed alone down the street. Finally, there was Nana, tall and square-faced, standing so straight no one would ever know how arthritis plagued her. In her hands, she held a covered cake dish. Cat smiled. Nana never went anywhere without an offering.

Cat rushed forward and helped her off the final steep step.

They hugged and kissed and Nana cried as the other passengers hurried by, picked up their luggage, and departed.

"My goodness, child," Nana sniffed. "Forgive me, but I knew I'd be blubbering once I caught sight of you."

Nana pushed Cat out to arm's length and gazed down at her. "Well, let me look you over, darling." Nana smiled. "You've changed. You look happier, prettier, not nearly so wary."

The notion surprised Cat. She had only recently begun to think in terms of happy or unhappy. Before, she had only considered safe and not safe, in place or on the run. "I am happy, Nana. Wait until you meet the family here and my friends."

Cat noticed that, except for a few more wrinkles, Nana's skin was still smooth and shone with the warmth of melted chocolate. Her halo of close-cropped curls only showed a few more gray strands. No, Nana hadn't changed much at all, but her clothes had. She was more dressed up than Cat ever remembered seeing her. She had on a classy-looking coat of navy wool. Where it hung open Cat saw that underneath she wore a rich green tweedy skirt and a hunter green soft knit cardigan. The gold cross that had once belonged to her sister, Samuel's mother, glittered against the white pleats of her blouse. Her best earrings, tiny gold balls, studded her ears. "Nana, you look beautiful," Cat said, hugging her again.

"I spent a few days in Beckley with Samuel and Letty. That Letty is a fashion hound. She took me to an outlet store and insisted on fancying me up to come see you. An early Christmas present. I told her she spent so much money she'd better count it as Christmas covered for the next ten years."

"She did a good job on you, Nana. You look real fancy."

"And look who's talking. Miss Fancy herself," Nana said.

Cat grinned. Kristen had gone shopping with her and helped her pick out the tailored khakis, navy-and-beige striped blouse, and soft cable-knit sweater of navy wool for this special day. Cat hadn't told Kristen that she'd never owned any pants that weren't blue jeans.

Cat picked up Nana's bag and led her to the truck. Nana chattered the whole way out of town. They hadn't seen each other for two years, but time had never been a barrier between the two of them. They were almost to the church when Nana said, "Samuel and Letty send their love. Samuel says to tell you that Bud's been by, but he hasn't told him a thing. It seems like Bud really might be sick. Samuel says Bud looks terrible, all yellow like, and he kept wheezing, more than usual."

Conflicting emotions of anger and pity surprised Cat. "Well, let's not talk about him today. It's a holiday and we don't need to darken it with thoughts of him."

"One more thing and then we won't mention it again. The reporter was around to see me. Said he thought I was part of some government conspiracy or something. I told him he was a fool. He said, 'Maybe so, ma'am, but you'll find I'm a persistent fool. And the little girl's rightful family—Bud Parker—well, he's worried sick about her. He needs her and she needs him, so neither one of us is going away.'"

Cat ground her teeth. Old Bud had sure fed that reporter a bill of goods. Uncle Bud was the thundercloud in her life. She could ignore him for a while, but every so often, regular as clockwork, she could count on him to let loose with a storm, complete with thunder and lightning.

EIGHTEEN

By five o'clock the warm aroma of the Thanksgiving feast filled the church hall along with the sound of laughter and chatter. Marty looked around. Only Cat and Nana were missing. Before she'd left home, Marty had phoned the bus station to be assured that the bus was due on time.

In one corner Duke and Aunt Bertie sat on the old plaid sofa. Aunt Bertie had never had so much as a civil word for her brother-in-law until recently. Lately, she'd been coming around more than ever, helping with the paperwork for the Center but then hanging around talking to Duke. She'd even skipped her usual Thanksgiving with her daughter Renee at Renee's in-laws to come tonight. Kyle claimed Duke and Aunt Bertie had been sweethearts before Duke dumped her to marry Mamma. He said Mamma herself had told him. All Mamma had ever told Marty was that her dad and Bertie had been feuding for ages. Now here they were grinning and laughing and practically flirting with each other.

Gayle slipped an arm through Marty's. "I keep hearing the sound of giggling from on high. I just know it's your mother."

"It's more serious than you know," Marty whispered. "As you can see, those are not the clothes Duke had on at the parade, and he even showered before putting them on."

Marty heard a squeal of laughter and Rachel raced by, chased by a smiling Jeff.

"Is this what it means to be the sandwich generation?" asked Gayle.

"Not quite, but it applies. I feel like so much dull old baloney sandwiched between all these layers of romance. Look over there," Marty nodded toward Kristen, who spooned a taste of her cranberry salad into Kyle's mouth.

"Ah well," Gayle said, giving Marty's arm a squeeze. "To everything there is a season."

A swell of sadness rose in Marty's chest. Her season was over. It had been a little more than a year since Dan's death. She was getting better about it, fewer tears, not so many fears, but still she lay awake some nights missing him terribly. How long did it take a heart to heal? She couldn't imagine that it would ever be whole again, but she'd be content with "well enough" to let her life move forward unhindered.

Across the room, Cam Brady helped Amy and Joel carve the turkeys. They had a big job. Four turkeys lined the counter. Each family group had cooked one before coming to the church.

"Cam's a good man, friend," Gayle said, her voice soft and knowing.

"I know he is," Marty answered.

When they were kids she'd been too busy chasing Derry, Cam's good-looking, bad-news brother, around town. She'd almost made the same mistake again when Derry had rushed in to console her this summer, shortly after she'd moved back here. Derry was fireworks and bottle rockets, a guaranteed burst of excitement, but gone in an instant. Cam was soft sunlight, enough to warm her soul day after day.

"Cam cares about you."

"I know he does. But I don't have anything to give him right now."

"He'll wait," Gayle said.

"I hope he does." Marty smiled at her friend.

"Hey, here they are," Kyle hollered.

Marty looked up and saw Cat at the door carrying a casserole followed by a tall, square-shouldered black woman with a cake pan in her hands. Together Marty and Gayle rushed over. "Cat, you made it. Good!" Marty laid a hand on the woman's arm. "I know you're Cat's Nana, but she's never told me your real name."

The woman smiled, a broad, kind smile that crinkled the corners of her mouth. "Nana's not far off. I'm Nancy Faith Riley, but most folks call me Nan."

"Welcome, Nan. I'm Marty Harris and this is Gayle Morgan. We are delighted you were able to come."

"Once my girl asked, I only hesitated a moment. I certainly have been missing her."

"Here, Ms. Riley," Gayle said, reaching for the cake pan. "Let me take this while you slip off your coat."

"Nana brought her chocolate cake. It's famous back home," Cat said with a shy smile.

Marty started to reach for Cat's casserole, ready to prompt Cat into performing the introductions as if Cat were one of her children. But it had probably taken a lot for Cat just to agree to join this group celebration. Introductions would be torture. "Cat, why don't you put your dish over with the others, and I'll make sure Nan meets everyone."

Relief washed over Cat's face as she headed for the crowded counter with her dish. Gayle followed with the cake.

Marty made the rounds of the room with Nan. For one brief moment Marty wondered if Nan felt awkward being the only brown face among so many pale ones, but Nan's wide smile and casual manner banished any concern on that account. "Please," she told everyone, "call me Nan."

Even Duke and Kyle, who had been known to tell racially offensive jokes, and Aunt Bertie, who had been known to fret about "the problems with the coloreds," greeted Nan with genuine warmth.

"I understand you raised Cat, ma'am," Duke said, shaking

her hand. "Well, you must be real proud of her. She's as nice a young woman as I've ever met."

Cat joined them, and Nan put an arm around her shoulders, pulling her close.

"Well, I thank you, but I can't take all the credit," Nan said. "She was with me from babyhood until she was about five, after that only occasionally. The good Lord always did have his eye out for this sweet girl. Still, I do count her as my own."

Cat stayed relaxed and smiling, unlike her skittish reaction when anyone else touched her. It was obvious to Marty that Nan and Cat functioned like mother and daughter, and it was a comfortable relationship for both of them—which meant that whatever had damaged Cat occurred after the age of five.

Joel called everyone to attention and began a beautiful blessing, much like the one he'd said the night before. Marty's eyes filled. She looked around the table, realizing her tears weren't the only ones. Joel prayed, "And, dear heavenly Father, on this day of our abundance please be with those who do not have enough to eat, and share your grace as well with those who have plenty but have no one with whom to share it."

"Amen," everyone chorused.

"Time to eat!" Duke hollered, leading the way to the buffet table.

But as they ate, their plates heaped full, Marty sat between Nana and Gayle and listened to the conversation around them. Apparently everyone was as curious about Cat's background as Marty was, judging by the polite questions they directed to Nan. Marty's own curiosity deepened as the facts spilled out. Nan again said Cat had only lived with her for five years, and then only visited after that. It had been more than two years since they'd seen each other. Nana had worked as a midwife in the hills outside of Beckley, West Virginia, and still went out occasionally when a baby was coming fast and no doctor was around. She'd delivered Cat. Cat's daddy died before she was born, and her mamma, who had been sickly, left her with Nana before she died.

Then who had really raised Cat? Marty wondered. She'd lived more years after she left Nan than before. What had those years been like to make Cat so wary?

Marty watched poor Cat squirm on her chair. "Nan," Marty interrupted, "I wish you could have been here this morning for the parade. It was wonderful!"

The conversation turned to the funny stories and warm moments of the parade, and Cat relaxed visibly. Not that Marty didn't want answers about Cat, but she wanted Cat to enjoy herself tonight. Besides, Marty had a whole weekend to talk to Nan and find out more. Surely at some point she'd be able to get Nan alone. After all, the more she knew about Cat, the more she'd be able to help her.

Marty stood to clear the dishes.

Nan started to rise and Cat stopped her. "Nana," she said, "you just set. We'll take care of it." She joined Marty. "She's got arthritis in her knees and ankles. It gives her fits," Cat whispered. "Otherwise she'd be running around trying to outwork all of us."

Marty looked over her shoulder at Nan, who sat straight-backed and proud. No one would ever know she was in pain. But wasn't that the way with most people? Marty sure tried awfully hard not to let her pain show. At the sink, Amy Cramer smiled as she took a stack of dishes from one of the kids. Marty knew Amy had troubles that plagued her—including a miscarriage, an inability to become pregnant again, and the hurtful criticism of some of Joel's parishioners.

Gayle hurried by her with the jug of milk to refill the children's glasses. Gayle had confided to Marty that she and Mac had serious money worries. The Morgan farm, which had been worked by Morgans since the late 1700s, might not survive. Times were tough in the area and many of the old farm families had already sold out and moved on.

Marty turned her attention to the older generation. Duke, Aunt Bertie, and Cam's mom had all somehow survived the deaths of their spouses. They had to have been as damaged by the experience as she was. Like her, they too had to face loneliness, but they still managed to smile.

Marty took a long look at her father. Duke hadn't been doing too well when she first arrived home, but he did seem to be getting somewhat better. Of course, he had never functioned at a very high level, but he did the best he could.

She guessed she was more like Aunt Bertie and Mrs. Brady, who sat gabbing at one end of the table. Aunt Bertie had once told her that she had survived by handing her life over to the Lord. Well, Marty was still working on that one.

But what Marty most noticed about Aunt Bertie and Mrs. Brady was that they kept themselves busy, busy, busy. She did, too. It was easier than dwelling on her own problems. Besides, it was much easier to deal with other people's troubles. She was trying to get better about not butting in where she didn't belong, but sometimes other people's problems seemed so much worse than her own, like poor Cat's. Whatever lurked in that child's past still haunted her.

Cam, carrying a handful of sodden paper cups and napkins, reached around her to put them in the trash. "And what thoughts have brought such a serious expression to your face?" he asked, the dimples flashing beside his beard.

Marty forced a smile. "I was just thinking that everyone has troubles of some kind."

"That's a cheerful thought for the holiday," he said.

"I know. I can't help myself. Sometimes I get maudlin."

"Actually, sometimes I do, too. But the way I look at it, the

Lord knew that there were plenty of rough places in this world. That's why he created friends, so we'd help each other over the bumps," he said, squeezing her arm, before heading to the table.

She turned around and watched him gathering more plates. And Cam … what were his sorrows? He never leaned on anyone. Not that she knew of. Did he, too, carry a load of loneliness?

She set her jaw and turned back to rinsing the serving plates. No way. The next thing she knew she'd be trying to fix his problems, and that might not be good for either of them, at least, not now. She had to get her own house in order first.

Cat handed her a handful of silverware.

This poor child, for instance, needed lots of love and care. Yet Cat gave so much to all of them, especially lately to Jeff. Jeff had seemed more calm, more content, since he and Cat had been playing music together. Duke was right; music was one of God's healing graces. Lately, Marty had come to see that the Lord provided for all kinds of healing. She just had to trust that sooner or later he'd get around to her. Marty shut her eyes and prayed, *Lord, heal us all in any way we need to be healed. And, as always, help me to remember that it is "thy" will, not "my" will be done.*

NINETEEN

Cat held her apartment door wide and ushered Nana through. Sadie gave a yip and came running from the bedroom. She slid to a stop and growled when she saw Nana.

"It's all right, Sadie," Cat said.

Sadie's stubby tail wagged so hard it shook her whole rear end. "So this is the Sadie I've heard so much about," Nana soothed. She handed her coat to Cat and sat on the sofa, bending over to hold her hand out to the dog. Sadie wiggled forward and allowed Nana to pet her. Nana winced as she sat back upright, but in spite of the pain, she smiled. "My goodness, but this place is lovely."

"Thanks," Cat said, pleased. "Everyone here is real good to me, Nana."

"I can see that, honey. They're good people. I liked each and every one of them, especially Marty."

"Me, too," Cat said.

They had a lot of catching up to do. Caring conversation filled the air. They talked about the things that seemed too unimportant to share over the phone, the details that create the fabric of everyday life.

"You're still my little magpie," Nana said with a laugh. Cat had stopped to catch her breath after telling the story about helping Duke set up the zoo room and how the raccoon had escaped and run to her.

"With you I am," Cat said. Nana would be surprised at how little she usually talked. It seemed that when she was with Nana, everything she'd been keeping dammed up burst free. But Cat was sorry to see how much more she had to tell than Nana.

While Cat's life was expanding, Nana's was shrinking. Nana's arthritis and waning eyesight had begun to limit her in real ways.

"I wish I lived closer," Cat said. "I could be more of a help to you."

"No, child. You're where you should be. I'm doing just fine. Samuel and Letty call regular. And Mr. Johnson up the road checks on me nearly every day. Don't you worry."

But Cat did. She'd tried lots of times to use her gift on Nana, but the Lord had never seen fit to ease Nana's pain. Nana always said, "God has his reasons, child. He must want the pain to teach me something."

"I love you, Nana," Cat blurted. "I wish you really were my mother." It's what Cat used to tell Nana when she was little, but she hadn't spoken the words out loud in years. There were some things too important to talk about over the telephone. Cat went to sit by Nana on the sofa. Nana put her long arms around her and held her just as she had years ago.

"I guess I'm as much mother as you've got, baby."

Cat leaned her head against Nana's shoulder. "That's why when I made up my new name, I made it O'Reilly. Riley for you. The 'O' and the different spelling to throw Uncle Bud off."

"Well …" Nana said, pausing before going on. "All things being as they should, your last name *is* Riley."

Cat sat up and looked at Nana. "My last name's Parker. At least, that was Mamma's name, seeing as how she was Bud's sister. It took 'til I was older, but I finally figured out that she never married my daddy, or my name would have been something else. But what are you telling me now?"

Nana sat silent, looking at her big hands, gnarled from work and affliction. When she raised her eyes, her face looked sad. "Bud threatened the daylights out of me about this. He made me promise not to tell you anything about your daddy or he'd never let me see you again. So all I told you was your daddy was named Nate and he died before you were born. Well, he did die before you were born. That part's true. The old folks say that's why you've got the gift. A child born never seeing its father will likely be a healer."

"Nana, you always said my father was in an accident, a car accident, coming home from Beckley on an icy night."

Again Nana looked down at the hands that lay limply in her lap. Her shoulders rose and fell with a deep sigh. "Lately, I've been haunted by all the lies. Part of the reason I came up here was to tell you the truth. These aren't the kind of things I can talk about over the phone."

Cat's chest muscles squeezed so tightly she wasn't sure she'd be able to talk. "Nana, you never lie to me, never."

"Not about most things, no. I just felt a little girl doesn't need to grow up knowing the whole ugly reality of things. Besides, Bud gave you enough to deal with. And I was probably being a tad selfish. I couldn't bear the thought of not ever seeing you again."

"Nana, please. Tell me what you've got to tell me."

"Your daddy took to drugs and died of an overdose. He truly did marry your mamma, but he'd run off. She hadn't heard from him for some while when it happened. His name was Nate Riley and I knew that boy inside out, for good and bad."

"Riley? My last name is Riley—same as yours?"

"That's right, my girl. Your daddy's daddy and my daddy were brothers. I may not really be your mamma, but we're blood. I'm your cousin."

Cat turned her face away from Nana's, hiding her eyes that were fast filling with tears. If she sat real stiff and still maybe they'd stop. But confused thoughts and feelings wouldn't stop racing through her brain. She had family, people connected to her by blood and history. There was Nana, and Samuel and

Letty and their boys, and Samuel's sister Jeannie. She didn't really know Jeannie, but Cat was going to count all of them. She'd almost forgotten Nana's cousins—the old ladies Betty and Marie. She felt a shaft of joy, pure and sweet.

But there was sadness, too. All those years of not knowing. All those years of feeling all alone, unconnected, with no blood ties to anyone she cared to claim. Always having to fight every battle alone.

And anger ... that was there, too—mainly at Bud. He'd been mean, always taking care of his own self and not caring one whit about anyone else. He'd smacked her and shouted at her and called her names till she felt like a worthless piece of trash. But this was the meanest of all. He'd orphaned her more completely than her parents' deaths had.

And Nana? Was she angry at Nana, too? She stood and stomped to the kitchen. Bet your life she was!

In the kitchen she jerked open a cupboard door and took down a glass. She filled it with water and downed it. All those years of not knowing! All those years! She slammed the cupboard door and slapped the glass down on the counter. She had to get out of there.

She stormed into the bedroom and got her barn coat. Shoving her arms into the sleeves, she raced by Nana.

"Now don't go running off, Katie. We need to talk about this," Nana said.

"I always run off! I've had a lifetime of it because I never thought I had any other choice. I never knew I had anyone who could help me. But you could have, Nana! You could have fought for me! And you didn't." Cat rushed out the door, slamming it behind her.

She stopped inside the arena. Cat could feel her anger swelling, threatening to fill the cold, cavernous space. She stormed into the shadowy barn, barely lit with low-voltage night-lights at ground level. She tore past several empty stalls until she came to the hay stall. She pulled the door shut behind her and crawled onto a bale of hay in the corner, hugging her knees to her chest, curling herself into a small tight ball. She squeezed tighter and tighter, trying to contain her rage. The way it was howling and tearing around inside her, she'd be torn apart if she didn't stop it.

She heard a scratching and sensed, more than saw, a slight motion above her. Before she could make out what it was, the thing leaped right at her. Cat struck at it, her fists connecting with soft fur. A yowl. A thud as the creature hit the wall. A scramble as it took off up the bales and over the top of the stall. Only then did she recognize Lucky.

She bolted to her feet. "Lucky," she called. She scaled the hay stack and looked into the next stall. Max looked back at her, but no Lucky. She had to find him. She'd hit him hard and he could be hurt. Maybe bleeding inside. Maybe dying.

The back of her eyes stung as she scurried from stall to stall, calling his name softly. A shadow too dark to tell if it was Lucky or one of the other kittens slipped around the corner into the arena. Cat followed, flipping on the arena lights. Lucky cowered in the corner by the office door.

"Lucky, I'm sorry. Oh, I'm so sorry," she murmured. She started toward the kitten, who shrank away as if preparing to run. Cat stopped. "I didn't mean it, Lucky," she said with a lowered voice. "Let me make sure you're okay." The kitten froze, one paw extended. Cat took a step. The kitten took two. Cat stopped. "Oh, Lord," she breathed, "let me catch her." It was more of a wish than a prayer, but as she inched forward the kitten stayed put. "I didn't mean it, Lucky. Honest." Cat was within grabbing distance, but she didn't want to scare the kitten off. Lucky rolled over onto her back and surrendered.

Cat scooped the tiny calico up into her arms. She could barely see to examine the kitten, but as near as she could tell Lucky was fine. She cradled the kitten against her chest, rubbing her chin against the soft fur. Lucky began to purr.

Cat turned out the arena lights and slipped back to the hay stall. She took a deep breath trying to get ahold of herself. Breathe in. Breathe out. All the way in. All the way out. Holding the kitten gently but close, Cat began to rock. She thought she was trying to comfort the kitten, but when she looked down she saw a baby in her arms, a baby with her own face.

TWENTY

Cat rocked herself until calmness returned. She always had been able to take care of herself. She gave Lucky a kiss and lowered the kitten to the ground. She felt stronger, but anger still rumbled in her belly.

She stood stretching, feeling every muscle. Now that her wrath had waned, she'd work the rest of it off. No doubt, the water buckets could use a topping. She hauled out the hose and dragged it to the first stall.

She would have told anybody that Nana had never lied, not to her, not to anyone. But she had, and it had been an ugly toad of a lie, a lie that had changed Cat's life. Cat set her jaw. How different her life would have been had she known she had a family. Not that it would have changed the reality of her day-to-day living. Uncle Bud still would have dragged her off, like some performing seal for his circus. He'd have still treated her rotten. She'd have still had to run off and hide out. But she wouldn't have been so desperately lonely and afraid. So many of her decisions, especially the ones that had turned out badly, were determined by that bleak well of loneliness. Had she known she had a family, her life would have been different.

She heard the splashing of water into straw. She'd overfilled the bucket. "Sorry, Max," she whispered. She moved on to the next stall. Grandma nickered a hello.

But would her life have been better? In some ways, yes. In others, no. She didn't remember a lot of the details of her early life with Nana except that it was warm, loving, and safe. But her time home with Bud was another story.

Bud had plopped a trailer down on that little bit of land that had been Mamma's just down the road from Nana's house. She slipped away to be with Nana whenever she could, more often than Bud knew. A lot of the time he was off about his business, whatever shady deal he happened to be working on, and didn't pay much attention to where she was. When he was drunk, he'd start howling for her, but she usually managed to escape him. Then he forgot all about not finding her by the time he came back to his senses.

Other than Nana, she hadn't really had anybody back home. Oh sure, Samuel and Letty and the cousins when they came by, but they didn't live there. She never had any friends her own age. School, the few months of the year she went, was a misery. Most of the other children avoided her. Most treated her like some kind of weirdo. She didn't mind those kids so much. Had she been looking out of their eyes, she might have thought the same. It was the others. The ones who thought she was a witch, a child of the devil. She'd heard the talk. She could see the fear in their eyes.

Worst of all were the kids who tormented her, especially the ones who lived nearby. She rarely made it from the school bus home without being pushed down, pelted with mud balls, or spit on.

She moved on from stall to stall, filling the water buckets, remembering….

"Katie, look at you. You're covered in mud," Nana said. "Let's get you cleaned up."

"I hate them, Nana!" Katie clenched her fists. If she were bigger, she'd whip all of them, all those kids who thought they were so great.

Nana pulled Katie's sweat shirt off over her head. "No. No, darling. Don't ever hate anybody. Hate hurts the hater more than the person hated."

"I don't care! I hate them!" Katie screamed.

Nana wrapped her arms around her, rocking her back and forth. "People around here can be ignorant, sweetie pie. Those youngsters are just parroting their parents' evil notions. See, it's hard for people to accept that God chose you for such a special gift and not them."

"Well, they can have it! I don't want it!"

Nana laughed, a sweet sound of comfort with no hint of mocking. "Well, sometimes the Lord doesn't give us a choice about the gifts he gives, and no matter how much we kick and squeal, they don't go away. I don't always understand it either. And I know it's hard for you sometimes what with some people thinking you're a liar and a fake and others thinking you're a child of the devil and some just plain confused and scared because you've got something they can't understand."

"But I don't understand either, Nana."

"Me either. That's where faith comes in, darling child. Just trust that the Lord knows what he's doing and one day it will all be clear...."

But Cat never had understood. Not then and not now. She'd have been pretty angry at God if she hadn't been afraid of what else he'd do to her. It had been bad enough that he'd visited her with this curse that Nana called a blessing. She sure didn't want to call anything else down on her head. So she'd prayed, at first simple childish prayers for deliverance, later more mature pleas for understanding. As far as she could see, God hadn't answered any of them. Not back then he hadn't. And now?

Dragging the hose, she moved on to the next stall. Red nickered and lipped at her fingers where they held the hose. Cat gave his neck a pat.

And now?

Well, she'd prayed for a family to love who would love her,

too. All the time she had one. She just hadn't known they really belonged to each other. God hadn't prevented that; Uncle Bud had. And Nana? Why hadn't Nana told her? Nana alone had known how much she needed to know, known what it cost her being so alone. Cat had never let anyone but God and Nana see how bad she hurt.

Cat filled the last bucket, rolled the hose up, and marched back to the apartment.

Nana sat on the couch just as she'd left her.

"Why didn't you tell me?" Cat demanded.

Nana looked up and held Cat with her dark eyes, eyes kind and warm and sad, so sad. "I was scared, Katie. Scared that Bud wouldn't let me see you anymore if I told. Scared that not just my life, but yours, too, would get a whole lot worse if we couldn't be together, at least sometimes. I still don't know if that was right or wrong. Samuel's been after me to tell you since last spring. Once you hit eighteen…"

"Is that how old I am really?" Cat snapped.

"Well, of course, you know that. We always did celebrate your birthday right. May first, a May Day baby."

"No, I didn't know that, not for sure. Uncle Bud told me and everybody else I was born on Christmas Day. Used to say I was like Jesus—a gift from God to help heal mankind. Made me sick, 'cause I knew that wasn't my birthday. But Bud was always making me younger. And at school they kept putting me back in with younger kids. I got confused."

"Well, he's got no hold on you now. And I'd have told you sooner, but I couldn't just blurt something like this out over the phone. I needed to tell you face-to-face."

Cat searched Nana's face.

Nana's eyes turned proud and bore right into Cat's. "Now you understand this, Katie. Hear me clear. I am proud of who I am and the blood I carry. We come from good people. But Bud sure didn't think so and sometimes—not lately—but back then ... well, he was the only person who ever made me doubt myself and then only because of you. And now you've been passing so long ..." Nana stopped and looked away again.

"What do you mean passing?"

Nana glanced at her, looking surprised. "For white, girl. What did you think I was talking about?"

Cat fell back into the chair. "Oh yeah. I guess I'm not a white girl anymore, am I?" She needed some time to sort all this out. All these revelations. Who in the world was she? "I mean, I never imagined a lily-skinned blond family somewhere ..." Cat said. "I always knew I was darker skinned than most white kids, but I figured maybe my daddy was Italian. I even thought that maybe that was why Uncle Bud didn't like him. You know ... I figured if he was Italian he was probably Catholic and Uncle Bud sure doesn't like Catholics. Me being half black makes more sense. I mean, Uncle Bud hates blacks even more than he does Catholics."

Nana's laughter erupted, deep and hearty. She began to rock back and forth patting her chest. "Oh my goodness, I'm going to burst," she gasped. Tears streamed down her cheeks. She pulled a hanky from her pocket and dabbed her eyes.

"It's not funny, Nana. This is just one more thing that makes me different from everyone else. I'm not black. I'm not white. I don't fit in anywhere."

"Only people like Bud with deep and nasty prejudices care about the color of someone's skin or what kind of blood runs through a person's veins. Who cares if you're black or white or purple? You're Katie or Cat or whatever you want to call yourself. You are still my darling girl, the same one I've loved all these years. And as for the blood you carry ... well shoot, you've got a bit of everything. Your daddy's mamma was half Delaware Indian. You got her silky dark hair and high cheekbones. You're a rainbow child with red, black, and white blood roaring through your veins. You're from an 'everybody' family. We've got Catholics and Presbyterians and Baptists and just about every Christian faith you can think of in our family tree. We've even got one branch that's Islamic."

Cat moved over to the sofa to sit close to Nana. She took one of Nana's big brown hands in one of her own small tawny ones. She turned them over, studying them. She lifted Nana's hand to her lips and kissed it. "I'm glad we're family, Nana, not just pretend but for real, no matter what, forever."

Nana held her close and kissed her forehead. "Just remember, good people come in all sizes, shapes, colors, and faiths, Katie love, and so do bad, but that's not ours to determine. Only God knows the heart of a person. That's why the Bible tells us that judgment belongs to the Lord. The rest of us just aren't smart enough or wise enough. You remember that when you think someone is judging you."

"I love you, Nana," Cat said, holding on to Nana lightly enough not to hurt her, but wrapped in a joy so strong she was sure it would never be broken.

TWENTY-ONE

The joy lasted for two days. The next day everyone pitched in to help Cat finish the barn work. In the afternoon, she and Nana went shopping in Washington, then out to dinner. Cat had saved money for a special dinner at the Century Inn, east of town. Nana was real impressed with the grand old inn. She grinned all through dinner. Cat loved being able to treat her.

That night they talked until late. Cat learned more about her family.

"Your daddy wasn't a bad man," Nana said. "He got caught up with drugs and boozing, and it changed him. He'd always been a sweet boy, and he really did love your mamma as much as he could love anyone. The trouble is he didn't love anything more than the next high. That's the way with addicts. So if you want to know about him, I'll have to tell you what he was like before it got ahold of him, 'cause none of us knew him after."

And the stories warmed Cat. They were all about a regular boy growing up like all the kids grew up around home. He fished and hunted, played basketball and baseball in high school. "He was too skinny for football," Nana said. "But he was handsome and the girls loved him. You've got his beautiful dark eyes, you know."

Cat smiled. She had never known she looked anything like anybody. And when she went to bed that night next to Nana, she curled up against the older woman's back. When she was tiny and afraid in the night, or when an icy wind blew off the mountain and made the house too cold to stay in bed alone, she'd run to Nana's bed. Now Nana was sharing hers, and neither of them had any reason to be afraid, and the apartment was snug and warm.

The joy was still there the next morning when Marty called to ask if she and Nana would have dinner with them that night. Nana insisted on making her special cake and Marty came up to watch and get the recipe. That night at dinner, the whole family joked and teased, including Cat and Nana joining in the fun. Cat almost felt normal, like any other eighteen-year-old girl home with her family for the holidays.

She and Annie offered to do the dishes. Jeff grudgingly agreed to dry. Kyle escaped to pick up Kristen for their regular Saturday night date. Cat smiled as Marty and Duke guided Nana into the living room for coffee. The living room was so beautiful with its oriental rug and honest-to-goodness original paintings and all those books.

When they had cleaned the kitchen and had it sparkling, Cat joined the group in the living room.

"Yes indeed, it has been an important time for my girl and me," Nana said as Cat entered the room.

Cat's breath caught in the back of her throat. What had Nana been telling them? They all looked too comfortable for Nana to have blown the cover off any of Cat's many lies. How she wished she'd told them the truth long ago. Then she'd be able to share the good news now and tell them she and Nana really were family.

"Thank heavens, you have each other, Nan," Marty said. "With no blood relatives, Cat is certainly lucky to have you. And as we've told her, now she has us, too."

"And I can see she's blooming here. That does my heart good," Nana said.

"How did you two ever bear all the years apart?" Marty asked.

Cat's heart started to pound. Marty was at it again, nosing around, digging for information. Cat shot a look at Nana hoping she understood. Nana just looked right back at her, a look that was asking something Cat couldn't read. "It was sure hard," Cat blurted. "And if you don't mind, I think we'd best be getting back. We don't want to overstay our welcome."

"Now, Cat, let Nan finish her coffee," Duke said. "Besides we old folks are enjoying ourselves. Jeff, why don't you run and get your guitar. Cat, you get your mandolin. I'll put another log on the fire and the two of you can give us some music." He lifted Annie from beside him on the couch onto his lap. "And maybe our princess here will sing for us."

"No, I ..." Cat began.

"Come on, Cat," Jeff said. "Let's play that song we've been working on. I'll even run up to your place and get your mandolin. Okay?"

Before Cat could answer, Jeff headed for the door. The ring of the phone stopped her protest.

"I'll get it," Jeff called.

A moment later Cat heard him opening the kitchen door.

"Who was it, Jeff?" Marty asked.

"Wrong number. Some guy looking for someone named Katie."

Cat's stomach seized, and she thought she was going to lose her dinner. When she looked at Nana, she saw her staring back, alarm in her dark eyes.

But Duke took up the line of conversation, switching the subject to music and addressing many of his comments to Nana. Cat sat listening only to her heart pounding, hoping the phone wouldn't ring again, praying it had been some other Katie the man on the phone had been searching for. It had to be. How could anyone have traced her here now ... after all this time?

Jeff returned with her instrument and ran to get his own. They played, not brilliantly but passably. The others sang along whenever they knew the words. On any other night, Cat would have enjoyed it. Everyone else seemed to. She just felt too creepy, like the time she'd sped past a police car and knew that right around the turn another one was waiting to flag her down and give her a ticket.

No. She was being silly. There were lots of Katies in the world, probably hundreds and hundreds right here in Washington County. She wasn't going to worry about it. "Jeff, let's play 'I Saw the Light,'" she said.

"I'm not too good on that one yet," Jeff said.

"It's one of Nana's favorites. Give it a try," Cat insisted.

"How about you play it and I help sing?" Jeff suggested. Cat forced a smile for Nana, who had straightened her chair, no doubt ready to belt out the song. Cat tuned her mandolin and began to play.

"I saw the light,

I saw the light,

No more darkness,

No more night," they sang, Nana louder than any of them, softly clapping her hands to the rhythm. Annie was the only one not singing. She probably didn't know the words. Cat tried to catch her eye on the second verse to help her along, but Annie jumped to her feet. She started to clap her hands and jump around.

"… Praise the Lord, I saw the light …"

The phone rang.

"I'll get it," Annie said, dancing her way toward the kitchen.

Cat found it hard to play while at the same time straining to hear what Annie was saying. Cat missed a note but saved herself on the next one. The song came to an end just as Annie came back into the living room.

"Who was it?" Marty asked.

"Some man asking for a Katie Parker. I told him there was no Katie Parker here. He asked to talk to an adult and I told him that wouldn't make any difference. None of the adults would tell him there was a Katie Parker here either, because we've never heard of anyone by that name. He got kind of angry then and slammed down the phone."

Marty laughed. "That's my girl, but it's getting late. Way past your bedtime, so off you go."

Annie protested, but Marty gave her a look, and after making her rounds of the room to give everyone a hug, Annie headed upstairs to bed.

Cat avoided Nana's eyes, sure she'd see a reprimand there.

"Well, I'm going to call it a night, too," Jeff said. "Rachel's not allowed to get phone calls much later than this, and I promised to call her."

With Jeff and Annie gone, Cat looked first at Marty, then at Duke, and finally at Nana. As she expected, Nana was giving her a look that said, "Well?"

She had to tell. She had to trust them. Not easy for her. Life had taught her only caution, but then she'd never known a Marty before. But Cat waited, hoping Duke would leave, too, but knowing he wouldn't. If she could trust Marty, why not Duke? In some ways, he was more forgiving and understanding than Marty, not so prone to jump to conclusions. She took a deep breath. "Marty, there's something I have to tell you."

Marty wrinkled her forehead, her eyebrows knitting in a scowl. "You're not allowed to quit. I need you."

"No, no, that's not it," Cat started.

"Wheew. Then whatever else it is, it can wait until I tuck Annie in," Marty said, rising and heading toward the steps. "I'll be right back."

Duke and Nana chatted and Cat tried to keep her breathing regular. Maybe it wouldn't go any farther than a few phone calls. Maybe she didn't really need to tell them. What if they wanted her to leave? Worse yet, what if they insisted she stay and then started treating her like a stranger?

Finally, Marty returned. She settled herself back into her chair. "Now, Cat, what did you have to tell me?"

"Nothing," Cat responded, instinct taking over. She bit her lip. That one had bypassed her heart and come straight from her head. "No … no … I …"

"Darling girl," Nana said. "Would you like Duke and me to withdraw to the kitchen, so you can talk to Marty alone?"

Cat shook her head. She looked into Nana's eyes, which held her in a steady, loving gaze. She didn't have anything to fear, especially with Nana here.

Cat turned and made herself look straight into Marty's green eyes. "I have to tell you …" She took another deep breath. "I am Katie Parker."

TWENTY-TWO

Marty didn't understand. "Cat, I don't know who Katie Parker is except that someone's been calling here for her."

Cat squirmed uncomfortably on her chair. Nan looked teary eyed. Duke seemed as puzzled as Marty felt.

"I know that name," Duke asserted. "And not just because of those phone calls. Now why do I know that name?"

Cat's lips trembled as if she was trying to say something, but nothing came.

"Cat?" Marty prompted.

Cat shot a look at Nan, a pleading look, and Nan answered. "The name Katie Parker was pretty well known in some circles a few years back. See, Katie Parker is a healer, but unlike most, she discovered her gift as a very young child, not more than a baby really. One day when she was almost three a bird flew into our window and was knocked senseless. Katie and I were outside. The minute we walked over to the poor thing I knew it was dying, lying all twisted up like it was. But when Katie took it in her hands, the little thing righted itself and flew off into a nearby tree. Now, I wasn't too surprised. Back home we believe that the Lord often uses people to spread his healing grace, especially if that person is born with a caul over her face, or has never seen her father. I delivered Katie. She had the caul, and her daddy died before she was born." Nan's voice rose and fell during the telling as if she were giving testimony at a prayer meeting.

Now Marty squirmed. This was pretty weird stuff. Superstition verified by coincidence. The poor bird was probably just stunned and recovered as the child touched it.

"I've heard of such things," Duke said. "Always wondered about them."

Marty sighed. She didn't need Duke adding to the confusion. If Marty knew him, he'd soon be buying all this lock, stock, and barrel. Somebody had to stay rational around here, and she guessed it would have to be her. "Now, Nan, I don't..."

"Please, Marty, hear us out. Katie, would you like to take it from here?" Nan asked. Cat shook her head, never raising her eyes to look at any of them. Nan went on. "We had some minor healings like that. I twisted an ankle and was sitting with it elevated. Katie kissed it and right away all the pain disappeared. Things like that. But about a year later I was called to deliver a baby for a woman up the road. Her husband wasn't home to get her to the hospital and they didn't have any insurance anyway. The baby was coming fast. There wasn't time to get someone to watch Katie, so I brought her with me. When we got to the place, I left Katie out front and told one of the woman's older kids to keep an eye on her. Inside things weren't going well. The baby hadn't turned right. It took a lot of time and effort, on my part and the woman's, to get that baby born. The baby was fine, but his mother was bleeding bad. I used everything I knew to stop it, but the blood just kept coming. They didn't have a telephone, so I called to the older boy and told him to run back to my place and phone an ambulance. But I knew no ambulance would get there in time. I hit the floor by that bed and bombarded heaven with my prayers. The next thing I knew, there was Katie standing by me. I was all ready to shoo her out when I saw this strange look in her eyes. Before I could stop her, she crawled right up on the bed and laid both her hands on that woman's belly. She lifted her tiny face toward heaven and said, 'Lord Jesus, please stop this flow,' which is what I'd been saying when she came in. The bleeding stopped. Against all reason, but by the Lord's grace, the bleeding stopped."

Cat nodded as Nan talked. Obviously, like Nan, she believed this spontaneous healing story, but surely other explanations were possible—natural explanations like the bleeding was stopped by normal body functions. Even if it had stopped through divine intervention, a prayer answered doesn't make someone a healer.

"Marty, you have disbelief written all over your face," Nan said. "Can't say as I blame you. All I can tell you is, word got out and people started coming to Katie, mostly women with headaches, monthly problems, bad backs, or sick children. Sometimes nothing happened, but more often than not Katie Parker gave them a cure."

"It wasn't me doing it, Nana," Cat blurted, her voice soft and sad. "The Lord did the healing, not me."

"I know, child," Nana said. "These are people of God. We don't need to spell it out for them."

Now Marty looked away from Nan's probing eyes. This wasn't the God she knew. Only once—when Annie was sick—had she very dramatically and powerfully felt the presence of God. He certainly hadn't given her a miracle for Dan, even though she'd pleaded, begged, and bargained. She didn't doubt God's presence in her life, but he was always just out of sight, just beyond reach. It was faith that kept her traveling toward him. Even her firm belief that all the wonderful events of the past months were the result of God's goodness was based on quiet faith rather than any thunderclap of recognition or tangible evidence. "I'm afraid this isn't a side of God I know," Marty said. "And I am going to need a bit more explanation, because, frankly, I'm not real comfortable with any of this."

Cat looked as though Marty had slapped her. Then her face went hard and she set her jaw. Marty wished she'd spoken more gently.

"Well, to be honest, at first I wasn't either," Nan said. "So that next summer I loaded us up and went to spend some time with an old healer woman I'd heard about way back in the mountains. She said she recognized the gift in Katie the minute she laid eyes on her. We stayed most of the summer and by the time we left, the woman had taught Katie some helping verses from the Bible and passed on as much as anyone could to a five-year old. The problem was that when we returned, the news of Katie's gift had reached her Uncle Bud, her mother's brother, who lived a few miles away. Bud was always real good at smelling out a dollar, and he saw plenty of them in Katie. Since he was her blood uncle, I didn't have a chance when it came to the law. He took her from me and hit the tent circuit with her, offering miracles for a price."

The rest of the story was pretty much what Marty would have suspected—lots of prearranged "miracles" with paid plants in the audience and enough spontaneous recoveries of psychosomatic ailments to make it all seem believable.

"Uncle Bud never understood that I didn't do the healing," Cat said, her voice shaking. "So I'd get a real thumping when things didn't go well. That's why he started fixing his own phony cures, so that no matter what, we'd look good and the people would keep coming."

"Now I know where I heard of Katie Parker," Duke said, his eyes round. "You were in my newspaper, Cat. A big article about missing prog … progenies … whatever they call them … you know, wonder kids. You ran off from your uncle and he's been looking for you." Duke struggled to his feet. "I'm sure I still have the paper somewhere. Let me go and get it."

"No, Duke, I've seen it," Cat said. "That night Annie brought you the paper. I saw my picture on the front and bought one."

"So I'm willing to bet that the call earlier was either from that reporter or your uncle. The story said your uncle was sick and trying to contact you," Duke said.

Marty didn't know what to say. As Jeff said, some things were just too weird for words. She stood and walked to the window. The porch light allowed her to see in only an arched circle of gold stopped by a greater darkness beyond. She filled her lungs with air and exhaled slowly, searching for the right words. She turned back to find Cat staring at her, her jaw still set, her dark eyes hard as onyx.

Cat stood. "Come on, Nana. We've outstayed our welcome," she said. "I'll give you a week to find someone else. Then I'll be out of here."

"Oh, Cat, no." Marty rushed forward, reaching for Cat to hug her, hoping it would comfort them both. When Cat shrank from her Marty stopped. She slowly extended a hand as she would to a frightened colt until she touched Cat's arm. "Cat, I don't want you to leave. Not as long as you want to stay. Please just give me a few minutes here to absorb all this."

"Time won't make any difference," Cat snapped, her voice harsh and unrelenting. "I can see it in your eyes, Marty. All my life I've watched people watching me. Some don't believe I have the gift and think I'm a fake and a liar. Others just can't deal with it because it's too strange for them. You're somewhere in the middle, aren't you? And nothing will ever be the same here for me, not now that you know."

"Cat, I care about you, honestly and truly," Marty said. "I'm a very rational creature. I like things in neat packages. I need observable evidence. I don't step easily into the unknown. Even plain everyday faith has been a struggle for me. Now you drop this on me. I just don't know what to think. Please, be patient with me and don't make any hasty decisions."

Cat's arm relaxed a bit under Marty's hand. "Talk to your pastor, Marty. Joel Cramer knows me."

Yes, Joel had said that the day Sassy got hurt, Marty remembered. And Cat had taken off. Marty had been perturbed that day because she and Cam had needed Cat's help. And Sassy …

those X-rays. "Sassy *did* break her leg that day in the field, didn't she?"

Cat nodded.

"And me," Duke said, his voice cracking, his face crumpled as if he was close to tears. "It was you. You healed me, too."

"No, God allowed me to help you, Duke," Cat said. She gave a wry smile. "You weren't doing so good."

"I told you!" Duke gave Marty a triumphant stare. He wiped his eyes on his shirt-sleeve. "I knew I was brought back from the brink of death." He scurried across the room and scooped Cat into his arms. "How can I ever thank you?"

"By not squeezing me to death," Cat said, looking very uncomfortable.

Marty returned to her seat and sank into it.

"Are you all right?" Nan asked.

"I don't know. Nan, how did you deal with this?" Marty asked.

Nan chuckled, her face folding into long laugh lines. "Well, it hasn't been easy, but then the Lord didn't promise us 'easy,' did he?"

"I'd settle for comprehensible, but I guess that's also too much to ask," Marty said. She watched Cat comforting Duke, who was giving full vent to his emotions. As much as she cared about Cat and valued her, she did judge her differently now. She was wary of her. She prayed that Cat would never notice. And if the Lord felt like answering her prayers today, maybe he could clue her in on just how she was supposed to respond to all of this.

TWENTY-THREE

Cat pulled her battered suitcase from the shelf in her bedroom and threw it on the bed.

"Now what do you think you're doing?" Nana asked.

"Getting out of here," Cat snapped, pulling open a drawer and throwing underclothes into the case. "I won't stay here as the resident weirdo. Besides, you know as well as I do, Bud's on his way. If not tomorrow, soon enough."

Nana shut the suitcase and stood in front of it. "Get ahold of yourself, girl. You can't just keep taking off every time something goes wrong."

"What about Bud? I can't let him catch up with me. Even if he has no legal rights, he'll do his best to mess up my life like he always does." Cat heard her voice, shrill and loud, but seemed not to have control over it. Sadie whined and pawed at her feet, but Cat ignored her.

"Bud's pretty pathetic. If you'd see him all yellow and shriveled up like he is, you'd know he's not the one you're running from. Hasn't been for some time. I know you think different, but he's not. Sometime, Miss Katie, you're going to have to stop running and face it." Nana turned and hobbled out to the living room.

Nana didn't understand. She didn't know how Bud ate into Cat's soul, making her scared and crazy. Cat emptied the drawers into the old suitcase and then went to get some garbage bags from the kitchen for the rest of her stuff. "Nana, you'd better call Samuel to make sure he knows to meet your bus tomorrow. I'll see you off before I go."

Nana humphed and hauled herself to her feet. "You have to

give these folks time to find someone else to fill your job," she scolded as she dialed. "The last thing you told Marty was you'd be staying."

"I changed my mind," Cat said. Why couldn't Nana see? She couldn't be around Marty anymore, not for another day. She'd thought Marty was different, not like other people. Marty wouldn't stop caring about her, no matter what. Well, she'd been wrong. Cat had risked everything here, and lost.

When Nana talked to Samuel her voice was as sweet as honey-suckle, telling him all about the great time they'd been having and the nice people up here and how well "their Katie" was doing. "Yes, Samuel, I told her we're her family ... No, your little cousin doesn't want to talk right now. She's in a mood. Seems Bud is closing in again ... No ... You're kidding me, boy? ... The nerve of some people ... Uh, huh ... Yes, I'll tell her ... Yes, she sends her love to you, too. See you tomorrow like we planned. You check with the bus line to make sure it's on time."

Cat heard Nana replace the receiver in its cradle. She didn't look up from her packing when Nana entered the room.

"Samuel sends his love. Letty, too. Say they're real glad they can openly claim you. Told them you were, too."

Cat just nodded.

"Katie, listen. Bud and that reporter fellow have been all over them like flies on honey, even interrupting their holiday dinner. Seems the reporter was spying when Samuel put me on the bus. He checked with the bus company and found out how far my ticket went. That and the fact that Samuel had been mouthing off to Bud about how you had this good job working with a therapeutic riding stable made you pretty easy to trace."

The phone rang. Cat froze, her hand poised over a bag.

"I'll not answer it, Katie love," Nana said. "Go ahead and pick it up. You've got to start dealing with your life." Nana retreated to the living room.

The phone kept ringing and ringing and ringing. But it couldn't be Bud. Her number was unlisted. Still unsure, she crept toward the phone. She couldn't believe Nana, putting her down like that. She glared at Nana sitting smug and silent on the couch. The idea of her—implying Cat couldn't take care of herself. Shoot, hadn't she been doing it all these years, since she'd been a little kid? She jerked the jangling phone off the hook. "Hello." Her voice wavered in spite of her trying to sound calm.

"Got you, Katie Parker!" a voice responded.

"You have the wrong number," she sputtered.

"Oh, I don't think so. See, Nancy Riley was going to visit Katie Parker and she just called her nephew from this number, asking him to meet her at the bus tomorrow and she said she was with Katie. So no, I don't think so. In fact ..."

Cat slammed the phone in place. They'd tapped Samuel's phone. She should have suspected that. Almost immediately the phone began to ring again. Cat tore the receiver from its cradle and then slammed it down again, breaking the connection. This time she took the phone off the hook, letting the receiver buzz and dangle to the ground. She stomped back into the bedroom and continued to pack.

She had most of her stuff bagged and boxed when the knock came. Sweat oozed from her forehead and back. On shaking legs, she wobbled to the bedroom door. "Don't answer," she whispered to Nana.

Nana's hand already reached for the knob. "Now you're being downright silly. They had to be calling from Beckley, and no one can make it from there to here in a half hour." Nana opened the door.

Joel Cramer stood on the stoop, a look of understanding and compassion on his face. "Marty called after you left. I thought you might want to talk. I tried the phone, but..." He shrugged.

"Come on in, pastor," Nana said. "She doesn't know it, but, yes, I do believe my girl needs to talk to someone 'cause I'm not getting anywhere with her. Now if you two will excuse me, I will turn in."

Cat slumped into the armchair, and the pastor without so much as a "may I?" took the couch. Cat crossed her arms across her chest. She suspected the inquisition was about to begin, much as she'd felt when she'd first met Joel Cramer and his whole posse all those years ago.

"Cat, Marty called right after you left. I told her everything I know about you and about that night you healed me. I'd been having those headaches off and on since I was a youngster. The doctors said my sinuses were misshapen—couldn't drain properly—and I'd probably have problems with them my whole life. I'd been in such agony with repeated infections that I was actually contemplating surgery. When you touched me that night, your small hands on my temples, I felt a searing heat shoot through my head and then the pain was gone. It's never come back."

Cat nodded and looked away from him, glad that she'd been able to help this nice man.

"Of course, you know about the healing, but what you don't know is that I was suffering from more than physical pain—I was in a full-blown faith crisis. Had been for some months. Walking back to my car that night, I was arguing with God. It was easy to see you were being used badly, that you were just a front for your uncle's greed. It was also easy to see that you, in all your dear innocence, believed in your gift. I didn't. I was railing against God for letting someone as sleazy as your uncle exploit you, for letting well-meaning people from my parish be duped by him. I was telling the Lord that I sure hadn't been seeing any of the wonders of his kingdom lately and that he'd better give me a sign because I was real close to bolting for greener pastures, taking a job in the real world where honest actions produce good results that are seeable, measurable." Joel leaned forward and held out his hands.

Cat unfolded her arms from around herself. Joel Cramer had been kind to her on that night long ago. Again tonight she needed that kindness. She extended her hands to him. When he took them she felt a wave of comfort.

"You didn't just relieve me of pain, Cat, you also gave me my faith back."

"It wasn't me. I didn't do it," Cat said softly.

"I know, but you let the Lord use you to do his work. That's all any of us can do, you know? And he gives us a choice. We can agree to let him work through us or we can turn our back on him and refuse. I thank you for not refusing."

That was the first time Cat had heard such a notion. "I never thought I had a choice in the matter."

"That's because you have a good and an honest heart. Although I know your gift has caused you pain."

Cat looked at him hard. He did understand.

Nana came to the bedroom door wrapped in the fluffy terry robe Cat had bought her last Christmas. "Please talk some sense into this child, pastor."

"Nan, join us," Joel said. "I think Cat needs the support of your love right now."

Nana sat next to the pastor on the couch. "I love that child with all my heart. And she is my child, more than she's Bud's."

Cat shook her head. No more confessions, not tonight. She was worn out with them.

The old woman shook her gray head right back. "Katie, there have been too many lies already in your young life. Most of them you couldn't help, but now is the time to make it all fresh and let the truth start healing you." Cat sank back against the cushions and Nana continued. "Like I told Katie tonight, we're related by blood. Her daddy, though she never knew him, was my first cousin. That may not be as close a relation as an uncle in the eyes of the courts, but the courts can't touch her now. She's not a child anymore. And when you add all the love I feel for her to the blood tie, that makes her my child. Though she didn't know that during all those years when loneliness and fear were tearing at her. There's never been much I've been afraid of, but I know a thing or two about loneliness and what it can do to a person."

"I'm sure you do, Nan," Joel said, his eyes sincere and with a nod of his head that urged, "tell me more." And Nana did. She spilled out the whole long story of her life and all about the girl named Katie Parker.

The actual events of the story had no surprises for Cat. The ones she hadn't already heard, she'd lived. There was still lots that Nana didn't know. She'd never told anyone about some of the scary times, like that time in Kentucky when she was fourteen and she got herself picked up for vagrancy. She remembered twisting free from the policeman and running, running, running until she thought her heart would burst. She'd been too afraid to go back to her truck. She'd slept in a wooded park under bushes, wrapped in paper from the garbage can. All that frigid night she'd been as terrified of freezing to death as she had been of being found. In those days she'd carried a knife ... just in case. She'd never had to use it, but more than once she'd had to pull it on some bum and threaten to cut him if he didn't leave her alone. But none of that was as bad as the time in Erie when she almost didn't get away. She'd known lots of scary times like those, and if she had her way, no one would ever know.

When Nana was all done talking and crying and carrying on, she turned to Cat. "Honey, you've got to let go of all that garbage you've got packed inside you. It's the only way you'll ever stop running. Now admit it, it feels better having the truth in the open, doesn't it?"

Cat shrugged. She didn't know how she felt. She didn't feel so restless or jumpy, but she sure didn't feel good. She'd learned long ago that hauling out your feelings and trying to sort through them didn't do anybody any good.

"Cat, you've been hurt by all this," Joel said. "The things you've gone through would damage anyone, but if you ask him, God will heal you, too."

Cat turned her face away. She rarely called on God unless someone else needed his help. Most of the time she tried to stay out of his way.

Joel rose. "I've got to be going. Cat, I'd love to see you in church tomorrow. You know the Lord can work through all of us, letting our lives touch each other in healing ways. They may not be as dramatic as the gift he's given you, but they can be very effective nonetheless. So how about it?"

Cat shook her head. No one said anything. Finally Cat turned back to face the pastor. He stood smiling at her. "I don't know … maybe … I'll have to see," she said.

"Just please don't go running off," Joel said.

"I think Marty wants me out of here," Cat said.

"Oh, for heaven's sake," huffed Nana.

"No, she doesn't, Cat. She really cares about you," Joel said.

Maybe she did care, but it wasn't the same as it had been. None of them saw that. Joel's eyes searched her face. Cat frowned. "I won't take off tonight or tomorrow, probably not even Monday, but I'm not promising I'll stay forever," Cat said.

"None of us can promise that. Finally how long we stick around is up to the Lord," Joel said as he went out the door.

Later, wide awake in bed next to a softly snoring Nana, Cat regretted her promise. She was packed and it was time to go. She needed to just bolt before she thought any more about it, because as the time rolled on toward dawn, the thought of leaving was becoming more and more painful. It was her own fault. She'd let her guard down. She'd become involved with these people. Now all those intertwining feelings, of what she felt for them and what she believed they felt for her, had wrapped themselves around her and anchored her to this place.

TWENTY-FOUR

The next morning as Cat carried the feed bucket to Daisy's stall, the little goat bleated, as she did every morning. And when Cat opened the stall door Daisy bumped her triangular head against Cat's leg, her tail switching fast in her excitement. This, too, she did every morning, but this time it made Cat's heart ache. Just like Grandma's nicker, and Sassy's nuzzle, and the kittens' milling around her feet were nearly unbearable, because she was going to lose it all. She couldn't stay.

Marty had called early and been strangely formal. She'd said she wasn't going to tell the children yet, but she had told Kyle. She didn't think the children would understand, as if it were some nasty secret too dirty for them. Then she'd asked if Cat wanted to go to church with them. Marty had only pushed "church" at her a few times before and then backed off when Cat had said she was looking for a Baptist church to attend. Now it was obvious that she and Joel were in cahoots and had decided that church was just what the strange girl needed.

Worst of all, Duke showed up to help her with her morning chores. Duke, who normally slept until the sun was high in the sky, followed her around as if she were Jesus, and he was trying to get close enough to touch the hem of her garment. When she'd asked him what in the world he wanted, he'd just flashed her a silly grin and said he thought she needed some help. What she needed was everyone to go back to being normal, the way they were before they knew about her.

After the second time she'd turned around and bumped into him, on his way to do a chore she'd already done, she sent him back to the house. "Please, Duke," she said. "I need to be alone this morning. You know, to do some thinking and to sort things out."

"Well, sure you do. How about if I finish up and you take the morning off."

"No. I need to work this morning. It helps me to think."

When he finally accepted that she really didn't want him around, he got this pitiful frown on his face. She almost regretted her words, except she really did need to be alone with the animals she'd come to love. Her animals never judged her or made unreasonable demands: they always lifted her spirits. Or at least they usually did, when she wasn't facing leaving them.

Her chores were soon done. Sunday mornings required just the basic care and feeding. Marty insisted on keeping Sunday as much a day of rest as a farm allowed. Cat wasn't ready to go back and face Nana, who was also sure she knew what Cat should do. She settled herself on the bench outside the tack room and watched the kittens play with Sadie. The kittens only tormented poor Sadie so because they knew they could outrun her. Still, when Sadie yipped and charged them, seeming to love the game as much as they did, it made Cat smile.

Cat heard the door at the far end of the barn bang shut, but she didn't look up. She wasn't up to dealing with Marty's pressuring her about church. Or Duke's annoying attentions. Or Kyle, who would no doubt tease and torment as his way of dealing with the disturbing story he'd heard about her.

"Katie?"

Uncle Bud!

Cat spun toward the hated voice. "Get away from me," she shouted, leaping to her feet and backing away from Uncle Bud, who already stood way too close. Beside him a fleshy-faced, younger man smirked.

"That's no way to talk to your uncle, girl," Bud said, in that oily voice that signaled he wanted something.

"Whatever you want, I'm not giving it to you." Cat saw Bud's eyes go hard. He set his jaw, thrusting his pointy chin at her. She stared back at his face with its acne scars and harsh angles. Hatefulness oozed from the man. That look had always made Cat cringe, but not today. Today he didn't look so fierce. The skin hung loose and yellow on his cheeks and neck. His eyes had gone dull. And the man who had always seemed so big and tall was really nothing but a short, banty rooster of a man who now looked old and weak and sick. Cat squared her shoulders and planted her feet, ready to do battle. She and her uncle locked eyes. But Bud glanced away, his expression crumpling.

"Now, Miss Parker," the younger man began.

"My name's not Parker. That's his name, not mine." Cat turned her glare to the man. "You're that reporter, aren't you? The one who printed those lies about me."

"Hey, I only print what I'm told, miss," he said. "From what I hear it's no lie that you've got the gift, you can heal people with a touch. Well, your uncle here could use some of your magic, and I'd like to watch if I may. Hey, a little well-placed news coverage never hurt anybody." He looked around the barn with a sneer. "You should be doing more with yourself than mucking out stalls. I'm willing to help you." The man pulled a cigarette pack from his breast pocket and made an elaborate show of lighting one. He winked a small piggy eye at Cat as he took the first long drag.

"No cigarettes in the barn," she snapped. "Get that thing out of here."

"No problem," he said, throwing the cigarette onto the ground and grinding it out with his foot. "Now can we talk?"

Cat spun away from them and stomped off. She could hear them scrambling behind her to catch up, but she didn't turn around.

"Katie, please … stop, I'm begging you," Uncle Bud wheezed.

Coughing strangled the remaining words.

Cat turned around. Bud leaned against a stall door, his face now grayish yellow as he gasped for breath. Her instinct directed her back to him, but she willed her feet to stay planted.

"You really are sick," she said flatly.

"Terrible sick, Katie. I need to talk to you."

"Then get rid of him," Cat said, nodding at the reporter.

The reporter spat, then scowled. "I'll wait in the car, Bud. As for you, Katie Parker, I'm going to print a story with or without your help. If I were you, I'd cooperate so your side'll be heard."

Cat glared after him. What a fool. As if he could do her any more harm than he'd already done.

When the man had gone, Bud extended a hand. "Katie, I've got cancer. It's eating me up inside. You're the only hope I've got left."

Cat stared at him. She'd never turned down anyone who had asked for her help, but surely not even God would expect her to help Bud. She saw tears pooling in the corners of his rheumy eyes. He turned away from her, covering his face with his hands, his bony shoulders shaking with his sobs.

"Oh, quit your crying now," she said. "And sit down here a minute." She led him to the bench. She'd give it a try. She had no choice. Besides, he was probably too far gone. God could have healed Bud without her help if that had been his plan.

Bud reached to hug her and she recoiled. He plopped down on the bench, his arms still reaching for her. "Come on now, girl. Give your old uncle a hug. We only have each other."

Bile rose in the back of her throat. Another image that lurked in her nightmares surfaced, the memory of nights he'd stumbled drunk into her room, calling her name soft and creepy. She'd always been too quick for him, and in the mornings he never seemed to remember. There'd only been a few of those nights, and only when she was older, but they'd been enough to haunt her. The first time she'd run off was after he'd sneaked in and then passed out across the bottom of her bed before she'd even known he was there. She was never sure if he was up to any nasty stuff or not, but she didn't want to stick around and find out.

She slapped at his hands. "No. And you're not all I've got. I've got Nana and Samuel and Letty. I wouldn't claim you at all if I had any choice in the matter."

"So the old darkie squealed, did she? After all these years."

Cat clenched her fists and her voice came as a roar. "Don't you ever use that word around me or my family, ever again!" She remembered his voice harsh and ugly from years before, telling someone she was his "little half-n——." It had hurt only because she'd known he'd meant to hurt her, but back then she hadn't understood that it had, in his eyes, been true. Now that hurt less, but made him more despicable.

He cackled and slapped his knee. "Well, that sure changes the ground rules, don't it?" She could see him scheming right there in front of her. "Look now, Katie, you better face it. You still need me. Those people don't stick by their own."

"All these years Nana and Samuel and Letty—all of my daddy's family—stuck by me better than you ever did. So you'd better shut your mouth, you hateful old man, or you'll be sorry!" She stiffened her body, but rage still shook her knees.

"I'm sorry. I didn't mean it." He stood and started toward her. "Just do your thing and heal me—for old time's sake alone." He stopped and lowered his head, no doubt expecting her to lay her hands on him.

"No! Not now! Not ever!" she screamed, her whole body shaking.

He looked up in surprise. He grabbed her arm in a clawlike grip that was unexpectedly strong. He raised his other hand to strike her. "You do as I say or you'll be sorry, you ..."

Cat shoved his arms away. He'd never hit her again. She clutched his temples in her hands, squeezing hard. His eyes shot open in surprise. If she could heal, why couldn't she kill? She felt a fearful coldness start at the back of her neck and begin to spread.

Bud shut his eyes and whimpered.

"Cat!"

Cat thrust Bud away from her and spun toward the sound. Kyle stood by the door.

"Get her away from me," Bud screeched. "She's crazy. I'm telling you, she's crazy."

Cat glared at her uncle, then lunged for him.

Kyle reached her just before she got to Bud. He threw his arms around her, whispering, "Don't, Cat. Don't." She allowed his strong arms to contain her. She collapsed against him.

"I know who you are, you worthless sack of skin," Kyle snarled at Bud. "And you better go while you can still walk out of here. Cat's no longer some little kid you can push around. She has people who care about her."

Bud shuffled toward the door. "Well, you all better lock your doors at night. She's crazy, just like her mother was."

"My mother wasn't crazy. She wasn't. She loved me enough to take me to Nana before she died. And if you'd have left me there ..."

Bud sat down on the bench sneering, acting like his old cocky self. "Your mother was sick all right, sick in the head. I don't know what fairy tales that old woman's been telling you, but your mother was nothing but a nig... " He gave a cruel, mocking laugh. "... Nothing but a negro-loving tramp who finally got one to marry her. 'Course when he found out how crazy she was he run off, leaving her knocked up with you. And I'll tell you how much she loved you. She loved you so much she tried to torch the house while you were still in it. If Nan Riley hadn't been coming by, the both of you would have burned to death. As it was your loony mother run off into the woods and hung herself."

All Cat heard was her own voice howling. She screamed and struggled with all the pent-up rage and pain of her eighteen years on earth. She could feel Kyle's arms tighten around her, but still she thrashed. Then the light dimmed until she saw only darkness and felt nothing but icy coldness.

TWENTY-FIVE

Marty knelt by the bed, her forehead against her folded hands. "Dear heavenly Father, show me how to help this little one. She's the healer, not me. I don't know what to do," she whispered. She raised her eyes. In the dim glow of the night-light she watched Cat, who lay with her face buried in the pillows, her body curled and her knees drawn up like a baby in the womb.

Hours before, Kyle had carried a semi-conscious Cat down to the house. As frightening as that had been, Marty was completely unnerved by Cat's long, shrill wail when the girl at last came to. Cat screamed and sobbed so long that Marty was becoming frantic.

Nan sat, holding Cat close. "Just give her some time now," Nan said. "She'll come out of it. Won't you, my darling girl? Her whole lifetime she's been pushing back these tears and now the dam's broke, that's all." But it went on too long. In desperation, Marty called Joel. By the time he arrived, Cat wasn't just screaming and crying, she was pulling at her hair and scratching her face. Kyle tried to hold her hands, but whenever she could she jerked one away and tore at herself. Joel called Doc Harbison.

Dear Doc. A lot of doctors would have called the ambulance and had her taken straight to the psychiatric floor of the hospital. Instead, he listened to everyone's version of the story before trying to talk to Cat. She didn't even seem to hear him. "Over the last few days, this kid's world has been turned inside out," Doc said. He patted Nana's shoulder and smiled at her. "Some of it for good, but today was bad, real bad, considering the image she'd carried of her mother. I'm going to tranquilize her rather than cart her off. I'd rather not add more terror to this day. Let's get her upstairs to a bed and see if some sleep helps. If nothing else, it will give her a break from herself and maybe the strength to pull it together."

Upstairs in the room Marty shared with Annie, it took three of them—Kyle, Marty, and Jeff—to hold Cat down while Doc injected her. The shot didn't take effect right away, but soon the screaming became sobs, and then quiet tears. Marty ushered the men and a wide-eyed Annie out of the room. She and Nana stretched Cat out on the bed and undressed her. By then she was as limp and passive as a sock puppet. Marty slipped one of Annie's sleep T's over Cat's head. Cat shivered and whimpered.

Finally, covered in three of the softest blankets Marty could find, with Nan gently rubbing her back and singing to her, Cat fell asleep.

Only then did Marty leave the room. With Nan holding vigil beside the bed, she went to talk to Doc, who still waited, sipping coffee in the kitchen. He looked at Marty over his half-glasses. "Well?" he asked.

Marty cleared her throat of unspilled tears before she answered. "She's sleeping now, Doc, but what do we do when she wakes up?"

"If she's still hysterical, we may have to hospitalize her," Doc said.

Kyle slammed a hand down on the table. "I swear by all that's holy, if I had that miserable no-account uncle of hers here now I'd kill the lousy…"

"Kyle!" Duke snapped. "That kind of talk isn't going to do anything but add to all the confusion around here."

Kyle's wide jaw began to work and he took a kick at the table leg.

"Your father's right, Kyle," Doc said. "You're all going to

have to try to keep everything around here as calm and quiet as you can."

"Big chance of that," Jeff muttered. "This place is chaos central."

Marty shot a glare at Jeff. When she saw the pain and confusion on his face she softened her look. "Jeff, are you all right?" He nodded, swallowing hard. "Annie, how about you?"

Annie jumped off her grandfather's lap and ran to Marty, throwing her arms around her and burying her face against her stomach. Marty lifted Annie up and held her close.

"Is Cat going to be all right, really?" Annie whispered in Marty's ear.

Marty took the seat that Joel offered her and looked at Doc. "Annie wants to know if Cat's going to be all right."

Doc shrugged and gave a grim grin. "I don't know. I'm not a psychiatrist. From the stories I've been hearing, our little lady upstairs has lived a very irregular life. In fact, I'm willing to bet that none of us has any idea about how much she's been through. I'm going to leave some pills for when she wakes up, just a mild sedative and only if she needs it. Now this is assuming she wakes calmer. Offer her something light to eat. Let her sleep as much as she wants. Don't make her talk if she doesn't want to. You hear that now, Marty?"

Marty scowled at Doc, the man who had taken care of her medical needs since babyhood.

"I know you, young woman," Doc said with a smile. "No prying. She'll talk when she's ready, and then she's going to need professional help. At least, that's my recommendation, and I hope she takes it. Now, this is all assuming she doesn't wake up screaming like a banshee. In which case, she's out of our hands and straight to the hospital. All right?"

Marty nodded.

Kyle had kicked back his chair and stomped out of the house, letting the door slam behind him.

And then there'd been hours of waiting. In the early evening, Cat had woken. Marty had looked over and found her watching her through a flood of silent tears. Nan had spoon-fed Cat some noodle soup, with Cat sipping and making small mewing sounds like a wounded kitten. Then Cat had turned toward the wall, curled around herself, and buried her face in the pillows. Occasionally, a violent sob had racked her small body, but the hysteria seemed to be over.

When the tears and the soft mewing cries didn't stop, Marty had given her one of Doc's pills. Marty had insisted that, since Cat was in her bed, Nan take Annie's. Marty and Annie had moved into the big double bed in Jeff's room, and Jeff had set up the cot in Kyle's. As for Kyle, Marty had no idea where he was, but guessed he was in some bar, drowning his anger in beer.

Now as Marty watched, the illuminated clock beside the bed crept on toward 1:00 A.M. Still Cat slept, although fitfully. Every once in a while she shuddered and whimpered, burrowing deeper under the covers.

Marty again bowed her head. "Cradle her, Lord, in your loving arms and let her sleep. Let her awaken in the morning peaceful and well," she prayed silently. She rose to her feet.

"Marty, that you?" Nan whispered from Annie's bed.

"Yeah, Nan. I couldn't sleep." The meager light revealed deep lines of worry across Nan's brow as she looked toward Cat.

"I keep falling asleep and waking up and then falling back asleep," Nan said, pulling herself up to rest her back against the headboard. She pulled her feet aside to make room at the foot of the bed. "Sit a minute, dear, if you've a mind to."

"Thanks," Marty said, easing herself onto the bed.

They sat in silence for some moments, Marty just watching Cat sleep, assuming Nan was doing the same. "It doesn't seem right, Nan," Marty said.

"Oh, lots of things don't," Nan agreed. "But which one of them are you referring to?"

"The Bible tells us that God never gives us more than we can handle with his help. Well, if I accept Cat is a healer ..." Marty took a deep breath. "And I do. I mean, it's a real leap for me, but I'm sure she must be. Nothing else makes sense, even though that doesn't make a whole lot of sense either. But anyway, if God gave her this gift, why wouldn't he take care of her better? She was just a baby, really. Where was he when she needed his help?"

Nan sighed. "I used to wonder the same thing, but over the years I've done a lot of thinking and praying on it. God gave Katie her gift sure enough and he stood by her. For a while she led a good life and it seemed to all of us then that God's grace shone from that child. What happened to her after wasn't God's fault. It wasn't all Bud's either, I don't believe."

"I don't understand, Nan. Something happened to her, something awful."

"What happened was Bud pushed an innocent baby out into the world and did nothing to protect her from it. Everybody she met, especially Bud, wanted something from her and nobody gave anything in return. And most of the time nobody was there to remind her, as she took to hiding deeper and deeper inside herself, that she should leave a door open to let Jesus come inside with her. So she shut the Lord out, too, only turning to him when she needed his help for someone else. Somehow it all got confused in her head, and I think she got too scared to ask for comfort for herself. In fact, I think she might have been as afraid of the Lord as she was of Bud. I don't really know, but that's what I think. Maybe when she comes out of this she'll tell us."

"Oh, Nan, I pray she comes out of this," Marty whispered.

Nan reached across the blanket and Marty took the hand she offered. "And praying is the only thing we can do for her right now," Nan said. "Our Father ... come on, Marty, say it with me. Right now I'm pretty scared, too, and hearing another voice besides my own calling to him would be a comfort."

Marty cradled Nan's hand in her own, bowed her head, and joined in the prayer, hoping it would ease not just Cat but also Nan and her and all of them toward a better morning.

TWENTY-SIX

Marty slipped between the sheets as quietly as possible, trying not to wake Annie. Her body ached for sleep, but her mind, racing between concern and agitation, prevented it. She laced her fingers together behind her head and stared at the blank darkness of the ceiling.

She didn't need this, not now. Her riders would start back on Tuesday. She had a full week of lessons. Everyone was depending on her, and she'd been depending on Cat to be there to help her. If the kid was really a healer, why didn't she zap herself?

Marty's eyes stung. Work wasn't worrying her; she'd handle the lessons, asking more of the volunteers until Cat got back on her feet. But what if Cat didn't? "Oh Lord, forgive me," Marty prayed. How could she resent that poor child?

She didn't, not really, but she was feeling powerfully agitated and resentful and ... what? Helpless—totally helpless, clueless, and inept—as she'd felt toward the end with Dan when she knew her prayers weren't going to be answered, that he would die and there was nothing she could do to prevent it.

And here was this young girl, a healer. As hard as that was for Marty to get down, she knew it must be true. And presumably God had given Cat this incredible gift. But where was God when Marty had needed a healing for Dan? Why couldn't he have sent Cat into her life sooner? Even if God refused to hear Marty's prayers for Dan, maybe he'd have listened to Cat, who had to be special to him. Resentment crystallized into a pinpoint of recognition. She was angry with God.

Instantly, fear gripped Marty. Wrath was a serious sin, one of the seven deadlies; when it was directed at God surely it was even more heinous. She eased herself upright to sit leaning against the headboard. "My Lord Jesus, I'm so sorry," she whispered. Annie stirred in her sleep. Marty continued her prayer silently, yearning with all her soul toward her God. *I know how much you've done for me, especially when Annie was sick.* What she didn't understand was why some prayers are answered and others not—why Cat had been given such an extraordinary gift and she'd been left to muddle along as best she could. *Lord, please forgive me my anger and confusion.* A tearful sigh shook itself free from deep in Marty's chest.

Annie snuggled closer to her. "Are you crying, Mom?" she asked.

"No. No, darling," Marty said, sliding down next to Annie and wrapping her in her arms. "Just fretting."

"Is Cat better?"

"I don't know, honey. She's still sleeping."

"Jeff said he heard everybody talking and that Cat can cure people. I don't understand. Is she magic?"

Marty kissed Annie's forehead. "You know what? I don't understand either, but as near as I can figure out God gave Cat a very special gift. Sometimes, when God wills it, she can lay her hands on someone who is sick and God will work through her to heal that person. That's not magic, sweetie; it's grace."

Annie was quiet a moment. "I think I get it now, Mom. And that means God will take care of her and we shouldn't worry, right?"

"I hope so, Annie."

Annie snuggled closer. "He will, Mom. I know he will." Before Marty could think of an answer, Annie was asleep and softly snoring.

Marty sighed. She wished for a faith like Annie's, so willing to accept, even when she didn't understand.

She turned on her side and willed sleep to come. Instead, she was bombarded with every worry she'd had in the last six months, the resolved as well as the unresolved issues. She flopped back over and sat upright with her back against the old headboard.

She had to get ahold of herself. She needed to get some sleep. She'd be of no use to anyone tomorrow if she was exhausted. And the way things had been going around the farm, who knew what tomorrow held?

The answer hit her right in the solar plexus—no one. And fortunately no one expected her to know. The thought brought a certain calmness and with that came the confidence that somehow or other, as she always had, she'd get through tomorrow whatever it brought. And how had she gotten through all these last months of tomorrows? By trusting the Lord enough to follow him, even when she couldn't see where he was leading her. By believing, as she'd told Nan earlier, that God wouldn't give her more than she could handle, not with him there to help her. Nothing else made any sense to her. She knew no other way to live. Besides, surely one day God would give her the answers she sought.

TWENTY-SEVEN

Marty swung her feet over the side of the bed. She still couldn't sleep, but she did feel better. Maybe she hadn't been sent a visible sign like a burning bush or a lightning bolt, but her prayers had, at least, calmed her.

The illuminated face on the digital clock shone the time— 3:35 A.M. Maybe Mamma's remedy of chamomile tea would help. She grabbed her robe and headed for the kitchen.

As she tiptoed to the top of the stairs, Marty heard the door downstairs swing shut. No dogs barked, so it had to be Kyle sneaking in. He staggered onto the landing and spotted her.

"Sis! I'm sure glad someone's up. I really need to talk," he said, his voice overloud in the quiet house.

"Shhh!" Marty scurried down the stairs and steered him back into the kitchen. "Now be quiet, so you don't wake everyone."

Kyle flopped onto a chair. "I'm not as drunk as I look," he said. He ran his hands through his hair, holding onto his head a moment as if steadying himself. "I'm not saying I'm sober, but I'm not smashed."

Marty bit her tongue. For a long time she'd been writing a speech in her head for him. Her little brother drank too much, and in her opinion he needed to get help for it. But tonight wasn't a night for speeches. Marty filled the teapot and put it on to boil.

"Sometimes I hate the world," he spat. He put his elbows on the table and buried his face in his hands.

Marty didn't answer, but he didn't seem to require one. When he didn't continue, Marty said, "I think Cat's doing a little better. At least, she's resting in relative peace."

Kyle lifted his head and then slumped back against the chair, exhaling a noisy breath. "Good. Good." He shook his head. "It was really awful this morning. I mean in the barn. I went up because I wanted to tell her that I didn't care if her name was Katie or Cat or Tigerlily, I still thought she was a good kid and was awfully glad she'd come to us. I didn't believe that healing stuff, but I figured, heck, if she needed to believe it, so what? We all live by some kind of delusion and sometimes it's the only way life's bearable. But you know..." He squeezed his eyes shut and swallowed hard. When he opened his eyes they looked haunted. "She was honest to goodness trying to kill her uncle and she believed she had the power to do that. I've never seen anything like the look on her face and if you'd have seen the expression on his, you'd know he believed it, too. Man, it was the scariest thing I've ever seen."

"Are you saying you think if you hadn't shown up when you did, she would have actually killed him?"

"I don't know ... I mean ... I may not be a churchgoer like the rest of you, but I do believe in God and Jesus, his Son. And if Cat has a gift ..." He looked at Marty, one eyebrow raised, questioning.

"As incredible as it seems, I think she probably does, Kyle."

"Well, then, I believe that a gift like that is God working through her and I don't believe the God I know would have allowed her to kill her uncle. Even though all of us may think the lousy pig deserved it, I don't think God works that way." Again he looked at Marty.

"I don't think so either, but I have to be honest, I'm really confused by all of this."

Kyle shook his head. "Well, don't look at me. I don't understand either. Cat was coming around so well ... opening up to everyone, starting to smile more. That first day she came here and you sent me up to show her the barn, she reminded me of

Brandy when Mamma first gave her to me. Remember?"

"I remember Brandy, but not when you first got her. I was in college and wasn't around then, Kyle."

"You should have seen Brandy as a two-year-old. She was the prettiest little blood bay filly I'd ever seen. She'd been abused and was terrified of everything and everybody. Mamma said that if I could make her trust me, I'd have the best horse I'd ever owned. It took me nearly two months of just sitting quiet and talking to her, before she'd let me touch her without her squealing and striking at me. It took nearly two more months of gaining her trust before she let me touch her head, another three months before I could easily get the halter on and off her. You know, that next year when we finally started training her to saddle, she was amazing. She threw me more than any other horse I've broken, but once she got the hang of it she was the best horse I've ever owned. But I always had to take care to keep her trust. I could correct her, but never by hitting her. She'd freak out and go after anyone who raised a hand to her. That first day, Cat reminded me of Brandy. She was so scared. I reached toward her to pat Red and she nearly climbed the walls."

The kettle whistled and Marty rose to make their tea.

"Make mine instant coffee, please," Kyle said.

"It wouldn't sober you up, you know. That's just a myth," Marty said, and then instantly regretted it.

"So humor me," Kyle answered.

Marty heard footsteps on the stairs, too heavy to be one of the kids. She reached for another cup, assuming it was Nan, and was surprised to see her father shuffle, bleary-eyed, into the kitchen.

"How about a cup of cocoa for me," he said, taking his chair at the head of the table.

"What are you doing up, Dad?" Kyle asked.

"Got up to go to the bathroom and couldn't go back to

sleep. I checked on the little one, just peeped in the door. She's still sleeping."

Marty fixed Duke his cocoa, Kyle his coffee, and then poured herself a cup of herbal tea. They sipped in silence for some minutes.

"What's going to happen to her?" Kyle asked.

Duke shrugged and shook his head. "Darned if I know," he said.

"What do you mean, 'happen to her'?" Marty asked.

"What if she wakes tomorrow and the pill wears off and she's as hysterical as she was this afternoon?" Kyle said.

"Doc was pretty adamant about getting her to the hospital if that happened," Marty said.

"Over my dead body," Duke insisted. "They'll get hold of her and that will be the end of her. They'll drug her senseless and just keep her that way. You can't trust those places."

"Dad, be sensible," Marty said. "Modern medicine does a bit better than that these days."

"Sure, Marty," Kyle said. "I can see it now. Cat finally comes back to her senses. She starts telling them the story of her life and how she can cure people by touching them and praying … yeah, right, I can hear the doctor now: 'She's completely delusional. More medication.' Modern medicine doesn't deal real well with supernatural events, Marty."

"So what do you want me to do, Kyle? I'm not the healer, she is. I don't know what will happen. I don't know what to do."

"Now, Marty, calm down," Duke said. "I didn't mean to put you on the spot and I don't think your brother did either. Cat wasn't screaming and yelling when she woke up earlier. Let's just hope she's still calm in the morning."

"And let's pray she gets well enough to continue on with her life here," Marty said.

"Yeah, but…" Kyle stopped, looking puzzled.

"But what?" Marty demanded.

"Well … maybe … I don't know. I'm not sure what I'm trying to say here," Kyle said. "But maybe she shouldn't stay."

"Kyle, I'm surprised at you!" Marty said. "Cat's got a job here as long as she wants it. I really care about her and I thought you did, too."

"I do, that's not what I meant."

"I think I know what you mean, son, and I'm not sure I've got the words either," Duke said. "Marty, Cat's a healer and…" He rubbed his chin and looked thoughtful.

Marty studied first her father then her brother. The two of them were softer touches than she was. Neither of them would think of sending Cat away. Slowly their meaning sunk in. "You mean if we care about her, we should want more for her … that maybe if she truly gets well—I mean better than she was when she came here—it might not be right for her to stay?"

"Yeah, something like that," Kyle said.

"She's only been here because she's been hiding, Marty," Duke said.

Marty bent over her tea. She inhaled its fruity sweetness. She lifted the cup and took a sip, letting it warm her. Too often she underestimated her dad and Kyle. "I love you two. Do you know that?" she asked.

Kyle grinned at her and winked. "What's not to love?"

Duke just smiled.

"Okay, no hospital unless she's a danger to herself and we absolutely can't control her. And then we'll see if we can give the world back one of its special children and, with God's help, put Cat back into the world—hopefully somewhere that's a bit gentler than the places she ran from."

Duke sniffed and wiped his eyes on the sleeve of his robe. "'Course I wouldn't care if that took us a while. I don't think she should be in a rush about it."

Marty reached over and squeezed her father's hand.

TWENTY-EIGHT

Upstairs in Marty's bed, Cat walked a forest path, the dank earth cold on her bare feet, the sharp wind biting her legs and face and blowing through her thin night dress. The full moon shone through the skeletal branches. Eerie shadows wavered all around her. Her heart raced. She had to hurry, but she couldn't see well enough to run. And why weren't her legs working right? Braces—metal braces—hindered her legs.

A huge winged shadow crossed her path, the eagle seeking its prey. She cowered against the trunk of a black-barked tree. Was the eagle what she ran from?

As soon as she was sure it was gone she ran again for the path. She had to hurry or it would be too late. No, she wasn't running from the eagle, she was looking for someone. Ahead of her and to the right the eagle passed between her and the moon. Cold terror struck her heart. The eagle glided on, either unaware or baiting her. She was running from the eagle *and* trying to find someone. Was there a connection between the two? She didn't know, but time was running out. Of that she was sure.

She lumbered down the path. With every step the braces seemed to get heavier, her legs less responsive. The ghostly white-trunked sycamores scattered among the other trees served as road marks, guiding her on … to where? She didn't know.

The path became less evident as the trees grew closer together. Still she dragged herself on, believing that whatever she was seeking lay just on the other side of this forest. Now briar bushes grew from between the trees. They tore at her arms and legs and the hem of her gown. The path turned and as she rounded it, clawlike hands shot from the bushes, grasping and scratching.

The turn became a corkscrew folding in on itself. The hands shoved her and pulled at her hair. Above the howl of the wind, wailing voices called her name.

"Katie … Katie, where are you?"

"I'm here, Nana," she called. "Right here."

"Cat, don't go," Marty pleaded.

"Marty, I have to find something. Then I'll be back," she answered.

The rest of the voices overlapped and mingled, with only a word here or there recognizable. They sounded as though they were coming from around the next turn. An unseen hand shoved Cat to the ground. She struggled to get back up, but her legs wouldn't move. Annie cried. Kyle shouted. Duke called. Other voices—Jeff, Samuel, Letty, Joel, Kristen, Sam, and Lisa—all cried out to her. She pulled herself along the forest floor, dragging her leaden legs. The ground became damp and then soggy until it sucked at her body as she hauled herself through it. The voices still called.

"Where are you?" she screamed. A mocking cackle floated in. Uncle Bud. She put her hands over her ears and screamed. The pitch of the wind rose to a deafening whine, covering the familiar tones. The trees bent toward her, their branches like talons reaching. They spun—slowly at first and then faster—in a tight orbit around her. She squeezed her eyes shut. The ground beneath her pulled away, tossing her into space. She fell, landing on hard-packed sand.

Cat opened her eyes. The forest was gone. Before her a rocky, barren plain led to a cliff where a lone tree loomed. Someone was in the tree. Everything in Cat yearned toward that someone. She pulled herself to her feet. The braces fell away and she began to run. The more she ran the farther away the tree seemed.

She sensed a presence behind her. Still running, she looked

over her shoulder. The eagle skimmed the edge of the forest, heading toward the plain where she would be easy prey. She pumped her legs harder. The tree seemed closer. She ran even faster. She seemed to be skimming the rocky surface and flying toward the tree.

She again looked over her shoulder. The eagle glided a safe distance behind. She would reach the tree before it caught her.

She willed herself on. She recognized the figure in the tree. "I'm coming, Mamma," she cried. She focused so intently on the tree that she almost didn't see where the ground stopped and the cliff face fell away.

The tree rose from the unseeable bottom of the canyon below. And in the tree her mother sat on a branch, her long hair over one shoulder, playing her mandolin. "Mamma, it's me!" Cat cried. Her mother raised her head. The roaring wail of the wind came from her opened mouth.

Just as her mother's eyes met Cat's, the branch broke. Mamma fell. A rope looped around her neck jerked her to a sickening stop. The roaring wind ceased, replaced by a deadly silence. Mamma spun at the end of the rope, her head lolled to the side like a broken doll.

Cat screamed. Her scream became the wailing and the wind rushed to meet it. A winged shadow fell over her. She saw it reaching for her. Before it could snatch her away, Cat jumped into the abyss....

"Easy now, darling," Nana soothed. "You're all right, child. You're just fine."

Cat felt the long arms wrap around her and pull her close. She buried her face against Nana's shoulder, still not wanting to open her eyes. Her teeth chattered and she shook all over.

"There now. You were having a bad dream."

Cat clung to Nana.

She felt Nana's lips brush her forehead. "Well, it's over now. Open your eyes." Cat shook her head. "Come on, now, open 'em."

Slowly, Cat opened her eyes, but when she saw that she was in Marty's bed, the memory of the day before returned, its reality as horrible as the dream. Her eyes filled with tears which coursed over her cheeks.

"Sweet child, don't start this again," Nana pleaded.

Cat slumped back against the pillow, unable to stop the tears, not sure she wanted to.

The door opened a crack and Marty peeked in. "Hi," she said, her voice soft, her face pale. "I heard her screaming," she said to Nana.

Nana rubbed Cat's hand between her own. "Just a bad dream. I think she's doing a bit better than yesterday."

Marty smiled. She nudged the bed away from the wall and sat opposite Nana on the other side of the bed. She took Cat's other hand in hers. "So ... are you doing better?"

Cat squeezed her eyes shut and shook her head.

Marty kissed her hand. "You may not feel better, but you are. Yesterday you didn't respond to us at all."

Again Cat shook her head. Her pain was still unbearable; she'd never be better. Cat opened her eyes to see Marty smiling at her. Marty reached across her and plucked a tissue from the box on the bedside table. She wiped Cat's cheeks with it. Still Cat couldn't stop more tears from spilling over.

"How about a cup of tea, with milk and plenty of sugar?" Marty asked.

Tea? Cat didn't care about tea.

"I think that would be just the thing for her," Nana said.

Marty headed toward the door. Cat, watching her go, saw Jeff's face peering through the crack. "Mom, is she okay?" he whispered.

"Why don't you ask her yourself?" Marty said.

Jeff slipped into the room, followed by Annie holding on to his shirttail. They stood as if poised to shoot right back out again. "So, are you ... okay, I mean?" Jeff said.

No, she wasn't, but they looked so worried. Cat didn't trust her voice to answer. She nodded.

Annie crept forward, her eyes studying Cat's face. "Really, Cat?" she asked.

Cat tried to smile, but the tears only came faster. She managed another nod. Annie climbed up on the bed and hugged her around the neck. "Please get better, Cat," she said. She gave Cat a quick kiss on the cheek and then fled the room with Jeff following her.

Cat rolled onto her stomach and sobbed into the pillow. She'd scared the kids ... and herself. She was still scared, maybe too scared, maybe so scared she'd never get out of this bed. How much did they know? Did they know she had tried to kill Uncle Bud? Part of her wished she had, most of her was horrified that she'd even tried.

He'd said such awful things. She still wasn't sure if what he'd told her about Mamma was true. The dream image of her mother hanging from the tree seeped into her mind. She squeezed her eyes shut and pulled the sides of the pillow up to hide her face. She'd been having that same dream for years with the eagle chasing her and Mamma in the tree, but in the old version Cat had always awakened with Mamma singing sweet lullabies and the eagle circling the moon. Of course, Marty and the family and her new friends hadn't been in the old dream calling her back. Is that what they'd been doing? Calling her back from the edge of the cliff?

She heard someone enter the room, heavy footsteps on the hardwood floor.

"Hey, kiddo," Kyle said. "Man, haven't you done enough

crying?" A clumsy hand ruffled her hair. "Tell you what, I'll go and get you a pop or something."

"Your sister just went to fetch some tea, Kyle," Nana said.

"Then I'll go help her." His steps hurried across the floor and down the hall.

Nana chuckled softly. "Men have a lot of trouble giving sympathy, child."

She didn't want sympathy. She wanted to be left alone. Really she wanted to be left alone to die. She was tired of running and she couldn't stay, not anywhere, not after yesterday. Maybe if she went back to sleep and into the dream, she could hang by her neck like her mother from the tree. That would be fitting. But then there were lots of ways to die. Who knew that better than she did? She'd seen so many sick and dying people in her life. All it took was the stopping of the heart.

She didn't know how to stop her heart. Maybe she could stop her breathing. She tried to hold her breath, but just when she thought her chest would burst, she turned her head to the side and gasped, sucking fresh cool air into her lungs.

"That's good, Cat," came Duke's gruff voice. "Breathe deep, open up those passages. You'll feel better." He dropped down on the bed with a bounce that tossed her upward. "She's doing better today. I can just tell. My wife, good woman that she was, used to say that every so often a good cry was just what she needed. Where's Marty? Does she know Cat's awake?"

"Indeed she does," Nana said. "She's gone to fetch a cup of tea."

"Well then," Duke said, patting Cat's back. "I'll pop some bread in the toaster and be back up in a jiffy. There's nothing quite like tea and toast when you're not feeling well." He stood and the bed dropped back to horizontal.

Cat sniffed back the tears. Well, maybe she couldn't suffocate herself, but she didn't have to drink or eat. She wondered how long that would take and if that was a painful way to die.

"What dear people," Nana said. "With all of your running around over these last years, girl, I think you're mighty lucky that the Lord brought you here for this chapter of your life."

Before long, they all trooped back in. Marty led the parade with the tray, laden with tea, toast, jam, and an apple cut in wedges. Cat heard a whine.

"I brought somebody who's really been missing you," Kyle said. He stepped from behind Duke and laid Sadie on the bed. The tiny terrier was so excited she wiggled all over as she jumped right onto Cat's chest to lick her chin. Cat took Sadie in her arms and curled her body around the still-wriggling dog. Cat kissed Sadie's head, right between her little ears where it was softest.

"Now, if we can get Sadie to calm down, I could give Cat her tray," Marty said, with that bossy tone that always brought everyone to attention.

Cat patted the bed beside her and Sadie snuggled into her side, still wagging her tail so hard that her whole body shook.

Duke handed a fluffy lilac towel to Nana, who spread it across Cat's lap. Cat fingered the towel's nap. She'd always loved that color. Marty flipped down the legs on the bed tray and laid it across the towel.

"I cut the apple," Annie said.

Cat tried to smile at her, but the effort only made her eyes water.

"Well, eat something," Jeff said.

Cat looked at Nana, who smiled at her and nodded. Then she glanced from Marty, to Duke, to Kyle, to the kids, all of them smiling and nodding. She picked up an apple wedge and took a small bite. She guessed with all of them watching, starving herself to death was also out of the question.

TWENTY-NINE

Cat couldn't eat everything on the tray, especially with all of them staring at her. Kyle and Jeff wandered away first. Then Duke. Annie crawled right up on the end of the bed and pulled Sadie into her lap. She petted and talked to Sadie, taking timid peeps at Cat. Even worse, Nana and Marty sat side by side on the other bed watching her. They didn't talk much, but smiled continually, as if their forced cheeriness would pull her out of her pain. As long as she kept eating they didn't expect her to talk, so she took small nibbles long after she'd had enough and until she thought she'd be sick if she took one more crumb.

"Oh, Nan, I called the bus station," Marty said. "You can exchange your return ticket whenever you need to."

Cat pushed the tray away and slumped against the pillows.

Nana stood and took the tray. "Well, I'd say our girl did just fine," she said, with a big smile.

Cat hadn't even remembered Nana yesterday. She'd made her miss her bus. She wanted to say she was sorry, but she was too worn out to talk. She pressed her eyelids together against the stinging of her eyes. Her nose began to run and she wiped it with a tissue.

Nana and Marty watched her with expectation, as if blowing her nose had some greater meaning. Cat grabbed a few more tissues and turned toward the wall, pulling the covers up to her ears. If they thought she was sleeping, maybe they'd go away.

Sadie yipped and pawed at Cat's back.

"Annie, I think Sadie needs to go out. Please take her for us," Marty said.

Cat felt Annie crawl off the bed and heard Sadie whine as she was carted away. Cat didn't want Sadie to go, just the rest of them. *Please bring her back, Annie.* Had she said that out loud or just thought it? She didn't know.

Neither Marty nor Nana responded, so she must have just thought it. She'd never realized how much energy it took just to form a single sentence. She felt gutted and drained. It was almost too much of an effort to breathe.

It seemed like a long time before Annie came back with Sadie, but maybe it had only been a few minutes. Sadie scurried right up to Cat's nose and gave it a lick. Cat reached out and pulled her in, nestling her against her chest.

"Well, we'll let you alone now to rest, Cat," Marty said.

Cat felt a hand smooth her hair. Another hand, much smaller, patted her foot.

"I'm going, too, darling," Nana said. "I could use a bite to eat. I'll be back up before long, but in the meantime, you rest well and call if you need us." Cat felt Nana's lips brush her cheek.

She lay, hollow and numb, holding Sadie to her. A ragged sigh broke her shallow breathing. She tried to match her breaths to Sadie's ... air in ... air out ... air in ... air out. Her heavy eyelids refused to stay open. If she fell asleep, maybe Sadie could breathe for both of them. She needed to keep breathing, if for no other reason than they all wanted her to.

When she woke, the sun slanted into the room from the opened shade. The bright light mocked the darkness inside her heart. Who had opened that shade? And after bugging her all morning, where were they now when she needed someone to close it? She would do it herself, but it was too far away. She did have to go to the bathroom....

She lay there a few more minutes. When it became evident that no one was coming, she eased her legs over the side of the bed. She drew in a lungful of cool air and slipped to the floor.

She knew the legs moving below her were hers, but they didn't feel like it.

On her way back from the bathroom, she stopped to peek out the window. Snow iced the creek bank and the hillside beyond. Along the edges the creek water was frozen solid, but it still rolled dark as slate through the center.

A rifle shot sounded from somewhere on the other side of the hill. A button buck leaped from the top, zigzagged down the steep hillside, splashed through the creek, and was gone. Buck season started today, always the first Monday after Thanksgiving. *Run, young buck, run. You'll be safe here. Get to the woods.*

Had they remembered not to turn the horses out this morning? Even though the farm was posted, a hunter could wander on. To an inexperienced, trigger-happy hunter, a brown horse could be mistaken for a deer.

A rifle boomed close by. She heard a whoop and a cheer and then Kyle calling, "Come look what I got in the front yard!" She'd forgotten Kyle hunted. He must have shot her buck. She pulled the shade over the window. Light-headedness sent her crawling back into bed. She heard footsteps on the stairs. She pulled the covers up around her ears and pretended to sleep.

She heard the door open and light footfalls quickly cross the floor. *Annie?* The other bedsprings creaked and then silence. No other footsteps followed. Minutes passed. Cat rolled over to find Annie staring at her, wide-eyed, from between the bedspread and the blanket.

"Kyle shot a deer. It's out there right in the front yard," Annie said softly.

"I know," Cat said back, her voice a rusty whisper.

"I'm not going to eat it. Not one bite," she said.

"Me either," Cat answered.

"Grandpap said he was going out to help gut and skin it. Can I stay here until they're done?"

"Sure, but let's not talk. Okay?"

Annie opened the drawer in the bedside table and pulled out a book. "I'm going to write about it in my journal. Sometimes that helps me understand things."

Cat nodded. She watched as Annie intently bent over her writing. Annie had such innocence and goodness in her. Cat wanted to tell Annie that lots of things in life seemed cruel and made no sense, but not to stop loving because of it.

Nana came to check on her. "My, but you two look busy. I think I'll leave you alone and come back in a little while."

Later Marty appeared again with a tray. Cat still wasn't hungry, but the whole-wheat bread and cheese tasted good. And the sweet acidic orange juice soothed her strained throat. This time when she finished and pushed the tray away she managed a feeble "thank you."

Marty patted her cheek. "You are more than welcome."

In the late afternoon, after Annie had long been gone and even Sadie was outside romping with Cody, someone knocked on the door.

"Come in," Cat answered.

Jeff walked into the room carrying Herman. "I thought he might cheer you up."

Couldn't any of them see she didn't want to be "cheered up"? But when Herman waddled up to the head of the bed, sat down, and chittered at her, Cat smiled in spite of herself. She pushed herself up against the headboard. He crawled into her lap. She picked him up. His humanlike hands played with strands of long hair that had pulled from her braid. He sat on her chest and examined a long strand. He sneaked it into his mouth and then pulled it from side to side with his paws.

"Raccoon dental floss," Jeff said.

Cat giggled as she retrieved her soggy lock. Jeff reached in his shirt pocket and handed Cat some raisins. He showed her how to make Herman sit up and beg for them. But Cat didn't want to make him beg for his treats. She preferred to watch him pluck one raisin from the bunch in her hand and pop it into his mouth. The eyes behind his bandit's mask looked so thoughtful as he chewed. He hesitated before he reached for another raisin, as if he were asking her permission.

When Nana returned with Sadie at her heels, the possessive terrier growled and took off after Herman. Jeff scooped up his timid raccoon, who climbed from his arms to his shoulder and chitted angrily at Sadie on the floor far below.

"I better put him back in my room," Jeff said. "Stumpy usually stops by the window ledge to look for treats sometime before dinner. If you want I'll call you."

"Maybe," Cat answered. It had been a long time since she'd seen the tailless squirrel who visited Jeff's windowsill for treats. But she was too tired to walk that far.

Marty and Nana tried to talk her into going downstairs for dinner. "I'm not really hungry," she said. More than that she just wasn't up to the whole family dinner thing.

When Marty brought her a steaming bowl of vegetable soup her stomach growled its appreciation. Cat ate every bite and two of Nana's homemade biscuits. She even managed an entire piece of the chocolate pie Aunt Bertie had dropped off, knowing it was one of Cat's favorites.

After dinner Duke came by with a deck of cards and insisted she play him a hand of hearts. Halfway through she realized that he was letting her win.

"Hey, play fair or I quit," she said.

He gave a shoulder-shaking chuckle and won the next two games.

And so Cat reentered the world slowly, aware of each step in the journey. She and Nana moved back to her own apartment on Tuesday night. Cat would have gone in the morning, but

Marty had fussed and bossed her into staying. Besides, Nana and Marty seemed to honestly enjoy each other.

Sam and Lisa came to see her Wednesday afternoon and brought her a box of chocolates. And although Sam and Marty had insisted Cat take the rest of the week off, she persuaded them to let her help get Grandma groomed and saddled. They agreed, but only if she took the first ride. When the other afternoon lessons showed up, she retreated back to her apartment, not yet ready to face just anybody.

On Thursday she was almost back to her old self. She simply refused to think about Uncle Bud. And as for what he'd said about Mamma ... no, she couldn't think about that either. When she felt stronger, she'd ask Nana. Then a letter from Uncle Bud arrived in Thursday's mail.

THIRTY

Nana came in from taking a short walk around the barn with the letter in her hand. "Katie, this came for you. Marty wasn't sure we should give it to you, but I think you need to know I'll always deal square with you." She handed the envelope to Cat.

When Cat saw the "B. Parker" at the top of the return address, her hand shook. The realization that she had really wanted to kill him washed over her. And he had known it, too. She'd seen it in his eyes, but still she hadn't stopped. Would she have stopped if Kyle hadn't grabbed her? She thought so, but she didn't know for sure.

She tore open the letter. The knowledge of her own awful sin hurt worse than anything he could possibly have to say to her. She read the letter:

Dear Katie,

I shouldn't have said what I said to you the other day. Whatever else your mother was, she was my sister. I shouldn't have bad-mouthed her like that. You may not believe this, but while we were growing up we were real close, your mamma and me.

I'd like you to think about coming home. I promise I won't say nothing bad about your mother or you or that old woman you care so much about. I really need you now. Like I said the other day, you're the only hope I got. I know you didn't really mean me no harm either, so just come on home and we'll forget all about it.

Cat crumpled the letter in her hand and tossed it in the wastebasket.

"Katie?" Nana asked.

"Nothing, Nana," Cat said. "He thinks by being pitiful he can get me to come to him."

"Did he say anything more about your mamma?"

Cat jerked back toward Nana. "How do you know about what he said?"

"Kyle told me," Nana said softly.

"I don't want to talk about it."

"That's fine, but I need to tell you that I loved your mamma. She was a dear girl who just never got a break in life. And whenever you're ready, I'll be happy to tell you everything I know about her."

Cat grabbed her coat off the hook by the door and, because it was still hunting season, her red wool scarf so no one would mistake her for a deer. She fled the apartment, Sadie at her heels. She needed a good long walk in the woods. She stomped off, her boots leaving dark, muddy imprints through the dusting of snow. At the edge of the woods, Sadie charged ahead of her after a rabbit on the path. Above her, wild grapevine ropes looped through the canopy of branches. No. She wouldn't go into the woods today. "Sadie, come!" she ordered and hurried back to the barn.

Inside the arena, Marty and Joanne stood by the mounting block with Michael, a fifteen-year-old boy who was mildly spastic. Robin, a perky, smiley eight-year-old with Down's syndrome, waited with her mother for her turn to mount. They seemed to be one volunteer short. Cat stepped forward. She didn't want to deal with people, but at that moment what she wanted most was anything that would distract her from herself. "I'll help," Cat said.

"Cat, you're sure?" Marty said.

Cat nodded.

"Great, then why don't you side-walk with Robin."

Cat went to stand just far enough away from Robin and her mother to discourage conversation. But at the sight of her, Robin got all excited and started pulling on her mother. The two of them disappeared briefly into the office. When they returned Robin broke away from her mother and charged, her head to one side, her tiny feet pumping in a rather crooked line to Cat.

"She made a present for you," her mother explained with a proud smile.

Robin tugged on Cat's jacket and Cat bent toward her. The little girl handed her a turkey-shaped sugar cookie covered with green and purple sprinkles. The cookie was wrapped in cellophane and tied with a yellow bow, no doubt her mother's contribution. "I saved it, 'cause I didn't see you on Thanksgiving after the parade."

Cat's throat filled and her eyes stung. "Thank you, Robin. Thank you very much." She laid a hand on the little girl's fine blond hair.

Robin looked up at Cat through round-lensed glasses that made her look impish. She smiled and hugged Cat's leg. "You're welcome, sweet pea," Robin announced.

Robin's mother's laugh sparked Cat's giggle. "Only her favorite people get called 'sweet pea.'"

Robin ran back to her mother and hugged her around both knees. "That's right, sweet pea," she said with a husky little laugh.

Cat felt slightly less honored when Robin kissed Max right on the nose and said, "And how are you today, sweet pea?" But still she was touched, and the child's affection melted some of Cat's reserve.

As Robin, with a little help from Marty, pulled herself onto

Max's back, Cat stepped into place beside her. Another volunteer took the other side. "Side-walkers," Joanne instructed, "I think she'll be fine with minimal support."

Cat held on to Robin's ankle and walked beside her as the lesson began. Cat felt no need from the little girl, as she usually did when she lay her hands on those who were sick or suffering. She decided to offer the prayer for her and see what happened. But no familiar warmth came, no healing grace.

Robin laughed and waved at her mother. Robin worked hard at her lessons, harder than many of the riders. She was a lot more willing to do some of the exercises Joanne suggested, especially when asked to steady herself with one hand and twist her trunk around to wave to her mother with the other. Robin's mother joined in by grinning and waving. "Hello there, sweet pea," she yelled to Robin.

Michael's mother waved and got as involved as Robin's mother did, but Michael, like most teenagers, tried too hard to be cool to take joy in such silliness. Instead of playing games, Joanne involved him by explaining the reasons for the different exercises and then got his full cooperation. Cat liked Michael. He was a good kid. He just demanded that he be treated with the dignity he considered appropriate for a near-man of fifteen. With his choppy gait and slurred speech, Cat guessed that respect was something he didn't often get from the other kids at school. She knew, as did all these children, what it was like to be the one who was different.

Cat walked around and around beside Max as he patiently carried Robin. She remembered Robin's first lesson. The little girl had required heavier support then, with a hand holding her knee and another her ankle. Today she bent and touched her toes, waved to her mother, and rode with both hands overhead, all signs of a dramatic improvement in her balance.

From the center of the arena, Marty encouraged her. "Robin, you're doing such a good job today."

Cat smiled. God hadn't given Cat this healing. This one was Marty's and Joanne's. Not a miracle cure of complete recovery, but perhaps a miracle nonetheless.

When the lessons were over, Cat watched Michael walk away and realized how far he too had come. Another everyday kind of miracle? It seemed so.

Cat waved good-bye to Michael and Robin and their families and then led Max to his stall. She'd been right all those months ago when she'd come here. This was a good place.

How she'd hoped then that Uncle Bud wouldn't ruin things for her! Sadness crashed over her, erasing all the good feeling of the moment before. But Uncle Bud had ruined everything … or had he? She leaned back against the stall, forgetting Max until he nuzzled her cheek. She freed him to go to his hay, and slid down the wall to sit in the straw beside him. Uncle Bud had come and gone and she was still here. He'd darn near destroyed her, but here she was up and working and, yes, feeling better.

Marty looked over the closed bottom of the stall door. "Hey," she said with a laugh. "Hiding out?"

"No, just thinking," Cat replied.

"Well, I wanted to thank you for helping even though you've been given time off. I've missed your help."

"Marty," Cat said, but the rest of what she wanted to say caught in her throat. She didn't know if she could bear to hear the wrong answer to the question she needed to ask.

"What is it, Cat?" Marty's green eyes had that warm glow of caring Cat had come to trust. Her sincere smile and squared shoulders promised that this was a woman who dealt straight and fair, as she had always dealt with Cat.

Cat pulled herself to her feet. She needed to see the answer in

Marty's eyes as much as hear the words she spoke. "Knowing all you do about me, do you really ... I mean ... deep down honest ... want me to continue to work for you?"

Marty's eyes held Cat's in an unwavering gaze. "Absolutely," she said. "I still don't understand your gift, but there's a lot in this world I don't understand. And I prize and respect you and can't imagine running this place without you. You have a place with us as long as you want to stay."

Cat grinned. "Thanks," she said. She didn't even bother to blink back her tears.

Marty dug in her jeans pocket and offered her a tissue.

Cat stepped out of the stall and took it. She wiped her eyes and blew her nose and didn't even care that Marty stood right there watching.

But as she walked back to find Nana, restlessness still gnawed at her. Marty had answered the way Cat had hoped she would and Cat believed her. She wasn't worried about Uncle Bud bothering her anymore. So why did she still have the sense that something was closing in on her and it was time to run? Maybe Nana had been right. Maybe all along she hadn't just been running from Uncle Bud.

THIRTY-ONE

Cat was feeling much better on Friday, nearly like her old self. She'd decided that in addition to not thinking about Uncle Bud and Mamma, she'd just ignore that restless feeling. If she were lucky, it would go away. She announced early in the morning that she was ready to return to work.

Still, she wasn't prepared to be ambushed by Nana, Marty, and Joel. But there they were, waiting in her apartment when she came in from the evening feeding. By the looks on their faces she knew she wasn't going to like what they had to say.

"What's wrong?" Cat asked.

Marty gave a hefty sigh. "Cat, last week … what happened to you …" She sucked in a lungful of air and then let it out. "Cat, you had a psychotic episode. Do you know what that means?"

Cat didn't understand all of it, but psychotic was plain enough. She looked to Nana to help her out. Nana just nodded. "I'm not crazy," she said. Her voice was hardly more than a squeak, hardly the assertive answer she wanted to give.

"No. No, Cat, none of us thinks that," Joel said. "Any one of us, given the right circumstances, can have an episode like you had. Episode means an isolated incident, but nonetheless we have to look at it as a sign that something's wrong."

"But I'm fine now," Cat said.

"Cat, we all thought you were fine before," Marty said. "But you never let any of us see all the fears and doubts you had rumbling around inside."

"I won't go to a mental hospital!" Cat screamed.

Nana went to her and put her arms around her. "Now, did you hear anyone say hospital? I sure didn't, so calm down and listen."

"Doc Harbison, who treated you last week..." Marty began. "He made me promise to talk to you about seeing somebody—a counselor who could help you work through some of this stuff. I've checked and our insurance policy through the Center covers counseling, so it won't cost you a thing."

Panic had already been sloshing around her ankles, but now the flood hit full force. "No, you can't make me. I don't want to talk to anyone. I'm fine. Why won't everyone just leave me alone?" She ran to her bedroom and slammed the door.

But there was no lock on the door and they just followed her in. "Cat, no one is going to make you do anything," Joel said. "We just want you to think about it. I know a counselor that I think you might like. She's a young woman who has an office in town, right in Washington. She'll fit you in whenever you decide you want to see her."

Cat glared at him. He'd been talking about her to this woman. "Did you tell her everything?"

"I told her you were a healer. She's a woman of faith. She accepts that God gives some of us special gifts."

"Cat, you don't have to give us an answer now," Marty said. "But please think it over. And, hey, whatever you decide won't make a bit of difference in how we all feel about you. We just want you to be well and happy."

Marty and Joel left. Cat turned on Nana. "I didn't hear you defending me."

Nana shook her head. "No, darling, you didn't. Because, you see, I agree with them. I know what Bud said to you, and if you don't get some help, you're always going to wonder if maybe you are crazy, especially after him telling you about your mamma that way."

It was true, then. "Come on. I'm hungry. Let's get something on for dinner."

"See, now there you go," Nana said. "You aren't going to

even ask me about your mamma, are you? Not ever. Well, that's not healthy, darling."

Cat stomped into the kitchen and began tearing packages from the cupboard and tossing vegetables from the refrigerator. She was no longer the least bit hungry, but anything was better than listening to any more of that nonsense.

But that night the dream came back, more horrifying than before....

She ran across the barren, rocky plain. The horrible eagle was close behind, but she would reach the tree before it caught her. She willed herself on. She recognized the figure in the tree. "I'm coming, Mamma," she cried. She focused so on the tree that she almost didn't see where the cliff face fell away. She stopped. The eagle was nearly on her. She jumped. "Catch me, Mamma," she screamed. But Mamma didn't even look her way, just kept singing and playing the mandolin. In one last grasping instant Cat grabbed the tree branch. With a loud crack, it snapped from the tree. As she fell screaming toward the canyon bottom she saw her mother jerked to a sickening stop as the rope snapped her neck.

She woke still screaming. Nana had her arms around her in a minute. "I killed her, Nana. This time I killed Mamma," Cat mumbled.

"Shh, darling child," Nana soothed. "It was a bad dream, that's all. What happened to your mamma wasn't your fault. You'd never willingly hurt anyone."

But she had. She tried to kill Uncle Bud. She'd wanted to kill herself. Now Mamma.

The next morning Cat called Joel and told him to make her an appointment with the counselor, although she told him she was sure it wouldn't help any. He called back right away. Dr.

Sarah Veld would see her at two o'clock that very afternoon.

Marty had lessons and couldn't go with them, so Nana and Cat went alone. Cat's heart pounded and her knees shook the whole ride in the elevator to the ninth floor of the big white building. Nana offered her hand and Cat clung to it.

When the elevator stopped, letting them out in the polished brass and wood-paneled splendor of the ninth floor, Cat pulled back. "This is stupid, Nana," she said. "Let's just go home." Nana again took her hand and led her down the hall like a little girl going to the doctor's for a booster shot.

But the woman who greeted them in the office was not as intimidating as her surroundings. She was young, not fat but rounded—all soft corners and smiles—and she had blue eyes that looked straight into Cat's and a deep, but gentle voice. Cat began to relax.

"Cat, would you feel better if Ms. Riley came in with you today?"

Cat nodded.

They followed Dr. Veld into her office, not more than a cubicle with a desk and three chairs, but with a huge square window that looked to the hills beyond the town. Cat took the seat facing the window.

"Joel Cramer told me about you," the doctor said. "I know you're a healer. I assume he also told you about me. I hold a divinity degree as well as a Ph.D. in counseling, so if you don't mind I'd like to start this session with a prayer."

Nana, of course, jumped right in. "That would be a comfort, dear."

Cat could feel her cheeks heating up. Nana had just called the doctor "dear." And furthermore, she didn't want to be forced into praying. She prayed privately when the urge came or when she needed God to help someone.

"Lord Jesus, we ask you to guide each of us today as we seek your healing grace. Amen."

Well, at least, it had been short. So far so good.

Dr. Veld opened a file and with her pencil poised, leveled a look at Cat. "Joel told me that Cat O'Reilly isn't your real name. If that's the name you want to use, I think it's a lovely name. But we're starting on a new stage in your life now. So what name do you choose?"

Cat thought awhile before replying, and not once did anyone try to hurry her answer. "I'm not Katie Parker. That was someone Uncle Bud made up. I like Cat O'Reilly better, but she's not real. Nana, what was my real name ... the one on my birth certificate?"

"You were named Katherine Ann Riley, but we always called you Katie."

"Then write down Kate Riley." Kate gripped the arms of the chair and prepared to dig deep enough to find out just who was this Kate Riley, and maybe more importantly find the root of her nightmare and make it go away.

THIRTY-TWO

Kate walked through the Washington Mall enjoying the brightly decked corridors and the twinkling lights in all the stores. She even smiled at the tall skinny Santa outside the toy store. She stood a moment at the life-size creche. No baby in the manger, but then there were still nine days 'til Christmas, so he hadn't come yet. She smiled at Mary, no blue-eyed blonde, but dark haired and tawny skinned, revealing her semitic ancestry. Kate approved.

After three weeks of counseling with two appointments each week, Kate was making progress. Part of that was a growing pride in the Riley side of her family. She sat down on the bench beside one of the nativity shepherds where she had told Nana to meet her. As Christmas approached she could feel Nana getting restless to go home. She'd only stayed so long because Dr. Veld felt it would be better for Kate. It had been.

Kate peeked into the bags at her feet. She had bought Samuel a boxed set of CD's, *The Complete Robert Johnson,* with a book about the famous blues man's life. That had been Jeff's suggestion. Letty was getting a pale blue blouse with a cut-work collar that Kristen had helped her pick out last week. She didn't know what to buy the boys. She had never really had toys when she was their age, except the occasional doll. She'd have to get Nana to help her choose something for them. They still had another week before she and Nana left for West Virginia—for home. This year she would have a real Christmas with her own family.

Nana hobbled toward her, the smile on her face hiding the pain she must be feeling in those poor gnarled feet of hers. Nana would love the present Kate had bought her—an electric foot bath and massager.

"Nana, you're empty-handed," Kate said.

Nana chuckled. "Hardly. The ladies from the synagogue are wrapping down by Penney's, so I just kept dropping my packages with them and said my strong-armed child would be by later to pick them up for me."

On the way home, the truck loaded with their gifts, Kate reached over and took Nana's hand. "Thanks for being with me all this time. I know it's been hard for you to be away from home."

"Oh, darling girl, I've cherished this time. Don't know how I'm going to get on not seeing you every day."

"Beckley's not so far. Now that I don't need to keep running, we'll visit back and forth more."

"So you're going to stay with Marty?"

"Sure, why not?"

"Well, Dr. Veld has asked you to think about what you are supposed to be doing with your life, what the Lord wants from you."

"I have been," Kate snapped, instantly defensive. "Marty needs me. All our kids are making such amazing progress. Julie is getting so much stronger. You should see how straight she sits on the horse. And Jim is talking more. And have you seen how much better Michael's walking?"

"But is that Marty's work or yours?"

Kate narrowed her eyes and watched the road ahead. The problem with this whole counseling process was that nothing was simple anymore and it all required more thought than Kate wanted to give it. Dr. Veld said prayer would ease the pain. The trouble was, whenever she tried to pray a soul-searching kind of prayer—anything more than her usual quick "Our Father"—the eagle came in the night.

Two days before Christmas she and Nana loaded up the truck to head to Beckley. Marty and her family had celebrated a special early Christmas with them the night before. Kate had given them her presents, just little things as they'd promised each other—a book on bluegrass guitar for Jeff; a cap with an embroidered rodeo logo for Kyle; for Annie a print for beside her bed with the Twenty-third Psalm and Christ as the Good Shepherd; for Duke a book called *Managing the Home Menagerie*. Everyone laughed when he opened that.

They had laughed even harder when Kyle gave Kate the present he'd picked for her. It was a sweat shirt. On the front, a long-legged heron had just snapped his beak shut on a big green frog, but the frog's legs hung out on either side. With his front legs the frog had a stranglehold on the heron's neck. Underneath it the caption read: NEVER GIVE UP.

She drove the truck to the farmhouse and helped Nana up the porch steps. Marty opened the door before Kate even got to it. "You all set to go?" she asked.

"Yes, I just wanted to say good-bye and show you..." Kate held her arms wide and turned around. Marty had broken the rules and given her a glorious new coat, a goose-down cotton duck jacket in forest green with a wonderful Aztec design on the back in beige, red, and black. It was the most beautiful coat Kate had ever owned.

Marty smiled. "You look gorgeous. I knew you would." She took Kate's cheeks in her hands and kissed her forehead. "And look at your hair."

Kate had combed her hair loose and had pulled some of it back from her face, using Duke's present to her, a silver and turquoise barrette. She marched into the kitchen to show Duke how much she loved his present. She opened her jacket and held the sides wide so Kyle could get another laugh at the sweat shirt he'd given her.

She assured Jeff she had his present, the Ralph Stanley bluegrass tape, in the truck ready to pop in the player the minute they hit the road.

"And, Annie, I have my new Murphy book in my suitcase."

She bent down and gave Annie a hug. "When I'm sad and missing you, I'll read it so it will make me laugh."

Marty pulled the gold disc on its chain from under her sweater. A dove in full flight was enameled on the front of the disc. On the back Kate had had engraved, "You gave me wings." "I treasure this," Marty said.

"I'm glad," Kate smiled. "We'd better get going." Enough sentiment. She could see by the glimmer in Marty's eyes that she was about to cry and she could hear Nana sniffing behind her. Things were getting way too mushy.

Everybody started hugging and kissing, except Jeff and Kyle. Jeff gave Kate's shoulder a punch. And Kyle tugged on her hair and winked. "Look here, kiddo, don't go getting all girly on me, all right? I don't want to lose a pal," he said.

Why did they all act as if she were going forever? "I'll be back before you all even miss me," Kate said, believing it to be true.

THIRTY-THREE

Marty stood with her family and watched the truck disappear around the bend in the lane. One by one, the rest of them went back into the warmth of the kitchen until only she, Annie, and Cody stood on the porch shivering in the icy air.

"Jeff says Cat might not come back," Annie said. "But she is 'cause she said so, right?"

Marty rested a hand on Annie's shoulder. "I know Kate wants to come back here, Annie. If she doesn't, it's because someone somewhere needs her more than we do."

"But we need her, Mom, and she needs us."

"We'll have to wait and see, honey. It's in God's hands." Cody whined and pawed at Marty's leg. "Poor old Cody is going to miss Sadie."

"And I'm already missing Cat. I mean Kate," Annie said.

"Come on. In the house with you," Marty said, ushering her into the kitchen. Marty opened the closet and grabbed her jacket, hat, and gloves from the closet. "Julie's coming for her make-up lesson in a half hour. I'd better get to the barn," she called as she headed back out the door.

On the porch, she gave Cody a gentle slap on the side. "Come on, big guy, keep me company." Together they climbed the hill to the barn. She hadn't been able to tell Annie what she truly believed—Kate wasn't coming back, not to stay. Joel had been trying to find something that offered Kate a chance to use her gifts. Kate insisted she wasn't ready to leave, but Marty believed differently. Kate had changed so in the last month, becoming strong and sure. And they were all wiser and stronger because of her. But it was time for her to move on.

Marty felt the gold disc lying against her breastbone. She sighed. She couldn't imagine the Center without Kate, but she couldn't give someone wings and then clip them, could she?

A gust of wind blew around the bend, rattling the bare branches of the trees. Cody took off at a run. Marty ran with him into the shelter of her barn.

Glory was ready and waiting when Marty heard the car pull up beside the barn. Jeff slouched on the couch in the office waiting to help. Joanne was busy at McFarland, so Marty was on her own with the therapist from the hospital. Since this was a make-up lesson and the only one scheduled for today, the three of them—Marty, Jeff, and the therapist—would go it alone.

Julie's dad came into the office first. "All right, Marty," he said. "Wait until you see this." He held the door wide. Behind him Julie walked, using only her crutches for support.

"Look at you!" Marty cried.

Julie's beautiful smile bloomed on her tiny face. "I'm getting strong, Marty," she said, without the strangled hesitation that had marked her speech two months ago.

"It's a miracle, Marty," Julie's mother said. "Until she started riding, every month she lost a little ground. Now look at her."

The therapist from the hospital arrived and the lesson began. Marty let the therapist take charge, while she side-walked and took direction. She had a lot to think about. Just three weeks ago she'd urged Kate to try to heal the children who came to the Center. Maybe God would grant them a few miracles.

Kate had said, "Marty, I already have, but it wasn't God's will." Marty had been disappointed; these children were so limited. It seemed so unfair.

"Marty, God offers all kinds of miracles," Kate had said. "Maybe it's your help he needs for these kids."

Marty had laughed at the time, but here before her was a miracle. Julie's miracle hadn't been an instant transformation.

Instead through her therapy, she'd grown gradually stronger until she had been able to walk into the barn without her walker, using only crutches. And she'd spoken clearly without hesitation.

Marty thought of the other children. All of her kids had improved, many of them dramatically. And God had let her be part of it. Of course, he'd also given her another mystery, since no one really knew why therapeutic riding was so successful. All the medical experts knew was that, for some reason and for some riders, the gains were greater than what they would be with more conventional therapies.

Marty watched Julie as they circled the arena. When she'd first come, her weak neck muscles had barely been able to support her head with the heavy riding helmet on it. Now she sat straight, her back and neck muscles so much stronger.

Marty glanced over at Julie's parents, who stood with their arms around each other, beaming at her. Like so many of the parents who brought their children to the Center, they seemed to have a special closeness to each other as well as to their daughter.

When the lesson finally came to an end, Julie was tired. It showed in her small face and in her sagging posture. On her crutches she struggled over to Marty, slowly walking high on her toes. She stood right in front of Marty, a small crooked smile on her pretty face. "Come … here … Mar-ty," she said.

Marty leaned her face level with Julie's. "What is it, Julie?"

Julie bent forward and pressed her lips on Marty's cheek. "Th-thanks, Mar-ty."

Marty blinked fast to hide the tears. These kids didn't need sentimentality, no matter how prone to it she was. "No, Julie. Thank *you*. You've worked very hard and made me very proud."

Julie smiled at her parents and started toward them. They waited for her to pass and followed her out of the barn. Her mother turned at the door. "See you next week, Marty, and thank you."

Marty laughed and shook her head. "Thank you for sharing her with me. Thank you for being the kind of parents who have allowed her to blossom and grow."

When they had all gone, including Jeff and the therapist, Marty walked the mare back to her stall. She thought about the children who came here. How ironic that she used to think of them as handicapped. Yet each and every one of them had given her more than she could ever possibly give them. So many of these children—regardless of what the world thought of their limitations—seemed to be mirrors of God's love.

It was as if God worked through all of them, letting their lives touch each other to create a circle of healing. Sure, she was supposed to be helping these children, but, in ways she didn't completely understand, the children and their families had touched her. Although she couldn't pinpoint the moment when it had begun, she knew she had started to heal.

She walked through the barn and out the far arena door. Lucky sat on the stoop to Kate's apartment, no doubt hoping Sadie would come out and play. Marty scooped him up and stood on the ridge looking out over the farm. "Lord Jesus," she prayed, "continue to use all of us as instruments of your healing love. And be with Kate and let her know our love goes with her."

THIRTY-FOUR

It only took Kate about four hours to drive home. Kyle had been working on the truck and had the engine running almost like new. As she turned off the main road onto the narrow one that wound back into the hollow, Kate's breath caught in her throat. Too many emotions raced through her.

She saw warm vapor rising from the flue of Bud's trailer. So he was home, was he? She took a deep breath.

"I hear he's not so good," Nana said.

The old white trailer was rusted in spots and sat crooked on its foundation. It was an even bigger dump than when it had been her prison. The porch pilings had collapsed on one side so that the front door wasn't usable. An end was dinged as if he'd run his truck into it. Kate turned her head away and stepped on the gas, skidding a little in the skim of snow on the road.

She turned off the paved road onto the gravel track that led to the cluster of houses where Nana lived. To her surprise, a fat pine wreath, studded with pinecones and red ribbons, hung on the door.

"That Samuel is something else," Nana said. "I asked him to check on the place, and look what he's done."

Inside, the house was as neat and trim as Kate remembered. Sadie bustled about getting used to all the new smells, running back frequently to check on Kate. On the mantel, pine boughs lay around Nana's nativity set. A note propped beside it read, "Welcome home, Nana and Katie. This will be our merriest Christmas yet."

Logs had been laid for a fire. Nana lit them, and the two of them sat in the twin rockers that had belonged to Nana's parents,

Kate's great aunt and uncle, and shared a pot of tea before they even unloaded the truck.

That night, snuggled into bed with Sadie under the old tick comforter in her childhood room, Kate lay awake. She listened to the sounds of the wind down the valley, owls in the woods behind the house, and dogs barking farther up the road, familiar sounds from long ago. She breathed in the smell of the place— old woodsmoke from the fireplace, cinnamon, cloves, and orange from the mixture Nana left in little bowls in every room, and a faint hint of menthol from Nana's liniments. She felt a stirring toward prayer, but wasn't sure what she wanted to say.

"Lord Jesus," she began, "I don't know what I want to say. Maybe thank you for bringing me home again. Thank you for letting me know my family and giving me friends like Marty who treat me like family. Dr. Veld says I should talk to you more, that memorized prayers are fine, but they don't always say what a person wants to say, but I really don't know what that is yet...." She thought but couldn't come up with anything else. She was sleepy and happy, very happy on the surface, but underneath, that old restlessness stirred. Dr. Veld said sometimes restlessness was God's way of moving us on toward where he wanted us. "Lord, help me to understand what you want of me," she prayed. "Amen."

That night the dream returned.

This time when she landed on the rocky, barren plain, Bud's shack stood at the edge of the cliff and the eagle soared faster, closing in on her. She had nowhere to turn but to that shack. She ran and ran until her lungs ached. The eagle was nearly on her when she reached Bud's door. It was locked. She pounded and pounded but got no answer. A voice inside screeched, "Go away. Bud's dead." In that instant she knew she had killed him. She could feel the air from the eagle's wide wings as he swooped toward her....

She woke with the scream still in her throat unreleased. She took a ragged breath. All night long she lay there thinking. The next morning she dressed quickly. She was writing a note when Nana came from her room, sleep wrinkles on her face, her hair in disarray.

"I thought I heard you moving about," she said. "Now where are you off to so early?"

"Before we leave for Beckley, I have to go see Bud."

Nana nodded. "I suspected you would. Sooner or later you always do get around to doing what's right. It's just your nature, child."

Sadie whined, scratching at the bedroom door. "I've already had her out. Just keep her in until I get back." Kate grabbed the truck keys and darted from the house before she could change her mind.

When she arrived at the trailer, her heart pounded against her ribs and it took all her courage not to turn back toward Nana's. In the early morning light, the trailer looked even worse than it had the night before. There were many more rusted places than she'd seen then. The yard was strewn with litter, probably from coons getting in the garbage and nobody ever picking it up.

Kate knocked on the back door. She heard a string of strangled curses and coughing, then bare feet thumped over the linoleum floor. Fear showed in Bud's eyes when he opened the door. The house smelled foul like human decay. Bud, gaunt and yellow, trembled in front of her.

"I'm here to try and help you," Kate said.

He threw his hands up over his face. He cried in weak little whines. He wiped his nose on his dirt-gray nightshirt. "I knew you'd come, Katie. I knew it. I just hope you're not too late."

She led him to a chair and pulled the only other one opposite him. "First off, I have to tell you I'm sorry I tried to hurt you before. That was wrong. No matter what you've done, I had no right."

"I ain't worried about that, just lay your hands on me, girl," he said, bowing his head toward her.

"Wait a minute, you've got to understand something," Kate said. She wanted to dump on him, to tell him what a lowdown snake he was, that he didn't deserve her help or anyone else's. She wanted to tell him that she was only there because she believed God wanted her to be.

"Come on. What are you waiting for?"

"Please understand," Kate said. "I'll pray as hard as I've ever prayed and as sincerely, but, Uncle Bud, I have never been the one granting the healings. It's always been God, so you better start praying, too."

Katie laid a hand on each side of her uncle's head and began to recite the healing prayer. Nothing. No sense of the Lord's presence, no familiar warmth. Maybe she'd said the words wrong. No. She knew them by heart. Maybe they didn't matter as much as what was in her heart. Uncle Bud whimpered and his thin shoulders shook. Tears came to Kate's eyes. She closed them and prayed, "Lord, please don't let me get in the way here. If it is your will, let this man be healed of his disease." Still nothing. She dropped her hands. "I'm sorry," she whispered.

"Just get out of here. You always were worthless," he shouted right into her face. His putrid breath made her gag. He stood and stumbled into the bedroom.

Kate followed. Bud rolled onto the bed, holding his abdomen and crying. His legs where they stuck out below his nightshirt were skinny as rails.

"Is there anything I can do for you?" Kate asked.

"No," he screeched. "Just leave me alone."

Kate turned to go.

Bud groaned. "Wait."

She hurried to the bedside. "What is it?"

"My pills ... for pain. I'm out. Could you get them refilled for me?"

She started to answer him, but instead, not exactly sure why she was doing it, she sat on the edge of his filthy bed and reached for his hands. They trembled when he gave them to her.

She prayed aloud, "Lord, if it is your will, take his pain and let him live his last days in comfort." She felt the warmth first deep in her chest where she believed her heart to be, almost as if the loving hand of the Lord rested there. She shut her eyes and bowed her head in awe as the heat radiated outward, traveling down her shoulders and her arms to her hands. It passed through her and into Uncle Bud. "Amen, my Lord, your name be praised," she cried.

Uncle Bud's eyes shot open in surprise. "Amen! Oh yes, amen! Katie, it's gone. That awful gnawing pain in my gut is gone! You cured me, girl!" He reached to hug her and she stiffened, but let him until she realized that he still hadn't gotten the reality.

Kate gently pushed her uncle away. She stood and pointed a finger in his face. "Uncle Bud, quit thanking me and hit your knees. You'd better start thanking the Lord and making your peace with him. You know as well as I do that you've just been given a stay of execution, not a reprieve. So you'd better make the most of it." He was still thanking her when she walked out of the room.

She only got a half-mile down the road before she had to pull off. Her vision blurred and turned inward. The world before her disappeared. As if she were seeing with her heart's eyes, she saw a light of golden glory all around her and felt the overwhelming presence of God. Her whole body was filled with the same divine warmth she'd felt back in Bud's trailer. She closed her eyes and let it carry her. She wasn't sleeping but the dream came....

She stood on the cliff with the tree in front of her. Her mother was gone from the tree, but as she watched, the tree burst into leaf. Behind her she heard the rushing wings of the eagle and became afraid. No one was there to help her. She could either throw herself off the cliff or face the creature in all its terror. She spun toward the thing. It was fearsome, but it wasn't an eagle. She only caught a glimpse of it, but as it rose into the sky, its white-feathered splendor brushed her face and she knew it for an angel.

Kate sat in her truck beside the road awhile, not wanting to disturb the peace she'd found. Surely, it would stay with her as she went. She started the truck and headed toward Nana's. The gray December sky promised snow before long. They needed to be on their way to Beckley.

A huge, dark-limbed locust stood stark against the sky just off the road. Kate slammed on the brakes. It was the tree from her dream, the tree her mother had hung from. Was this the actual tree? It was close enough to where the house had been, where Bud's trailer now stood. What had driven her mother to such a desperate act? Instead of panic, the question brought quiet and the knowledge that someday she'd understand even this.

She drove away, promising herself that sometime she'd ask Nana all about her mother and if that, indeed, had been her death tree. But not today. Today was Christmas Eve, so she hurried toward home and Christmas—to celebrate the coming of the Lord.

EPILOGUE

M arty went to the door when she heard the sound of Annie's footsteps thumping up the porch steps. Annie's face was flushed from her run from the mailbox on this warm April morning. She waved a letter high above her head. "Everybody come here," she called. "We got a letter from Cat!"

"Kate," Jeff corrected, reaching for the envelope.

"I know. I just keep forgetting," Annie said. She slipped away from Jeff and handed the letter to her mother.

Marty held it a moment before opening it. She knew it would only be filled with good news. In January, when Kate had returned from spending the holiday with her family, God's grace had shone from her. As Marty had expected, Kate had announced that she was leaving. She'd decided to go to Africa with Joel's friend, a minister who ran a worldwide relief organization.

Marty fingered the necklace she never took from her neck. Even though she'd been expecting the news, when the time came it had been hard to let Kate go. Someday she'd have to let Jeff go and then Annie. Funny. That didn't seem so scary anymore.

"Well, for heaven's sake, Marty, read us the letter," Duke said.

Marty looked around the room—Jeff, Annie, Duke, Kyle—all present. She opened the envelope and read:

My dear family,
   That's what I call you, because that is how I hold you in my heart. But then we are all supposed to be one in God's family. Sadly, it doesn't always work that way.

Poor Bud died last month, all alone in his trailer, but Nana tells me he'd gone back to church and had found some peace. I often wonder why God chose not to heal him. All I can figure is that if Bud had been given a cure, he wouldn't have changed. I remember Joel saying, "God will only answer prayers that bring us closer to him."

Nana sends her love. I left Sadie with her. They will be good company for each other, but I'll miss them. Nana said to tell you she has no intention of losing touch with you guys. I told her there was no danger of you letting her. You aren't like that.

Please pray for our mission here. Tomorrow we head inland to the village. Conditions are even worse than we'd been told. The years of near famine and then last fall's floods have devastated the land. We will be rebuilding the entire village from the ground up. There are twenty of us from many different Christian denominations. If we can keep from arguing over our differences in religious practice and focus on our common belief in Christ and the job he's given us to do, I believe we will be a powerful force for good. We will need to be builders, farmers, teachers, preachers, and healers, too. There is so much sickness. We have two doctors with us, a husband and wife. They are gradually getting used to the idea of me. Marty, the woman sometimes gives me that "deer in the headlights" look like you did when you first learned about my gift. If she has a heart only half as caring as yours, she'll come around.

I miss you all but am so excited about our mission here. Please be happy for me. I am finally where the Lord wants me to be or, at least, where he wants me now. Pray for all of us here and ask all my friends there to pray, too. I pray every day for all of you.

Love,
Kate

Marty looked around the room at her family. They sat quietly, rare for them.

Duke finally cleared his throat, breaking the silence. "I still think she should have stayed until summer. Given herself more time."

"Casey and I have to find another mandolin player to work with us. All those songs she taught us sound so much better when a mandolin plays along," Jeff said.

"I miss her," Annie said. "I miss Sadie, too."

"Now that Kate's not here for me to tease, I'll just have to pick on Annie more," Kyle said, scooping Annie up and spinning her around.

"All right," Marty ordered. "Lunch break is over. It's time to get back to work. We have eight riders between now and dinner."

Marty ushered her family out the door and up the hill. As she went she prayed for Kate, and for the others with her on the African mission. She asked God, too, to be with her and her family as they went about their business, helping them to keep their hearts focused on him.

When Marty whispered "Amen," worry still jiggled around inside her. She did so want to please God, but she was often uncertain about what he wanted of her. Hers was a quieter, less dramatic kind of faith than Kate's, but it was the only kind she knew. Unlike Kate, she had never felt the brush of an angel's wing or the overwhelming presence of God in a golden light.

It sometimes seemed as if God had put her down on this highway and said, "This is the right road, Marty. Just keep driving straight toward me." But God always stayed on the other side of the headlights beyond her range of vision, yet she never doubted his presence there. And the waves of love that came from that great unknown at times nearly dissolved her.

Maybe that's what faith was all about—love. It was like the

old joke, "If love is the answer, what's the question?" Maybe the question was "How do I best serve the Lord?" And maybe it took all of them loving in their own ways and according to their own unique talents to fulfill the Lord's plan. Marty didn't know. There was so much she didn't understand. She never did seem to get clear-cut answers to her many questions. But now and then she caught a glimmer of what was intended, and that was enough. She smiled as she climbed on up the hill to her barn to get ready for the afternoon's lessons. She placed one foot carefully after the other, digging into the damp spring earth to keep from slipping.